WHAT
LIES
IN THE
CORNFIELD?

WHAT
LIES
IN THE
CORNFIELD?

A JAKE AND MALLORY
THRILLER

IVANKA FEAR

LEVEL
BEST BOOKS

Author Photo Credit: Amanda Belec, thirteen13designsnphotography

First edition

ISBN: 978-1-68512-753-4

Cover art by Level Best Designs

This book was professionally typeset on Reedsy.
Find out more at reedsy.com

For my husband, Brian, in whom I trust everything
You light my path.

To our family
With all my love. You mean everything to us.

And to our little Lucky cat
who lives on in our broken hearts.

Praise for What Lies in the Cornfield?

"A tenuous marriage and the discovery of more than one dead body make everyone a suspect in this gripping, snappy suspense. With well-paced, punchy chapters and multiple POVs, *What Lies in the Cornfield* had me questioning everyone's motives. Not knowing who to trust and who might die next, I raced breathlessly to the heart-thumping, satisfying finish."—Samantha M. Bailey, *USA Today*, Amazon Charts, and #1 international bestselling author of *A Friend in the Dark*

"Ivanka Fear's *What Lies in the Cornfield?* blends suspense and emotion into a gripping story that follows deeply human characters."—Elle Grawl, Amazon Charts bestselling author of *One of Those Faces* and *What Still Burns*

"Ivanka Fear has written a fast-paced, tense crime thriller that will keep the reader turning the pages late into the night. I really enjoyed the crazy twists and turns, and finding out who was telling the truth. *What Lies in the Cornfield* is the second book in the series and doesn't disappoint. This is one crazy ride!"—Joseph Souza, bestselling author

"Fear has once again proven herself a storyteller of remarkable talent, blending mystery, drama, and emotional depth into a narrative that is as thought-provoking as it is suspenseful. This novel is a must-read for anyone who enjoys a compelling blend of psychological suspense and domestic drama, delivered against the backdrop of a hauntingly beautiful rural landscape." Gayle Brown, author of *A Deadly Game*

"*What Lies in the Cornfield?*, the second novel in the Jake and Mallory

i

Thriller series by Ivanka Fear, is a twisty, action-packed novel that keeps you anxiously turning the pages to the very end. It's a riveting read, with a storybook wedding thrown in for a nice contrast. Fear handles the various twists and reveals skillfully and leaves you wanting more. You just can't go wrong with an Ivanka Fear thriller!"—Kelly Young, author of the Travel Writer Cozy Mystery series and the Haunted & Harassed Paranormal Mystery series

"Packed with action and intrigue, *What Lies in the Cornfield?* will keep readers turning the pages, never knowing what to expect next. The plot is as complex as the relationship between Mallory and Jake, tainted with secrets and deception, but fortified by shared histories and uncontrolled passions. Trust is at the heart of this fast-paced thriller by Ivanka Fear, the second in a series. Who do you trust when no one can be trusted, not even your spouse? You won't want to put it down."—Lori Duffy Foster, author of the Lisa Jamison Mystery Series and *Never Let Go*, a thriller

"Deceit, mistrust and dead bodies showing up on your property, *What Lies in the Cornfield?* by Ivanka Fear is a wild ride that will leave you astounded and begging for more from couple Jake and Mallory."—Sandra Rathbone, author of *Skelee Boy: A Skelee Boy Book* and *Skelee Boy and the Demon King*

"Venturing back into the world of Jake and Mallory, *What Lies in the Cornfield?* unravels hidden truths from a tangled web of lies inside a subtle and deceptive plot that challenges the reader's expectations and leaves them guessing and second-guessing at every turn."—Renee Cronley, Canadian author of the upcoming poetry book, *Burnout*

Chapter One

"What was that?"

I bolt from our bed and peer through lined curtains. Jake continues to snore while my eyes investigate the source of the rumbling outside our two-story red brick farmhouse. A flash of light to the right frightens me back under the floral and plaid duvet.

"Jake!" I nudge him and he rolls toward me with a snort. "Wake up! I heard something outside."

"Yeah, it's windy," he mumbles.

"No, it's something else. And I saw lights. Go see what it is."

Jake moans, telling me to go back to sleep. And I would, if I could. But the sound gets louder, closer. My pulse throbs into my palm as I curl up, hands supporting my head, trying to do as Jake asks. The pounding of my heart against my forearm adds to the incessant roaring in my ears. Blood whirs through my veins, strumming a persistent rhythm.

Breathe, just breathe. Slow and steady. In and out.

It can't be good for the baby, having a panic attack. Over something as simple as a windstorm.

Jake's right, of course. I remember now. The nighttime weather forecast called for high winds and warned of damaging gusts amidst an early autumn rainstorm. The old windowpanes rattle as squalls batter their exterior, rain now hammering the roof. The flash must have been lightning. A boom cracks through the room, jolting me to a sitting position. But as long as there are no leaks, we'll weather the storm, safely cocooned in our century-old home that's been in Jake's family for generations.

Unless the basement floods. Or we get hit by lightning. Or the storm becomes a hurricane. Or a funnel cloud touches the ground, and we get whisked away to Oz.

Jake's unconcerned, his rhythmic breathing punctuated by raspy vibrations from his airways. I don't dare wake him again. He needs his sleep if he's going to work on the finishing touches to the family room addition in the morning.

With the baby coming and Jake's inheritance from his grandfather, we decided more space was in order. Or *I* decided. And Jake has been doing everything he can to make me happy after the blip our marriage suffered this summer, although he hasn't entirely gotten his head around the fact that soon there will be three of us. It's not as though there wasn't plenty of room in this old beauty of a home we're lucky enough to own, thanks to Jake's Mom for selling it to us at a decent price. But I envisioned the kitchen as the center of our cozy little family. Knocking down the back wall and deck to expand the kitchen with a family room/dining nook addition to make it the focal point of our home was *my* idea.

The wind has picked up, slamming against the windows. Just a simple storm. I settle back into bed, wrap my leg around Jake's, touch one hand to his back, and focus on his steady snorts and wheezes. Another flash illuminates the room, followed by a deep rumble. Eyes shut tight, I try counting sheep. Only they're not sheep; they're cats. Which reminds me. Where is Nellie?

She must be terrified. Why isn't she here with us?

I slip out of bed, careful not to disturb Jake, although if he's sleeping through this storm, nothing is likely to fully wake him. In the hall, the night light guides me to the staircase. Not wanting to risk a fall, I flip the switch, and a glow bathes the steps all the way down to the front door with its sidelights as I descend to the entryway.

"Nellie! Nellie! Where are you, sweetie?" My loud whisper draws no response.

She must be hiding in the living room. The curtains are drawn against the raging tempest, and the front door is secured. But it doesn't keep the monster at bay. No, it whistles through its gaping mouth in the spaces between the wooden entry door and the jambs. It flares and crackles, breathing fire into the hallway through the crystal lenses of the sidelights. Angry tears plaster the window and door, demanding to be let in.

BOOM! Its fist slams down in fury, the house trembling as a chill sweeps through the cracks. The rumbling in its bowels clamors for sustenance, a human sacrifice.

You're letting your imagination run wild.

I switch on the floor lamp. No Nellie on the blankie draped over the sofa.

Across the hall, the chandelier illuminates the dining room, but Nellie's not curled up under the table, either. Down the hall toward the kitchen, I tread, one foot in front of the other, calling for her, trying to stay calm when she doesn't materialize. I pass the closed powder room door. She must be in the laundry room, next to the back bathroom, a favorite hangout of hers.

"Are you in here, sweetie?" Flipping on the lights, I scan the area around the washing machine and dryer. She's not sleeping on the pile of dirty towels in the basket, nor is she using the litter box in the mudroom off the laundry.

I'm about to check the den, which has been repurposed as a meeting/work room, when another flash floods the nearly renovated kitchen still awaiting new light fixtures.

I scream at the shadow, unable to suppress my horror. Eyes glowing, back arched, hair standing on end, her dark silhouette against the bay window overlooks the back yard.

Calm down. It's just Nellie.

Still. Quiet. Watching.

"Nellie, what's going on, girl? What do you see?"

She responds with a short meow, then turns back to stare at the dark. Frightened, but curious enough to stay rooted in her spot when I approach.

I join Nellie on the window seat Jake built for me and gaze into the blackness. Whatever fascinates her, I don't see it.

"Was that other cat out there?" I stroke her black and white fur to soothe us both. "Want to come to bed?" As I scoop her up, the back yard brightens, my flowerbeds splashing a brief flash of color against the green lawn that stretches hundreds of feet to the garden shed. "Let's go."

We get as far as the hallway leading out of the kitchen when I freeze next to the basement door. The wind whistles a new tone. Different. Louder. Rhythmic.

Tornado?

Head to the basement, Mallory.

I can't leave Jake sleeping upstairs. How much time do I have to save us?

As I hurry toward the stairs, a roll of thunder spooks Nellie and she darts toward the laundry room. I follow. Nellie sits on the counter, gazing out the side window.

The wind whirs like a motor, the sound vibrating through the glass. It seems to have taken on two faces. One whistles and howls, slapping the house in anger. The other swishes and whips, rhythmically whupping the exterior walls. All together, it roars to a frenzy, threatening to blow us to smithereens.

As I try to scoop up Nellie once again, I venture a peek out and upward through the glass. Darkness ahead, the corn field eerie as usual in the night. And lights above, yellow, red, green, against ominous clouds.

Oh. My. God.

The shrieks send me scurrying down the hall to the stairs. Jake meets me halfway up, wrapping his arms around me, and I realize the terrified cries are coming from my own mouth.

"Mallory! Are you okay?" Jake cups my face. "Honey? What happened?"

Lightning flickers through the sidelights up the stairwell, shedding an unearthly yellow glow on my husband's face. For a second, a crazy thought goes through my mind. But I squelch it. Jake is many things, but an alien is not one of them.

Chapter Two

"I saw something..." The words I'm about to spit out sound ridiculous in my head, so I reconsider them before they slip out of my mouth. "I don't know what it was."

"Go back to bed while I check the house."

"No, I'm coming with you. I'll show you."

We walk side by side, my hand clutching his arm, to the back of the house. Jake hears it, too. He stops to cock his head, taking in the wind's violence underpinned by a continuous hum, a steady drone. It's as though something is coming for us.

A bomb? A missile?

"I'll take a look outside." Jake steps toward the back entrance and touches the doorknob.

"No, don't!" My hand reaches to stop him. "There's something out there. In the sky. A UFO or something."

Jake flips the outdoor switch, dispelling the darkness in the back yard. His blue-green irises meet my blue eyes, and he raises his brow. I wait for him to make some silly joke about the situation, or maybe laugh at my expense and call me batshit crazy.

But he does neither.

"Let's have a closer look. I'm sure there's a reasonable explanation." My brave husband turns the knob, unlatches the screen door, and a gust flings it wide open. He steps outside with me clinging to him like plastic wrap.

"Nellie! Don't let her get out!" I don't want to chase her around the yard in the middle of a storm while an unidentified object hovers above our

5

cornfield.

Jake closes the door and rain batters our backs, blasts of cool air pushing us toward the corn. My floral nightgown billows around my upper arms and flaps against my knees like a flag as the chill ripples through me.

Our eyes focus on the sky, the source of the unnatural sound and lights. Grey and black clouds swirl. Spots of light—yellow, green, red—break through the dark sky. A circular shape hovers above.

"What is it?" Surely, Jake will share that reasonable explanation he mentioned earlier.

He remains silent, staring upward.

"Jake?"

"A helicopter. That's what it is. I just don't know what it's doing here, above our property."

A helicopter? I suck in air and exhale slowly, setting free the tightness in my chest. Of course, it's a helicopter. *Not* a UFO.

As if to confirm Jake's answer, a bolt of lightning illuminates the aircraft. Below, dark stalks of corn wave, bend, and twist in its wake. The sky blackens again, triggering another round of panic as the rustling cornfield threatens to pull me in.

"Let's go back inside," I wail above the gust that nearly knocks me over.

Jake turns to guide me toward the house as another flash brightens the sky, giving me a glimpse of the helicopter logo. Something else catches the corner of my eye. An object has dropped from the sky.

I'm seeing things. Imagining UFOs and aliens in our cornfield. Jake will think I'm losing my mind. He's been treating me with kid gloves the last few months, my fragile mental health concerning him, though he hasn't said anything. He worries I'll snap. Never mind that he's the source of my anxiety.

Once inside, we stop in the back bathroom for a warm shower to draw the chill out of our bones. We linger under the drenching spray, Jake soaping my body and washing away the tenseness with the lavender scent. The blasting of the storm is nearly drowned out by the rainfall shower head but still in the background, reminding me it's not over.

I'm finally warm enough to head to bed, but Jake has other ideas. His lips claim mine, and his hands trace my curves, a little more pronounced in the last month. "You're so beautiful," he murmurs, running fingers through my long, wavy, blond hair.

Right back at you, husband.

Jake is a good-looking man with chiseled features, a chin dimple, and wavy brown hair. But it's his eyes that drew me from the start—sparkling like turquoise waters. I try not to be jealous when other women ogle him, and I remind myself he chose me. In fact, he begged me to be his wife. And he pleaded with me to take him back a couple of months ago when it looked like our marriage of three years was doomed to fail.

He's gentle with me now, since accepting the baby is his. As though I might break. No hint of the rage that sometimes came to the surface when things weren't perfectly the way he wanted them to be. His jealousy has taken a back seat to his love for me and our unborn child.

We've both changed. That's what marriage is about. Growing, changing, and accepting the new people we become.

After making love, Jake wraps me in a fluffy white bath towel and grabs one for himself, dropping the wet pajama bottoms and nightgown in the laundry room hamper on our way back to bed. He stops in front of the basement door and listens.

"I'm going to check the water level. Make sure the sump pump is ready if the rain doesn't let up. You go on upstairs."

I won't argue with that. I don't go into the unfinished basement with its bricked-in windows, beams and pipes hanging overhead, partial dirt floor, and evil fire-burning furnace. I've been there and survived, but it's Jake's domain.

After blow-drying my hair, I return to bed; Nellie lies curled up on my pillow. "That's my spot, sweetie." I remove my towel, slip in next to her, gently prodding until she agrees to move to the foot of the bed. The duvet pulled up to my chin, I snuggle in, waiting for Jake.

"It's all good." He climbs into bed minutes later. "The rain water's flowing away. No water in the basement. And the pump hasn't had to start up."

With his arm slung around my waist, Jake begins to snore before I get a chance to ask if he noticed the helicopter drop anything. If it's what I think I saw, someone's going to have a lot of explaining to do.

Chapter Three

"Jake, honey? Wake up. The power's out." The clock beside our bed blinks red. I pick up the phone to check the time. 9:42. He was supposed to be working on the new addition this Saturday morning. "Hmmm…okay…I'm up." He rolls onto his back and snorts.

I poke him in the ribs. "You were going to paint today, remember? Maybe you could hook up the generator?"

Instead of getting up, he rolls over on top of me. "Did I tell you how beautiful you are?'

"You did. Last night. Speaking of which… Did you notice anything fall from the sky just before we went inside?"

"Uh, yeah."

"You did? What was it?"

"A whole shitload of rain. We're lucky it quit when it did. With the power out, we could have had a flood. I'd be spending my morning bailing out the basement instead of painting."

He trails kisses along my neck, and I'm tempted to spend the morning in bed. But we have a lot of work to do before the baby arrives. Although the new addition is getting there, thanks to the contractors Jake hired, he wanted to handle the finishing details himself. I think it's because of his OCD.

Trim, paint, lighting, fixtures…there's still tons to do. And that's just one room. I've got lots of other plans for Jake.

"I'll put the coffee on," I offer, trying to extricate myself from him. The kitchen is still in functioning order, despite the renos, except for the sink.

"No, you won't. Unless you're going to light a match and start a woodfire outside."

Oh, that's right. The power's out.

Judging from the rays of sunlight coming through the edge of the curtains, I assume it won't be for long. The electrical crew will come along and get things up and running. Even on our isolated road.

"You're lighting a fire in me," Jake teases, pulling me on top of him. "Things are beginning to spark up."

I stiffen at the image he injects into my brain. It brings back memories of the fire that took my parents' lives five years ago as they slept in their own bed.

"That was a stupid thing to say. I wasn't thinking. How about some orange juice and cereal? Then, I'll get the paint mixed and ready. It looks like a bright enough day to work without power." He rolls out of bed and pulls on an old pair of jeans and a worn work shirt.

I know he worries about saying the wrong thing, doing something to trigger my anxieties. He wasn't always so sensitive to my feelings. My meltdown this summer has changed him. It's changed me.

Calling it a meltdown makes me feel better. But I'm not a child and shouldn't excuse my actions as a tantrum or an emotional outburst. I've seen plenty of kids who can't control their behavior. Managing overwhelming frustration is part of what I do every day in my kindergarten class.

What happened to me was...I don't really know. I snapped. I cracked. I popped. Into some alternate state where I didn't have to acknowledge my husband's disappearance and possible demise. Because I couldn't face it. The reality of living without Jake was too much. Without Jake, there is no Mallory. It's Jake and Mallory all the way.

I pull open the curtains to allow light to dance into our bedroom. Across the road, the forest stands, a nature retreat, so unlike the forbidding monstrosity it presents itself to be in the middle of the night. On our front lawn, robins hop in search of juicy worms brought out by last night's rain, and two squirrels chase each other around the maple trees.

In the kitchen, the morning sun sheds light on dust motes. We eat our breakfast at the table that Jake shoved into the corner, out of the way of the renovation crew. The kitchen has been expanded to more than twice its original size. To the right, a nook with double glass doors leads to a future wraparound deck. On the back wall overlooking the gardens, the bay window seat forms a semicircle, with floor-to-ceiling built-in bookcases lining both sides.

"The perfect place for you to enjoy both your flowers and books. And the drawers underneath will hold the baby's toys," Jake said when he surprised me with the window seat.

The primed walls are ready to paint a fresh coat of creamy white to match the new cupboards. And shiny silver appliances complement the fresh white background. I worried that it would be too clinical after I chose white. But the warm wood flooring and countertops maintain the country kitchen atmosphere. As I clear away our dishes, Jake rolls out the clear sheeting and covers the floor and countertops. I love to watch him work. Especially on this house, our *home*. We're building more than an addition, renovating more than a structure. It's our marriage we're rebuilding, patching up, adding our own special touches to.

By the time Jake pries open the paint can and gives it a good stir, the house begins to speak. A steady hum, the underlying life force of appliances and electrical gadgets, returns. It's louder than usual in the calm after the violent night.

"There we go. Back to normal." Jake winks to assure me that we survived another storm out on the old homestead. He tips the can, pouring the thick, white liquid into a tray, then rubs the roller back and forth on the ribs.

"Jake."

"What, honey?"

"What do you think that helicopter was doing last night?" I ask an open-ended question to give Jake a chance to voice an explanation before I confess what I saw.

He hesitates, then looks up from the paint tray. "I think it was a medical helicopter."

"Above the cornfield?"

11

"It was stormy. The pilot must have gotten disoriented. They were probably responding to an accident in the area caused by the wind and rain."

"And got lost in our cornfield?" I scoff.

"Not lost, just off track. I'm sure it's not easy flying in that kind of weather. Anyway, they're gone, so whatever problem they were having, it all worked out. Hopefully, they got to wherever they needed to be."

"Makes sense." But I know it was no medical helicopter.

Jake changes the subject. "So, you've got lunch and your dress fitting today. Beats watching paint dry."

"Yes. But I'd rather stay home with you."

I'm meeting my best friend, Vicky, and a couple of her workmates to try on bridesmaid dresses. I'm her maid of honor. Funny how things work out. Vicky dated Jake before I met him. The sharp pain of jealousy strikes me now and then when I see the two of them together. It's tempered with the guilt of having slept with Jake's best friend, Craig. Once. One mistake.

Not my only mistake, by any means. But the only one I made with Craig, Vicky's fiancé. If the same guilt plagues Craig, he hides it well. Our little secret. No point in upsetting Jake and Vicky over something so trivial in the big scheme of things.

"I miss you already. Maybe I'll call Craig to come over for a couple of beers and get him to give me hand with painting the trim."

Upstairs, I flip through the hangers in my closet. Some of my clothes still fit, but everything is snug. No matter what I choose to wear, Vicky will outshine me with her glamour. Long auburn hair, a svelte figure, and high cheekbones never fail to impress the men she encounters. I settle on a pair of black leggings with an elasticized waistband and a blue tunic sweater over top. Does it matter? *I'm* carrying Jake's baby, not Vicky. And Jake thinks I'm beautiful no matter what I wear.

The leggings aren't so bad, after all. I look casual chic. A light layer of makeup and mascara, a few twirls of the curling iron, and I'm set to go. "I'm off. Good luck with the walls." I blow Jake a kiss, not daring to get near the paint in my fresh outfit.

"Okay, hon. See you later." He flashes me one of his charming smiles. "You and the baby."

As I walk down the porch steps, I glance toward the cornfield before heading to my Toyota. My mind plays tricks on me, I tell myself. Nothing fell from the sky last night. Only rain. Like Jake said. Yet, I can't help but wonder if there's something hidden between the rows upon rows of tall stalks. Something that shouldn't be there.

Besides the marijuana plants my husband's associates cultivate.

Chapter Four

Today is about Vicky. Not me. During my half-hour hour drive to the city, I push aside my jealousy and focus on the positive. Jake married me, not Vicky. Vicky is marrying Craig.

Everything has worked out perfectly. We're all going to live happily ever after, just like in the romance novels I used to read as a teenager before my world crashed down to earth. Now, my mantra is: If anything *can* go wrong, you can bet it will. Jake believes he was born under a lucky star and that he'll glide through life on a winning streak. We're such polar opposites it's no wonder we're hopelessly drawn to each other.

I pull into the parking lot of Cucina Romana and glance at the clock on my dash. The Italian restaurant is expensive, but a successful lawyer like Vicky doesn't consider price when choosing a lunch venue. If Jake hadn't accepted his dad's generous gift of one-quarter of his grandfather's estate, we would be stretched thin to afford this meal.

The Maitre D escorts me to the table where three women are absorbed in a humorous conversation. Vicky is likely gossiping about me.

Poor Mal. She's so fragile. Can't even make lunch on time. Maybe it slipped her mind. What little there is of it.

Their heads turn as I approach, eyebrows raised. Vicky rises to embrace and air kiss me on both cheeks. "Mallory, you look great! Pregnancy definitely agrees with you."

The Maitre D pulls out a chair for me. As I'm seated, it's evident I'm underdressed for this occasion. The other three women have donned simple but elegant cocktail dresses for Vicky's bridal luncheon.

"Um, I…most of my clothes are too tight. The baby's grown a lot in the last few weeks and I haven't had time for shopping. Jake and I are busy with renos, getting ready for the baby. And to tell the truth, I've been tired. My doctor says it's perfectly normal when you're pregnant." I'm laying it on a bit thick with baby excuses, but I want to remind Vicky I've got something she doesn't. Besides Jake.

Baby Jakey or Jacoba.

We've decided not to find out the sex of the baby. Jake says it'll be a pleasant surprise. "We'll have fun going on shopping sprees for baby clothes, the three of us."

I'm just happy that Jake has accepted my pregnancy and is becoming as excited as I am about the baby. His doubts about being a decent father kept him from wanting children, and the loss of my own nuclear family brought out my maternal urges in full force. Now, we're finally on the same wavelength, and both want more kids.

"So exciting! I'm going to be an auntie!" Vicky gushes over me, insinuating herself into the role of aunt to our unborn child. "If it's okay…I'd like you to think of me that way, Mallory. We're as close as most sisters."

Being an only child, I wouldn't know. But Jake's brother's wife will be our child's aunt. Not Vicky. "Of course, Vicky. We'd be honored to have you as an auntie to little Jakey. You're family, you and Craig."

The other two women switch the conversation to Vicky and her upcoming wedding, putting me in second place. It's only natural. They're her friends from work. I barely know them, having only recently met them during our hunt for the perfect bridesmaid dresses.

"And the caterers?" Cindy's eyes move from Vicky to me in search of an answer. "Have you managed to find someone on such short notice?"

"Yes, lucky for us, there was a cancellation at Michael's. Otherwise, we would have gone with Plan B and had a backyard barbecue or pig roast and salad bar, maybe pizza delivery," I say.

Cindy and Moira stare at me open-mouthed, but Vicky laughs. "Craig would have loved that."

Jake and I were given the privilege of helping with the wedding planning.

Originally, Vicky had thoughts of an elegant holiday wedding in the conservatory of Stonehill Manor, followed by a reception in the great hall, catered by Chez Ramon, and a string quartet. White Christmas lights strung throughout, everything in white and silver, including decorations on freshly-cut Christmas trees.

But, when I jokingly remarked that I hoped Craig didn't get cold feet and back out before then, her plans changed. "If I were you, I'd tie him down sooner rather than later, with Craig being a self-proclaimed life-long bachelor, according to Jake. All this wedding fuss might spook him."

I didn't expect her to take me seriously, but a shadow fell over her face, and she said I was right. "We've broken up before. I don't want to lose Craig again."

Craig was more than happy to move the wedding up, especially if it meant keeping things simpler. When Jake offered our property for the nuptials, the four of us decided a late September wedding would be best. A tent out in our back gardens, hopefully before the frost hit, and the rest would fall into place if we worked together. We'd recreate our own wedding. To Vicky and Craig's tastes, of course.

"Our best friends will have the wedding we had," Jake said. "It'll be perfect."

I hope their union will be as happy as Jake's and mine. True, we've had some ups and downs. But in the end, our love triumphs. Because we're meant to be. Jake and Mallory. And so are Craig and Vicky.

"It's all coming together," I tell Cindy and Moira. "You wouldn't believe what you can accomplish when you're under pressure. Two weeks from now, Vicky will be a married woman. Mrs. Craig Dunsmere."

"Thanks to you, Mrs. Shelton," Vicky says. "You and Jake first brought us together when you guys got married." As our best man and maid of honor, Vicky and Craig hooked up. "And then you brought us back together for *good* when you went through that rough patch this summer."

Although I'm embarrassed to have Vicky bring that up in front of two relative strangers, I smile and pat her hand, not sure what exactly she has told them. Moira, pity in her eyes as she acknowledges my discomfort, raises her wine glass and makes a toast to Vicky, wishing her every happiness and no rough patches. I keep a smile plastered on my face as I clink my water glass against the other three glasses filled with white wine. I could use a drink right about now.

The waiter takes our orders and we relax, silent for a few moments, the classical music in the background gracing our ears. I excuse myself to use the ladies' room. "The baby…" I motion to my stomach. They nod in understanding, although they have no idea, all three unmarried and childless.

On my way back to our table, a voice calls my name. My head turns to the right, and I see my friend, Brad, with an attractive woman. I wave and head over to their table. He introduces me to his lunch date, and I tell him about my bridal luncheon with Vicky. Brad is part of my everyday life. He teaches Grade 6 at the school where I work as a kindergarten aide.

I won't tell Jake I bumped into Brad, even though there's nothing more than friendship between us. Although we dated briefly, we split up before I met Jake. Jake isn't keen on me spending time with him, even if it's work-related. Jake, on the other hand, doesn't see a problem with Vicky being a fixture in our lives, in spite of the fact that they were pretty hot and heavy before I came into the picture.

"She's your best friend. And my best friend's fiancée. Whatever was between Vicky and me is ancient history," Jake said. "I hope you can put that behind us."

Part of me is grateful that Vicky and Jake were a couple. I wouldn't have met Jake otherwise. Luckily, they split up, leaving Jake free to be with me.

Back at our table, the conversation continues to revolve around Vicky, Craig, the wedding, the new house they bought in the city.

"It'll be nice for Craig to have a shorter drive to work," Vicky says.

But, I'm wondering whether Craig will be suited for a city existence after living in a small town all his life. I moved the other way, from the city to the middle of nowhere, when I married Jake. I'm still not used to all that space.

"It's a gorgeous two-story in a new subdivision with a back yard. Lots of space to raise a family." Vicky glances at me. "Who knows? Maybe this time next year, we'll be celebrating a new baby, too. Wouldn't it be great if our kids became best friends like the four of us?"

"That would be amazing," I agree.

After our main course, I'm the only one ordering dessert. The others finish their meal with an espresso. "I crave sugar. The baby..."

Vicky nods. "You're entitled, Mallory. I'd join you, but I need to fit into my wedding dress."

An hour later, in the dressing room of White Wedding Boutique, Vicky stands before us in all her splendor. The spaghetti-strapped, form-fitting designer gown fits her toned hourglass figure like a glove. Straight, expertly styled auburn hair trails partway down her bare back. Intricate lace and bead details on the gown and a long train create a timeless elegance.

"Wow, you're stunning." I've seen her in the dress before; I helped pick it out. It's breathtaking. "Craig won't be able to take his eyes off you." Neither will Jake.

Next to Vicky, the three of us will fade into the background. But it *is* her special day, and that's the way it should be. The wine-colored bridesmaid dresses are less revealing. Vicky took my growing belly and my feelings into consideration when she suggested the double-strapped A-line style for all three of us.

The flowing skirt allows room for my small baby bump. I twirl in front of the full-length, three-sided mirror, pleased with the fit. My pregnancy isn't obvious, and it's pretty, but I wouldn't have minded a mermaid-style dress exposing my bulge. I'm proud to be pregnant.

"You're absolutely glowing, Mallory. The color suits you." Vicky compliments me and extends the same praise to Cindy and Moira when they finish their fitting and stand alongside us in front of the mirrors.

Vicky and I talked about colors first thing once she decided to go for a fall wedding. She knew the white/silver theme she had hoped for wouldn't work, so we substituted burgundy for silver. Vicky chose roses in the wedding colors for her bouquet, her favorite flower, and mine.

After the fitting, Vicky hugs and thanks us all. "I can't believe this is really happening. Two weeks from today."

Two weeks can be an eternity when you're waiting patiently for something. It can also go by in a flash when you have a wedding to finish planning. With the big event at our house, Jake and I are having a cleaning and landscaping crew come in a few days before to make sure everything is in tip-top shape. Jake doesn't want me straining myself over this.

As I pull into our driveway next to Jake's new Honda, I glance toward the cornfield. Craig's still here, his car behind Jake's. Stepping out of my own vehicle, I walk behind the other two in the direction of the corn. Jake has told me numerous times to stay out of there, but I haven't always listened.

All day, I've been thinking about the helicopter last night. What was it doing above our field? I don't buy Jake's explanation. But surely, my imagination was in overdrive because of the dark and the storm. I can't help but question what exactly I *did* see and whether Jake knows something about it. Given the fact that he has kept secrets from me before, I can't stop imagining the worst.

And the worst is too horrific to imagine.

Chapter Five

The storm has damaged the crops. I'm no expert in the field, but it looks like bent-over stalks and flattened rows won't likely recuperate from the wind's whipping last night. But what do I know? I'm a city girl. The field corn has bounced back from storms before.

I walk along the side of the road, my eyes open for any sign of unusual activity. The sun warms my arms through the yarn of the sweater tunic. Most of the rainwater has dried up along the narrow gravel shoulder, but the field remains muddy.

What used to be parallel rows of ripening stalks almost ready for harvest are now interspersed with flattened green and yellow swirls. Maze-like tunnels appear as I stroll along the edge. And again, my mind wanders to thoughts of aliens, UFOs, and crop circles.

I wonder what it looks like from above.

Under the night sky, the corn comes to life, an underlying buzz and hum emanating from the dark arms and hands of scarecrows reaching out for me. During the day, it's harmless. Relatively speaking. I won't get a better chance than now to explore the field. Whatever lies hidden within is better discovered by me than by someone else.

I trudge through the field, my black flats sinking into the ground. The wind has created a path to follow. Motionless stalks listen as I push along the muddy trail, my eyes on the ground. Once I'm far enough in, a new crop catches my attention. The weed. Jake promised this year would be the last. We'll find some legitimate farmers to rent our fields from now on.

The corn is disorienting, if not menacing, during the day. Green and yellow stalks, tassels, and silk-topped ears surround me. Downed stems crunch under my feet, but I could swear the corn talks without my help, crackling out a warning.

Getout, getout, getout.

Crackle. Crackle. Crunch. Squish. Swish. The stalks advance, trying to wrap themselves around me, and I shove them aside. It's ridiculous, like looking for a needle in a haystack. I've heard horror stories of kids getting lost in the corn. But it *will* be discovered when the crop is harvested, which I hope won't be until after the wedding. Marijuana first, then the corn.

I need to get out, or they may not find *me* until after the wedding. As I'm about to give up and turn around, I catch a glimpse of something that doesn't belong in the middle of the field. I keep trudging through, reminding myself not to scream if it's what I think it is. The last thing I want to do is draw attention to myself and what lies in the cornfield. Not that anyone would hear me.

Numbness and brain fog grip me as I stand and stare down at it. On the dirt, the stalks surrounding it still standing tall, it lies as if gently placed there. I would have expected it to be broken, lying in pieces, yet it's still whole. Not what I expected, in more ways than one.

Breathe, relax, breathe, think, breathe. MOVE.

When it's found, it's going to raise a lot of questions. Questions for Jake and me. It's our property. How did it get there? Where did it come from? Who left it there?

Police. Media. Nosy neighbors. People who can't stop themselves from gawking at the train crash of our lives.

Why is there marijuana in your cornfield? What happened to your husband this summer? Do you have any connection to organized crime?

The only good thing about this is that I didn't imagine what happened. I'm of sound mind. Something did fall from the helicopter. This...and something else. I'm sure of what I saw. And scared to death.

This isn't the only thing lying in the cornfield.

Chapter Six

et rid of it.

It's the only thing to do. If I don't, it *will* be found. Our whole lives will be exposed to the public. Every embarrassing, shameful, disgusting detail of our perfect marriage. All the immoral, illegal acts we've committed. I can't let that happen.

Pull yourself together, Mallory.

Not having breadcrumbs on me, I pull out my phone, set the timer, and begin the slow trek out of the cornfield. Walking at a normal pace, eyes on the ground, counting steps, I follow the path (hopefully) that brought me to this location. I focus only on numbers till I reach the road.

Seven hundred twenty-four. I record the time elapsed and the number of steps on my phone. Then I repeat the process as I walk along the gravel back to our home, pop open the back hatch of my Toyota and bury the object next to the spare tire. For now. If I decide to return to the cornfield for a more thorough search, I'll have an idea of where to begin.

Do I tell Jake? We don't keep secrets from each other. Not anymore. But can I really be sure he hasn't been lying to me? It wouldn't be the first time. Or the second. Or the…

What if Jake's involved in this somehow? It's his cornfield. His weed. His criminal buddies. He claimed it was a medical helicopter. He said he didn't see anything fall from it. He pretended it was normal to have a copter hovering above our property in the middle of a storm during the night when no one would be likely to see it.

I enter through our unlocked front door and shout out, "Honey, I'm home."

Jake greets me with a kiss on the cheek, keeping his hands and body at a distance. Paint splatters decorate his jeans and shirt, and his hands are stained creamy white. "Did you have a good time with the girls?"

"Yes, it was nice to get out. I see you've been busy with the paint. Did you get any on the walls?"

Jake chuckles and tells me to have a look. In the new kitchen/family room, Craig kneels on the floor, brushing paint on pieces of baseboard that Jake has precut to the right length. The walls look fresher. He *has* been busy. A handful of empty beer cans line the counter next to a pizza box. Jake notices my eyes on the mess.

"I'll clean it up later," he says with a wink.

He's trying. A month ago, his obsessive neatness would never have allowed him to wait till later to get rid of the clutter. It's something he's working on. We've both got issues to work through. Professional counseling and our support group are guiding us to a better marriage. Not that there was anything wrong with it before.

"How was the dress fitting?" Craig asks. "Vick texted, but she's not telling me anything. She doesn't want to even talk about the dress in case it jinxes the wedding."

"I don't want to be the one to jinx it either, but I will tell you this. She's absolutely gorgeous."

Craig smiles, his brown eyes lighting up. It's obvious he loves her. I don't know why I didn't see it when they were keeping their relationship secret. They told us they wanted to be sure their getting back together was going to work out this time before burdening us yet once more with their on-again, off-again status. Craig has commitment issues, according to Vicky. Jake says Craig was sowing his wild oats but given an ultimatum between Vicky and playing the field, he chose the woman of his dreams. That's what happens, Jake says, when you find the right woman.

"You didn't forget Group, did you?" My eyes scan the trim laid on the plastic across the new flooring and the paint paraphernalia surrounding the two men. "I don't want someone tripping on their way to the meeting."

Our support group, composed of co-workers at The Auto Supply Warehouse, where Jake works as a supervisor, meets Saturday night from 7 to 8:30 in what used to be our den, off the kitchen. Fold-up chairs set in a circle create our meeting area in the center of the room, the sofa against one wall. Jake is going to relocate his office here, with his desk in front of the window for both of us to use, me for schoolwork, him for bill paying and other business. The file cabinet and safety deposit box are going to the basement next to his workbench. No more personal office for Jake. He's excited to convert it into a nursery.

"No, of course, I didn't forget. We'll clean this up in a few minutes. The trim can stay put to dry. We'll just steer everyone around it." Very un-Jakelike. But that's the way it's been the last couple of months. "Why don't you lie down while Craig and I clear out this stuff?"

I won't argue with that. Up the stairs I climb, my mind on what's in the back of my Toyota, what probably lies in the cornfield, and whether I should say something to Jake.

No more secrets. No more lies.

Nellie moves from the foot of the bed to curl up next to me. "Hi, sweetie. Mommy loves you."

Forty-five minutes later, Jake joins us, a towel wrapped around his freshly showered body. He snuggles into me and nuzzles my ear. "We've got time before the meeting.

The bedside clock tells me people will start arriving in half an hour. "Later. Your mom and dad will be here anytime."

Gloria and Steve help us lead the marriage support group. If anyone knows about the ups and downs of marriage, it's Jake's parents. They've dealt with alcohol addiction, physical and emotional abuse, denial, threats, and a long separation. Now they're back together, problems solved. Love conquers all, or so they say.

"It won't take long."

I roll out of bed and sit on the edge, eager to have a serious conversation. "Jake? There's something in our cornfield we need to talk about."

"I know, I know." Jake waves his hand in the air. "It's all taken care of."

"It is?"

"Yes, like I told you. After the crop is harvested, it's over. No more weed, just like there's no more gambling and no more borrowing money to feed my bad habits. No more illegal shit. You and the baby are my priority now." He flings his towel onto the floor and pulls me back down onto the bed. "Just give me a couple more weeks to sort things. And don't worry your pretty little head about it."

After making love, Jake pulls on clean clothes, while I decide what I was wearing earlier is fine. We brush our teeth and head downstairs in time to greet Jake's parents at the front entrance. "Gloria, how nice to see you." I greet her with a hug and give Steve a nod. Jake tolerates his father's presence, finally, after twelve years, but there's no display of affection forthcoming anytime soon. I follow Jake's lead out of respect for my husband's feelings. Steve may have handed over a half-million inheritance to us, but Jake isn't ready to embrace him back into the family.

"We brought Timbits," Gloria motions to the large box Steve holds. "Do you have the coffee on yet?"

"No, we've been busy, Mom. I'm sure Mal could use some help in the kitchen. Just watch your step. The floor's a bit cluttered with plastic and trim." Jake leads the way to the counter, where Steve lays down the box of donut holes, and Gloria sets up the coffee and tea so it will be ready to go for break time.

I head to the dining room to retrieve the fancy plates, cups, and saucers from the china buffet and place them on the runner of our antique table. When I return to the kitchen, Jake and Steve are visible through the open door of the adjoining den, setting up the folded seats. No conversation, just the clicking of chairs.

It's not the ideal father/son relationship, but at least they're in the same room and not beating each other to a pulp. Progress.

The doorbell rings, and I welcome the first couple. "Janice, Rod. How are you? It's a lovely evening, isn't it?"

Rod, who shares my husband's sick sense of humor, comments, "Jesus Christ! What the hell happened in your cornfield? It looks like a fat lady had a roll in the hay. Flattened it right down. Hope it pops back up again before harvest."

Jake shows his face, slapping Rod on the back. "Hey, man. What's up?"

"Not your corn."

"We had a helluva windstorm last night. Shit happens." Jake shakes his head.

The doorbell rings again. Sid and Gail. Beth comes up behind them, without Jason.

"You won't believe what I just saw in your cornfield as I drove by," she says.

I'd believe anything at this point.

Chapter Seven

"A couple of coyotes running through the downed corn. Do they attack humans? Is it safe?" Beth is pale, looking ready to make a run for her car and head back to town.

I can't say I blame her. Usually, they stay in the woods, but sometimes they wander onto the road at night. Jake says to yell and wave my hands in the air to scare them off if one comes near.

"Probably munching on some of your corn," Sid says. "They're visible now because the wind blew through the rows, but it's likely not their first time in there."

That's very reassuring. Jake flinches next to me, and I'm sure he's wondering whether the coyotes are munching on some of his special crops, as well as corn kernels. In my mind, I envision them chowing down on something entirely different, and nausea overcomes me.

I grasp my stomach with one hand and place the other over my mouth, rushing to the powder room. I spit out the bit of food that has risen in my throat, trying to calm myself and keep the rest of my stomach contents where they belong. I've never had a coyote approach me, but the thought of them feasting next to our yard is unnerving.

"Are you okay, Mal?" Jake knocks on the door and I rinse out my mouth, then join our guests in the meeting room, where they are seated in a circle. They stop chatting when I enter, ready to officially begin the meeting.

Our sessions are informal, with Jake facilitating. "So, how was everyone's week? Everything good on the home front?" He turns to his right when no one answers. "Rod, do you want to start the discussion?"

"Well, we're still married. But, the old marriage bed hasn't gotten any warmer, if you catch my drift. She's colder than my mother-in-law's soul. And that's as cold as it gets."

Janice gasps and nudges her husband, red creeping into her cheeks. "You don't need to tell the whole world our private business."

Jake tries to keep things on an even keel. "It's okay, Janice. What's said in Group stays in Group. That's what we're here for—a safe place to express ourselves and offer support." He turns the floor back to her husband. "Go on, Rod."

"Well, a man's got needs, you know what I'm saying? And if he's not getting what he needs at home, then he might be tempted to look elsewhere. Not that I'd ever do that," he holds up a hand to assure his wife, "but I've got plenty of women eyeing me up at the bar. Beating them off with a stick, let me tell you. Why just last night…"

As vivid as my imagination is, I have a hard time with that image. Rod's balding head, small stature, and beer belly aren't likely to attract a queue of women, even the ones who've bellied up to the bar too many times. And the words that he spits out don't add to his attractiveness.

"Why don't we give Janice a chance to respond?" Jake interrupts before Rod provides details from last night.

When her face isn't beet red, Janice is still a pretty woman, even with graying hair and a growing middle. "You don't know what it's like," she sputters. "I spend all day at work, then come home to more work. I'm exhausted at the end of the day. Maybe if you'd get off the sofa once in a while…"

And that's how the back-and-forth bickering between Rod and Janice gets started, just like last week, monopolizing the conversation. Jake turns to me and raises his eyebrows, looking for suggestions. He's new to this; it's our second week in, and this marriage doesn't look particularly salvageable.

I'm too meek to speak up and tell Rod if he'd get his bottom off the bar stool and help his wife out instead of flirting with other women, he might be better appreciated at home. But Gloria reads my mind and offers her sage advice. "You know, Rod, women find men who cook and clean extremely attractive. Maybe Janice would be less tired at the end of the day if you helped out with the chores. Cook her a nice meal after work, let her put her feet up. Clean the house on Saturday while she reads a romance novel. It just might put her in a better mood. *If* you catch my drift."

"Since when do men do women's work?" Rod looks back and forth between the other three men, expecting support, but gets none.

"I do my share," Sid joins in, raising his hand as if for permission.

Thank God. Maybe we can steer the discussion away from Rod and his needs. Sid and Gail are around our age, thirty-ish, but they've been married for longer.

"Somebody has to do it. Gail's too busy drinking most of the time." He mutters under his breath. "Just like her mother. That woman's a great example to wives everywhere, passed out on the couch most of the time. You won't catch her doing housework."

"Just because I have a couple of glasses of wine to wind down at the end of the day doesn't make me a drunk. And my mom's under a lot of stress at work lately," Gail says. "Besides, I don't see you giving up your beer."

"We all enjoy a good drink," Jake says, siding with Sid. "You can't blame a man for cracking open a brewski at the end of the day."

"Like I said, men have needs," Rod agrees.

The bickering between Rod and Janice, and Sid and Gail, continues, and I zone out. I'm not sure how Group is going to make anyone's marriage stronger. But it does put things in context when it comes to our own marriage. Relationships are messy. I've spent too much time reading romance novels and watching romantic movies. Life isn't like that. Some people pretend it is. And I've been guilty of that myself. But that's over and done. And Jake and I are coming out stronger than ever now that we're facing our problems head-on.

I'm fed up with perfect people who live perfect lives and don't understand imperfections.

Jake squeezes my hand in a plea for help and breaks me from my reverie.

I stand and wave my arms in the air, yelling, just like Jake told me to do if a coyote approached. "If I could say something..." They stop arguing and stare at me, shocked that I've opened my mouth for the first time during Group.

Jake did the talking for us last week, our first, making it sound like our home life was a sitcom. You know. The stupidest things happen and get blown out of proportion, but when you look back at them, they're positively hilarious. "I hid a bit of money from Mallory for my own use, but she found it. She stole it, and I practically tore the house apart looking for it." Like Lucy and Ricky Ricardo in the old *I Love Lucy* show on Classic TV. Cue the laugh track.

In an attempt to turn the topic away from sex and drinking and the ensuing squabble, I focus on something else Rod and Sid said. "I just wanted to say thank you to my wonderful mother-in-law, Gloria, who has been so supportive of our marriage. And if I may suggest, maybe you could spend some quality time with your own in-laws, find things you have in common. It might bring you closer together. I'm so grateful to have a great relationship with my mother-in-law."

As I smile at Gloria, Steve looks down at his hands, and I realize I've hurt his feelings by omitting him. Not only that, I've given advice I haven't taken myself. No quality time, doing things we have in common, has transpired between Steve and me. I still hate him for what he did to Jake.

"Break time," I announce. Insert caffeine and sugar. That'll put people in a better mood.

As everyone makes their way to the dining and living rooms, Gloria and I stop in the kitchen to prepare the snacks and beverages. I pull Beth aside and ask her to give us a hand. "Beth, we didn't get around to you yet. I see Jason couldn't make it tonight. Hope everything's okay."

Beth heaves a huge sigh. "I'm not sure."

"Not sure? Is he ill?"

"I don't know."

"You don't know?"

"No. He didn't come home last night."

I catch Gloria's eye. Deja vu. Jake didn't come home one night in July. I didn't know where he was for days. We both know what Beth's going through right now.

Yet she doesn't seem overly concerned.

"Have you called the police?" Gloria asks.

"No. He's done this before. Been out all night. Sometimes two." Beth wrings her hands. "Because of his…you know, his problem."

I do know. Jason, like Jake, has an addiction. Gambling and drinking don't mix well. They can lead to some serious consequences. I dread to think of what's going on in Beth and Jason's marriage behind closed doors.

And what, exactly, has happened to Jason? My thoughts go to the helicopter with the logo I recognized.

Chapter Eight

The alarm assaults us at nine o'clock. Jake plans to finish painting the rest of the family room today. He mumbles, "Just five more minutes."

I hold the railing as I descend to the first level to brew a strong cup of coffee for Jake and herbal tea for myself. Opening the fridge, I search for eggs, cheese, and ham slices. An omelet and buttered toast will get him going for the morning. He deserves it after the work he put in yesterday. If he keeps this up, the room should be done by next weekend. Just in time for the wedding the following week.

I whip the eggs and milk in a bowl, shred the cheese and ham, and bend down to pull the frying pan out of the drawer. Jake bounds into the kitchen, dressed in his painting clothes. "Coffee smells great! I'm all set, hon. Ready to get down to…"

He stops as I pull out the skillet.

"Omelet?" he asks. Our eyes meet, his blue-green irises questioning. "I can do that, Mal. Why don't you sit down at the table, and I'll finish this up?" He gently pries the frying pan from my hand and places it on the stove.

"No, that's okay. You've got lots of work ahead of you today. It'll just be a few minutes. Why don't you check out your social media while it's cooking?"

"If you're sure, hon…"

"I'm sure." I scoop a pat of butter onto the skillet and wait for it to sizzle, then pour the egg mixture into it and pop bread into the toaster.

"I think Group went well last night, don't you?" Jake looks up from his phone. "Got a lot out into the open. That's good, right? Communication?"

"Jake, honey, I know you want to help other people, but I'm not sure we're properly equipped to lead a support group." The cheese I layer onto the egg mixture melts, creating a gooey filling.

"Sure we are, hon. Look at us. We went through hell and back this summer. And we're stronger for it. We're good role models."

"Are we?" The toast pops up, and I butter it, then flip the omelet.

"We are." Jake reaches into the cupboard for plates and cups and pours a cup of coffee for himself and hot water over my teabag.

"What do you think happened to Jason?" I set two filled plates on the table and join Jake.

"Nothing. Didn't Beth say he sometimes stays out two nights? It's been two nights. He's probably home by now." Stringy cheese trails from his fork as he lifts it to his mouth. "This is delicious, hon."

The morning sun brightens the roomy white and oak-trimmed space. "Do you think you'll get done in time?"

"Sure, no problem. I'll finish up the walls today. Get those taps put into the sink. And I'll get the rest of the trim up this week."

"What about the lights?" We've been without kitchen lights for a week now.

"Sure, I'll get to it, hon. Soon as I can."

Once I've cleared away the breakfast dishes, Jake prepares the paint can and roller. "Why don't you pick up Chinese food later? I'll take a break, and we can sit out back for a while."

With the coyotes next to us? And God knows who else? I don't expect to go near the cornfield again without company and Jake's baseball bat. "Sounds good. I'm going to read in the living room while you're working. Maybe go for a walk later."

I pass Nellie in the hall as she scampers to check out her food dish while I head upstairs to shower and change into loungewear for the day. A nice, lazy Sunday awaits. After spreading the drapes open, I lie on the living room sofa and pick up the romantic suspense novel I borrowed from the library. According to the reviews, it's in the vein of *Rebecca*. Very Gothic.

I try to lose myself in the story, but thoughts of my own ghosts interfere. My parents' deaths, never far from the forefront of my mind, my recent near loss of my husband, haunt me every moment. Something else occupies my thoughts, as well.

"Jake, honey. I'm going for a walk," I shout down the hall. "Get some fresh air."

"Good idea. Looks like a great day for it. See you in a while."

"Maybe I'll pick some wildflowers." I grab a cloth bag, a couple of plastic grocery bags, and my hoodie from the hall closet. Removing the spare keys from the holder on the wall, I head out.

Sun warms my shoulders, but it's no longer the heat of summer. The coolness of a fall breeze permeates the late morning air, and the color of autumn decorates the trees. It will warm up by afternoon, but the days are getting shorter. I stop on the driveway, turn my head in all directions, unlock my back hatch, and scoop the dreaded object into my bag. I've never held one in my hands before yesterday. In fact, I don't think I've even seen one except on TV until I came across it in the corn.

Shovel.

I can't bury it with my bare hands. Somehow, I need to get to the shed without Jake noticing me skulk past the patio doors and the huge bay window in the room where he's painting. The copse of evergreens next to the driveway follows the length of the back yard. A perfect cover for a wife who needs to extract tools from the garden shed without her husband asking questions. What I don't need is for Jake to open up the back door and offer to give me a hand.

Hey, hon. I'll dig up the weeds for you. You go on in and rest. What's in the bag?

I cut through the evergreens and walk along the other side where he won't see me. Just marching along the meadow. I did say I was going for a walk. It's not a lie. I stop now and then to pick wildflowers and stuff them into the bag. I'll put them in a vase on the kitchen counter, proof that I was telling the truth about my reasons for going out.

Once I'm even with the shed, I cross over to our back yard and open the shed door. Jake says there's no need to lock it; people don't always lock even their house doors in the country. But I'm from the city, and leaving doors open is just asking for a gang or a serial killer to make themselves at home. Everything is in its place in the shed. Jake cleaned it from top to bottom and restocked my gardening supplies after some things crashed down off the shelves and walls this summer. The large shovel hanging on the wall isn't what I'm looking for. It will look too obvious if I lug that down the road. Instead, I unhook the trowel from the wall organizer and slip it into my bag. As I'm about to exit the shed, I spy the gardening gloves Jake bought for my birthday sitting on the bench, and I grab them. I don't want to have to explain the dirt under my long, pink fingernails. It's a good thing I noticed them or I wouldn't have thought to bring them. My mind is too occupied with thoughts of getting caught.

Back along the other side of the evergreens, I tread toward the road, stopping to look both ways for traffic that rarely ventures down our desolate stretch of farmland and scrubland. Our farmhouse sits on the outskirts of town, far enough away to be isolated, yet close enough to walk to our small town for supplies.

No one will see me.

Still, I need to dispose of it far enough away from our property that it won't come back to haunt me. I cross the road and keep walking to the left, past the woods on one side and the meadow on the other, then come to Paul and Linda's house. Only one car is parked in their driveway. That's good. They're out for a Sunday visit to see their kids and grandkids, which means they aren't staring out the front window, watching me.

At the corner of our road, I pull the hood over my head and continue to the right, following the edge of the forest. Evergreens interspersed with a variety of deciduous trees—maple and birch are the ones I can name—beckon me to lose myself in their midst. Ever mindful of eyes on me, I walk briskly as though I'm out for exercise. A few cars pass and meet me on this stretch of road that connects with the country highway leading to the expressway and the city. Ten minutes down the road, I enter the woods and follow a natural trail, just wide enough to let me through without suffering too many scratches and bruises.

I wander far into the woods so no one will see me from the road and take several steps off the trail into the bushes. Donning my gloves, I remove the trowel from the bag, dig a shallow grave, and deposit the offending object into the hole. If anyone does happen to find it here, it's not my problem. Or Jake's. Nope, we had nothing to do with it. Or anything else associated with it that might happen to be lying around or near our property.

Once I'm back on the road, I cross to the other side and speed walk until I reach our small town. By the time I get to Fletcher's FoodMart, I'm huffing and puffing, my hoodie wrapped around my waist, sweat dripping off my forehead. The bench in front of the store is a welcome respite.

"Mallory!"

I whip my head around to see one of our in-town 'neighbors' heading my way, heels clicking on the sidewalk. Her designer jeans and full makeup make me feel like a drudge in my lounge outfit and face set off with nothing but sweat and, most likely, dirt. "Jilly! How nice to see you."

"Yes, it's been a while. How's everything with you and Jake out on the old farm?"

"Great! We're renovating again. Making room for an addition to our family." I pat my stomach. This is the type of gossip I don't mind spreading through town. And, if anyone can make sure it spreads, it's Jilly.

"Oh, wow! Congratulations! When are you expecting?"

We converse about the baby and the renos for a while. I politely ask what's new with Jilly, which turns out to be a big mistake, because she tells me not only what's new with her, but also with half the population of Idlewood. I really need to pee.

"It's been nice chatting with you, Jilly, but if I don't get to the bathroom right now, it's going to be embarrassing. Have a great rest of the day."

I wave goodbye and head into the FoodMart, where I ask the young part-time clerk, Kim, if I can use the facilities. "I'm pregnant." I indicate my stomach.

She nods and leads me to the back, through the storeroom, into the employee area. On my way out of the staff bathroom, with its outdated plumbing, I'm stopped by a young guy on his way to the storeroom. "Excuse me, Ma'am. I don't mean to be rude, but it's kind of a store policy to check in parcels at the counter before using the washroom. May I see what's in your bag?"

"My…uh…oh, of course." I open it wide. "I've been out for a walk gathering wildflowers, and I needed to use the washroom."

Satisfied, he allows me to leave the store without making a purchase.

Half an hour later, I'm back home. Jake is still painting, and he's got a couple of empty beer cans on the counter. "I'm starving," he says. "Where were you so long? I thought we'd be eating by now. How about I take a break, and we go out for supper?"

"Just let me put these in water." I head to the laundry room and select a large vase for my flower collection, fill it with water, then bring it to the kitchen counter.

"Something to brighten up our new space," I say. "Just let me clean up, and I'll be ready to go in fifteen minutes."

After surreptitiously depositing the trowel and gloves back in the shed, I take a quick shower and change into fresh lounge clothes. Anything with an elastic will do. Jake has cleaned himself up downstairs and comes into the bedroom looking for fresh clothes. "So, what did you do on that long walk?"

"Gathered flowers, silly. That's where the bouquet came from. Oh, and I went into town. Saw Jilly. I hope it's okay, but I think everyone will know about the baby now."

"Huh." A smile spreads across Jake's face. I had worried he might not want to announce it to the world just yet. "Well, it's getting a bit obvious anyway." He pats my round tummy. "Unless people think you swallowed a bowling ball."

On our way out the door, Jake says, "Why don't we drive down to the lake for a picnic instead? We can bring takeout from the diner."

"Do you have time for that? What about the paint?"

"I finished off the walls. Trim can wait till tomorrow. I'll get up with you. Do some *work* before going in to *work*."

After we pick up supper, we embark on the twenty-minute drive to the lake. As we pass the woods where I dug earlier, I turn to observe Jake. His strong, stubbled chin is formed into a whistle, keeping tune to the radio. Crystalline turquoise eyes meet mine for a second. He's calm. Happy. Happy-go-lucky.

Should I tell him what I've done?

Chapter Nine

What the hell is that smell? It's like something croaked down there. A raccoon? Possum? Skunk? That's all I need. As if I haven't got enough shit to deal with.

It's not the usual damp smell. Musty, moldy, yeah. But there's something stronger. Something rotting. Rotten eggs? Cabbage? Spoiled meat?

Best to check out the furnace. I descend the wooden steps, one hand on the rail, the other plugging my nose. The stone walls and concrete floor in the main section hold little other than several metal shelving units along the left wall for storage of crap that Mal can't bear to throw out. Besides that, the water heater and softener, and the old furnace sit against the back wall. My wooden workbench takes up space on the right-hand side, tools hanging from the pegboard behind it, and shelves filled with more tools, paint cans, and nails and screws next to it. It's a dry enough (most times), if not user-friendly, basement. Mal freaks out because of the bricked-in windows, despite the brighter lighting I've had installed.

I walk around the three sides of the furnace, exploring the metal ducts, listening for gas leaks. My nose sniffs the air around it. I'm no expert on furnaces, but I don't see a problem. Opening the panel, I look inside to find the pilot light blue. All good, I guess.

My other thought is to check the level of groundwater. The hole containing the sump pump indicates the water is down to a safe level, and I find no evidence of leaks along the walls or floor. Friday's storm, more wind than rainfall, hasn't left its mark on the old basement.

Whatever crawled in here and died, I don't see it. Unless it's in the other part of the basement. Nothing much but dirt floor and rubble in there. It'll have to keep rotting for now. I'm not digging around for a body when I've got work to do. I promised Mal I'd get the new room done by the weekend. I'd better move my ass, or she'll have one of her crying fits if she comes home to find I've done nothing all day, and I'll be in the doghouse. Again.

Back upstairs, I root out a can of air freshener from the cleaning cupboard and squirt a few puffs down the steps. I light a couple of scented candles in the kitchen, hoping Mal will smell cinnamon and vanilla rather than dead skunk when she comes home to fix herself supper. Armed with the spray can, I head back to the stench and empty most of the can into the basement. Eventually, the dead thing will decompose and stop stinking up the house, but that might take weeks.

I don a mask to keep out both the offensive smell and the disinfectant (kills 99.9% of germs) with its summer fresh scent. It's the other .1% I'm worried about. Mixed together, the sweet smell just about knocks me out. But I need to get the job done. Keeping the basement door open for ventilation, I lift a piece of pre-measured trim off the skids where they've been sitting and set it into the miter box. Safety goggles on, I saw through neatly at a perfect 45-degree angle and do the same with the adjoining piece.

Two perfectly cut pieces that don't join when I tack them around the patio doors. What the hell? I measured everything exactly, down to the nearest tenth of an inch. The canyon-sized gap won't do. Back downstairs to shave off the angle for a tighter fit. The second fitting isn't any more snug. Try number three still leaves something to be desired, but if I keep trimming off more, the pieces will be too short.

Caulk and paint. Fill the gap. Who's going to look that closely, anyway? I will.

After struggling with damn angles all morning, I've almost forgotten about the smell. The rest of my mitering doesn't go much smoother, but it'll have to do. What does Mal always say?

You're too much of a perfectionist, Jake.

I slap a coat of primer on the trim, the smell of paint mixing with cinnamon vanilla drowning out the stench of the dead thing in the basement. Not quite. I might have to call somebody to get rid of whatever's down there. Exterminators or something.

I snuff out the candles and take another walk around the basement before getting ready for my three to eleven shift at the warehouse. This time, I venture into the other section, where remnants of the old foundation lay on the dirt floor. No one's bothered to clean it out in the last century.

The smell is definitely stronger here. I flip the light switch, scan the room, and nothing jumps out at me. No rats with razor-sharp teeth, no crazed raccoons. An earthy smell. But not like usual. What the hell is that stench?

The cistern sits in the middle of the room. Why is there a rope hanging down from it? As I move closer to the old stone well, the smell intensifies. A dead skunk at the bottom of the cistern? Stinking up my whole damn house. Reminds me of a country song.

I hoist my arms over the top of the stone structure and peer inside the dried-up cistern.

Holy shit! Shit, shit, shit! What the hell?

Chapter Ten

No way. No, no, no! No effin' way. This can't be happening.

Mal is going to go ballistic. The new area rug she bought for the family room, which *was* rolled up in the laundry room yesterday, is now at the bottom of the blasted cistern. How did it get in there? *I* sure as hell didn't throw it in there. I only had a couple of drinks yesterday. Four, tops.

Mal? Maybe she decided against the calming muted blue and neutral cream and thought she'd prefer loud and bold accents. No. My pregnant wife didn't roll up the rug, lug it down the stairs, and hoist it up into the cistern. If she changed her mind about the color scheme in the family room, she'd just return it to the store and get a different rug. No one in their right mind would dispose of a carpet they didn't want in the basement cistern. Not even Mal when she's *not* in her right mind. Would she?

So, who else has been in our house since yesterday afternoon? Nobody. Nellie. She can definitely be ruled out.

Back to me and Mal. I was in the kitchen all morning and half the afternoon, painting. Mal was in the living room, then went out for a walk. The basement door was within my sight the whole time. I would have noticed a rug heading down the stairs. Especially if it stank like this one.

I plug my nose and take another look at the rolled carpeting. Yep, that's our family room floor covering. Muted blue and cream.

And black shoes sticking out the end of it.

A scream startles me, and I turn and run for the stairs. Once I'm in the kitchen, I slam shut the basement door, but the sound follows me. Halfway across the back yard, I realize I'm the source of the screeching. I clamp my mouth shut and turn in all directions to make sure no one has heard me scream like a girl.

And, wouldn't you know it, the guys come running out of the cornfield wondering who's getting murdered. "What the fuck, Jake? You tryin' to bring out the entire police force?"

They're harvesting the weed today. I told them it has to be gone by the wedding. The last thing I need is parents of the bride and groom strolling along the cornfield, peering through the windblown stalks, and spotting something hidden, like in a Where's Waldo? book.

I spy with my little eye something that'll get you high.

'What is that, Jake?'

'Is that what I think it is?'

'Where is that smell coming from?'

'I just called the cops. You won't believe what's growing in your field, Jake.'

"Hey, Jake. Man, you look white as a ghost. What's up?" The guy with the abs and biceps waits for my answer.

Can't let them know about the body in the basement. Think on my feet.

"Sorry, guys. Just practicing my singing for church. I'm thinking of joining the choir. They're auditioning for a soprano. I think I sprained my vocal cords, but I'm okay now. You can get back to what you were doing."

The three men shake their heads, shrug their shoulders, and head back to their illegal harvest. Muscle Man turns back and comments, "I'd cut back on the weed if I were you. You're losin' it." He taps his finger to the side of his head.

Not exactly best buds of mine, but when they approached me with 'a business opportunity' a few years ago, I could hardly say no. I needed the cash. Easy money, tax-free. All I had to do was rent the land and let them sublease it to their own corn growers, then sit back and collect the dough. Tons of it. I would have been an idiot to turn them down.

And I'm no idiot.

But Mal, finding pot growing amidst the corn, didn't think it was legal. Tried calling the cops. Till I stopped her by explaining it was a perfectly legit deal, verbal contract and all.

I whistle my way back into the house, cool as a cucumber. Through the mudroom, into the kitchen, down the hall, into the front entrance. I need to leave for work in about an hour. Mal will be home in two and a half hours. Two ships—me, a smelly, decrepit garbage barge, and Mal, a beautiful sailing ship—passing on weekdays. Should I text her? Leave a note?

Don't go in the kitchen, honey. The smell from the body in the basement might be a bit overpowering. Especially in your condition.

Maybe she won't notice. If I spray some more air freshener around, it'll cover up the smell. I glance into the hall mirror and let out another screech. The figure staring back scares the crap out of me. Shocked ghastly face, brown hair flying in all directions from raking my hands through it, blue-green eyes bulging out of my head.

I need to calm down. Can't show up at work like this.

I start to hum, then sing to settle my nerves. *There's a body in our basement, dear Mallory, dear Mallory... Then bury it, dear Jakey, dear Jakey...*

Where did the body come from? Who put it there? How? Why? Who is the dead guy? Or dead chick? No. Men's black shoes, Jake, men's shoes.

Think.

Who would need to get rid of a body? Who would dump it in my basement?

And it hits me. I slap my forehead.

Dom. Of course.

I pull out my phone and call his personal cell. He answers with a lazy, "Jake, old buddy."

"What the hell, Dom?"

"Excuse me?"

"What's with the...the...thing in my basement?" Not sure who's listening. Cops, government, security intelligence.

"The thing in your basement?" he repeats slowly, as though he doesn't understand the words.

"In my cistern. Rolled up in a rug. Smelling to high heaven."

"I have no idea what you're talking about." His voice takes on its usual assertive tone, reminding me I'm the minion and he's the Boss.

"Have you seen the movie, Dead Dude in the House? If not, you should check it out. It's a real hair-raiser."

Silence on the other end.

And then, he says, "No, I don't think I've ever heard of that one. But thanks for the recommendation. I'll keep it in mind." He's cool. Guess that goes with the territory. Rich casino owner. Illegally obtained wealth. Illicit activities. Devil may care attitude. Gets what he wants. "Is there anything else I can do for you?"

"Yeah." At the risk of having him send over one of his goons to improve my manners, I say, "I thought we were done, Dom. I paid my dues. So, what the hell is this?"

"We *are* done, Jakey boy. I've got other things to do besides discuss horror movies, so I'd suggest you find another date for this one." And he hangs up.

Now what?

I can't haul that body out of there myself, even with the rope tied around it. With my luck, it would slip out of the rug, and I'd be left holding a smelly, calming muted blue and cream rug, dead dude still in the cistern.

If Dom refuses to remove his body, I'm going to have to ask for help elsewhere. And, if he thinks I'm going to open up my cistern as a body disposal service, he can forget it.

Craig. He'll help me haul it out. Dump it out in the woods somewhere. What are best friends for?

I shower the dead smell off, get dressed, spray the rest of the air freshener around the main level of the house, and head for work like every other Monday. The first part of the evening drags along, wandering up and down warehouse aisles, chatting with employees, overseeing the operation from my upper-level glassed-in office, and flipping through paperwork. When supper break finally comes, I text Craig and tell him to get his butt into my office. "Hey, man, what's up?" he asks after climbing the metal steps, lunch pail in hand.

"It's not what's up; it's what's down. In my basement cistern." I lower my voice and tell him what I discovered this morning.

He stares at me, then breaks out in a loud guffaw. Not the reaction you'd expect when your best friend tells you he found a body in his basement.

"Okay, I'm listening. What's the punchline, Jake?"

"There is a frickin' dead body, long dead as in no longer alive, in my basement cistern, rolled up in my wife's new rug. And I need you to help me get it the hell out of there before somebody finds it and arrests me for, I don't know, maybe *murder*."

"Have you been sampling some of that weed in your cornfield? I don't believe this. With Mallory being pregnant, you're getting high. And driving to work in this condition. What's wrong with you, man? Didn't you learn anything this summer? You need to treat Mallory with respect. If you don't take care of your wife, someone else will."

I don't doubt Craig, my best buddy, would love to step in for me, and in other circumstances, I'd gladly connect my fist with his jaw, but that's not the issue right now. Dead guy in the cistern takes precedence over my jealousy.

I repeat what I've said for the third time, with a straight face, but he still shakes his head.

"Come home with me after work, and I'll show you. We'll grab a couple of beers and sit on the basement steps; let the smell convince you."

Craig agrees to come home with me and have a drink, maybe crash in the guest room if he's too tired to drive home or to Vicky's place. "I'll let Vick know I'll probably be staying over."

"Great, thanks. Let's eat." I open my lunch pail, and the smell of sliced roast turkey hits my nostrils. I won't let my mind go there. "Mal packed me a nice turkey sandwich today. Beats bologna."

Speaking of Mal reminds me to text her.

Hey, hon. Go to bed early, get some rest. Craig and I are going out for a beer to celebrate his last days of freedom. We'll be late. Don't wait up.

I need to make sure my wife doesn't catch us transporting the body out of the basement. It'll really do her head in if she sees her carpet ruined.

Maybe I'll get Craig to let me dump the body in his car. That way, nobody can trace it back to me. Nobody would ever think to look in his car for signs of a body. He's too straight-laced to get involved in something like this. "I wouldn't want anybody coming across the body during the wedding. It might spoil the festivities. So, we'll have to take it far away."

He stares at me and raises his eyebrows but says nothing more.

It's not every day your best friend asks you to dispose of a body. But he owes me. I know damn well he slept with my wife. He's just lucky I didn't kill him.

"Time to get back to work," I say. "Meet you at my place later."

"You'd better sober up by then, buddy. I'm not letting you drive home in this condition."

I breathe a sigh of relief after he leaves my office. Problem solved. Craig and I will lift the dead guy out of the cistern while Mallory sleeps. Nobody's going to see us load the body into his car at night, out on our isolated back road. We'll drive it to the woods, carry the body in and dump it. Oh, and wear gloves, of course. And get rid of the damn carpet. Burn it in the fire pit in the backyard. Then, we'll have a couple of beers and go to bed.

Having a plan makes it easier to deal with.

What could possibly go wrong?

A lot.

I need to concoct a Plan B.

Not sure what that is, but one thing's for sure.

It's going to take one hell of an exterminator to get rid of that dead skunk in my basement.

Chapter Eleven

A sickening aroma hits me when I open the front door. Air freshener? What did Jake do? Empty out the whole container? I'd rather smell paint than this. The summer breeze scent is overpowering, and my stomach dry heaves in response. Maybe it's hormones, but I don't think I'll be buying that scent again.

The house needs a good airing. I wander from room to room, opening every window and door to allow the cool breeze to waft through and dissipate the odor. In the kitchen, the smell is stronger but mixed with something else. Candles have been lit, and the sweet smell of vanilla and cinnamon still lingers. I relight them, hoping the outside air and smells of baking will get rid of the sweet, pungent stench that pervades our home.

What was Jake trying to cover up? The paint smell wasn't that bad. The house has smelled before, many times, when skunks have made their nests under our porch or deck. A couple of times, they weren't deterred by Jake's homemade repellents, and he had to pay for professional pest removal.

The first time eau de skunk permeated our home and the animal refused to leave, Jake suggested he go to our local hardware store and pick up a hunting rifle. I couldn't bear to think of the poor skunk murdered just because he stank, so I insisted he have it removed humanely. When the animal removal guys came, they found a nest of five babies under the front porch. They were so adorable I asked if we could get them de-scented and keep them. Jake and the animal guys shook their heads.

"There's no frickin' way we're keeping skunks, Mal. Are you nuts?" Jake wouldn't even hear of pets of any sort, so I guess I shouldn't have been surprised by his reaction.

"It's illegal to have pet skunks," one of the removal guys said as he pulled out a cage. "They belong in the wild. The mom will come back and relocate them to a better spot."

"As long as it's not our back deck," Jake said.

"We'll repair any entry holes and check out the back deck, but there's no guarantee she won't return."

Whether it was the same skunks or distant relatives, they were a recurring problem. Many nights, we couldn't sit outside because of the smell and had to close our windows.

But this is a different smell. And it's inside the house, not outside.

Why does the house stink?

I text Jake and immediately get a reply.

Sorry, hon. I didn't want to have to tell you. A family of skunks crawled into the basement and couldn't get out. Dead skunks now. Don't go down there. I'll take care of it in the morning.

As if I *would* go down there.

Another text comes through.

I'll pick up some more air freshener. Love you.

I text back to tell him I love him, too, and he should pick up two cans of air freshener, but not the summer breeze scent, maybe something more neutral.

Having been put off food for now, I decide I'll forgo making supper and get takeout again. Closing the kitchen door most of the way, which we rarely do, I head upstairs to change out of my leggings and flowing blouse into jog pants and a loose sweater. Nellie gets up from her spot on the bed and rubs her head against my legs, meowing for supper, and although the thought of going back down there doesn't appeal to me, I'm a good mom, so I head to the kitchen and open a fresh tin of her favorite chicken pate, and scoop it into the bowl.

Nellie waits on the floor, her mouth agape, ears back, and nose crinkled, wide eyes asking, "What on earth is that smell, Mom?"

Feeling sorry for her, I carry her supper and water bowl up to the bedroom, then return to bring her litter box to our ensuite bathroom, fully closing the kitchen door behind me, as well as the bedroom door. We'll dine in bed tonight. No point in subjecting either of us to that stink and having us throw up our supper.

I text Jake again.

Going to town for pizza. Leftovers will be in fridge. Picking up air freshener myself and deskunking spray at the hardware.

Leaving Nellie on the bed, I head out to my Toyota to make it to the hardware store before closing time. Henry Wilkens, owner of Wilken's Hardware, rings through my sale. "Skunks 'neath the porch again, Mal'ry?"

"They crawled into the basement somehow and died, smelling up the whole house. Jake's going to get rid of them in the morning."

"Ahh, that's a shame. It'll be a real bugger gettin' that stink out. You should try settin' around a couple pails of odor neutralizer. Got just the thing here." He heads down an aisle and returns with a couple of industrial-sized pails. "These'll absorb the smell like a sponge. And leave a nice light lemony scent."

I accept his suggestion. Anything to get rid of that smell.

Henry bags my purchases and says, "Thanks for shoppin' local. And tell Jake to give me a holler if he needs help draggin' out the bodies and buryin' 'em.

I throw my stuff in the passenger seat and cross the street to Tony's Pizzeria to order an extra-large pizza, three-quarters meat lovers' and one-quarter pepperoni and mushroom. While I wait, I stroll down to Becky's Buns. There are doughnuts still available—half price during the hour before closing. Too good a deal to turn down. And the baby wants sugar.

When I return home, the smell doesn't smack me in the face as strongly since I'm prepared this time. I deposit my hardware bags in the hallway and leave my supper on the dining room table while I retrieve a couple of bottles of water from the fridge. Lugging my supper up the steps, I settle into bed with my iPad and select a movie on Netflix. Nellie sniffs the air, and I peel off some pepperoni for her.

Apart from my trip to the fridge with the leftover pizza, the rest of the evening is uneventful except for the text from Jake telling me not to wait up. I don't need to be told. With Nellie curled up next to me, my eyes close long before the end of the movie.

They fly open at 10:46. Something has startled me from my dreams of Baby Jakey, but I'm not sure what. Sitting up, I listen, barely breathing. I don't hear anything unusual, so I close my eyes.

But I can't shake the feeling that I'm not alone in the house.

Chapter Twelve

Shivers wake me. The curtains billow.

And I remember.

I had left the windows open to air out the house. The back screen door is latched, but the window is up; only the screen is locked on the patio doors. Someone could have cut through the screens and entered the house.

Get a grip, Mal. People leave their doors unlocked all the time out in the country.

Parting the curtains, I gaze upon the front lawn. No security lights have been triggered. On the road, the streetlight sheds a bright circle, thanks to Jake's constant calls and complaints to the township about it not working half the time. The air is crisp, stars lighting an indigo sky above the shadows of the forest. No coyotes wander along the edge.

I creep across the hall to the guest room. Through the open window, the moon and stars, aided by the garden solar lights, partly illuminate the back yard. The cornfield looms in the background. No unusual sounds other than the chorus of insects. No serial killer running across the expanse of grass.

Nobody is in the house.

But I should go down and lock up before someone *does* break in. I lock Nellie in the bedroom to keep her safe. Staircase lights on, hand, gripping the rail, I descend to the entryway and check the front door. Locked up tight. I creep through the house, closing windows, locking the patio door, and ending up in the mudroom. Several crickets have made their way in from the grass and are stirring up a racket. As I rustle through the recycling bin for a flyer, they stop their chirping. With the paper, I scoot one toward the door, holding it open enough to allow it to escape, but it's intent on staying. I try again with another cricket when I realize something's wrong. More than one thing.

I didn't need to unlatch the screen door. It swung open with ease. I could swear I had locked it earlier when I raised the window to let the air in. Anyone could have walked right in unseen and unheard, with me being none the wiser, especially with the kitchen and bedroom doors closed.

More unsettling than that is the squeaking behind me on the other end of the mudroom. Locking the back door, I tiptoe toward the noise.

Slow and steady, it crawls to meet me. From the basement.

Cer...eak. Cer...eak. Cer...eak.

From behind the cellar door, a light is visible through the cracks.

Someone's coming up the stairs! Not Jake. He isn't due home yet, even if he were coming straight from work. Not for another fifteen, twenty minutes. Unless...did he take off early to get rid of the skunks? And he's the one who left the back door open so he could take them directly out?

Of course. The sound that woke me was Jake coming home, as he normally does. I just wasn't expecting him to be home early, especially when he told me he'd be late.

"Jake? Is that you?"

Cer...eak. Cer...eak. Cer...eak.

"Jake? Honey?"

The creaking stops.

I touch my hand to the doorknob and debate whether or not I should turn it. I hold my ear to the door and listen for a few seconds. No sound. Did I imagine it? Or are there more skunks, live ones, down there?

The door opens a crack, and I peek through.

Pee uw. Dead skunks.

The smell overcomes me, and I slam the door shut, but not before I get a glimpse of what's down there.

The overhead LED fixtures shed light on the wooden steps, their shadows splayed against the wall. My eyes take in the concrete floor and stone walls, then the back of the door as it closes.

The creaking rhythm resumes.

Chirrup. Chirrup. Chirrup.

Crickets. That's all I heard. Just imagining someone on the steps. Jake must have left the lights on before he left for work. Some crickets made their way downstairs when he left the basement door open.

I return to my room and pull the duvet over my head, Nellie asleep in the same spot I left her. The rhythm of my heart pounds in my ears, blood whooshing through my neck and head. I concentrate on my breathing, trying hard not to hyperventilate, then throw down the covers as the thought of suffocation rushes through my mind.

Everything will be fine. I'll wait up for Jake. Get him to shut off the lights and send the crickets outside. Check the basement, make sure none of the skunks are still alive, wandering around down there.

Several minutes later, I jump as doors slam, and a rumbling draws me to the window. A dark van, no headlights, cruises past the house toward Paul and Linda's house.

Then everything goes quiet. Too quiet.

It's the middle of the night, Mal. Of course, it's quiet. What else do you expect out here?

Nellie curls up beside me, purring loudly in my ear. Jake likely won't be home for another couple of hours if he and Craig went out for drinks. I drift off to sleep.

My eyes spring open. Someone's in the house.

Maybe Jake's home? I pull back a corner of the curtains and look toward the driveway. I can't tell if his car is there. I don't think so, but it could be on the other side of mine. No headlights, tail lights, no security lights. No, it's not him.

Yet, I hear the distinct sound of a door opening and closing. Quieter than usual. It must be Jake, trying not to disturb me from my sleep. I open the bedroom door and stand at the top of the stairs, looking down into the dark. The front door is closed. I flip the upstairs switch and hold the railing as I descend to the main level, mindful of the creaks beneath my feet, hoping not to alert an intruder (should it happen not to be Jake).

Halfway down, I stop and listen. Scuffling sounds. Muffled whispers. Someone *is* in the house.

Creeping back up the steps, I call 911 emergency assistance to report a break-in. From the walk-in closet, I retrieve Jake's baseball bat and begin the trek down the stairs again, pausing halfway, my ears attuned to the voices coming from the back of the house, behind the closed kitchen door.

And I wait.

How long will it take for the police to get here?

Chapter Thirteen

Something rubs against my legs from behind, startling me into losing my grip on the metal bat and nearly sending me hurtling down the stairs.

Clunk, clunk, clunk.

Down the steps, the bat rolls, coming to a stop in the entryway. Nellie arches against my ankles. I freeze.

Police. They'll be here soon. I need to unlock the front door for them so they can rush in with their guns when they hear my screams. No sooner do I get to the bottom of the stairs than the kitchen door squeaks open, an inch at a time. I open the front door, preparing my escape route, and grab the spare car keys from the holder. Any second now, I'll come face to face with the intruders, and they'll shoot me before I can run or the police get anywhere near here. I pick up the bat, ready to swing, and run toward the kitchen, hoping to take them by surprise with a couple of good smacks before running out the door.

The door swings open. The bat is wrenched out of my hands. Arms wrap around me, preventing me from moving.

"Mallory! What are you doing?" Jake loosens his grip, and his eyes meet mine.

"Jake?"

Craig stands next to him, the bat lowered. "Mallory. We thought you were sleeping."

"I was. But I heard noises."

"Just us, Mal," Jake says. "Sorry we scared you."

"I thought you were going out for drinks."

"We decided to come home and have a couple of beers and polish off that pizza instead."

"I didn't hear your cars. And why didn't you come through the front door?"

"Left them down the road. Came in the back. Didn't want to disturb you, hon."

If my blood pressure wasn't through the roof already, my husband might just send it off the charts with his stupidity. "So instead of waking me, you thought you'd park on the road, sneak in the back door, scare me to death, put the baby at risk, and get whacked by your baseball bat?"

Jake has no response.

Craig raises his eyebrows, and his eyes flicker between Jake and me. "This wasn't such a good idea. Maybe I should go home. Leave you guys to sort this out."

"No!" Jake speaks up. "Everything's okay. Mal, we're just going to wind down after a rough day at work. Go back to bed. I'm really sorry we scared you, hon. I didn't want to wake you and the baby. You're sleeping for two now." He escorts me toward the stairs and pecks me on the cheek before heading back to the kitchen.

"Oh, no! The police!" I exclaim.

Jake whips around, mouth open, staring at me.

"I called 911 when I thought you were breaking in. They'll be here anytime."

"You did what??" He paces back and forth in the entryway, fingers running through his hair. "Called the police? Give me your phone."

He redials 911, explaining it was a false alarm, only to be told they need to check it out anyway. His eyes bulge out of his head, his face now pale, as he continues to pace, pulling at his hair.

"Jake? Are you okay?"

He raises his hands to his face, pulls them down, and they slide to his sides. "No, Mallory, I'm not okay. What the hell did you call the police for?"

"I thought you were intruders." I can't believe this. He's upset because I called the police to report a break-in?

"You have no idea, Mal." He says it with resignation. So unlike Jake. I'd expect him to get red in the face, insult my intelligence and mental and emotional state. I'd be prepared for him to yell, raise his hand to me, then stop himself in time and beg my forgiveness. But I don't expect him to stand there with drooping shoulders, looking defeated.

And I know, without a doubt, that my husband is keeping secrets again. Hiding something from me. What is it this time?

I glance at Craig, who has been quiet throughout all this, looking out of place as though he doesn't want to be here. His eyes don't meet mine. He's in on it, whatever *it* is.

Before I can get the truth out of them, a car pulls into the driveway. The security lights come on. The doorbell rings.

The police are here.

Chapter Fourteen

O*h, shit.*

How the hell am I going to explain this?

Oh, wow! Are you serious? I had no idea there was a body in my basement, Officer. No, I can't imagine how it got there. We've had skunks before, but never a human. This is our first. Maybe it came with the house?

If they search the house for intruders, they'll search the property. Illegal crops, grown to finance my illicit loans, which stem from my association with a mobster. And that's nothing compared to some of things my sweet little wife has done.

Mallory, fortunately wearing loose pajamas and not a silk nightie, opens the door for two uniformed officers. "Thank you for coming so quickly. Please, come in." She invites them to enter our home like they're guests coming over for a visit. "Officer Heinz, Officer Rombough. I'm so sorry to have brought you out. I called by mistake. It's just a false alarm."

Does she know these guys? She acts like they're friends.

"We're glad to hear everything's okay, Mrs. Shelton, but we're required to check things out when a call comes in." The older, graying guy with a bit of a paunch brings his hand up to his nose. He turns to Craig and nods. "Mr. Dunsmere."

Gazing at me, he says, "You must be Mr. Shelton? Jake?"

"Yes," I say guardedly, narrowing my eyes. "May I ask how you know us?"

"We responded to a call from Mrs. Shelton this summer. Actually, there were a number of calls to the station about you, Mr. Shelton."

Eyebrows raised, I put on my best wide-eyed, innocent look as though I have no idea what they're talking about. "Really?"

"Yes, we're glad things worked out for you."

So am I. "Yep. Had a lucky break."

The other cop, a young, tall blond guy, sniffs the air and turns his attention up the stairs, having heard a thump. "Anybody else here? Mind if we take a look around?"

"Nope, just the three of us. Ah, sure, knock yourselves out, but the place is a bit of a mess with the renos ongoing. Still painting trim." Maybe they'll assume it's the paint fumes stinking up the place.

I follow them upstairs. Halfway up, Nellie darts between their legs, nearly plowing them down. They check out our bedroom, bed rumpled from Mal tossing and turning, the ensuite and walk-in closet, then head across the hall to my office, the bathroom, and guest room. Satisfied no one is lurking there, they head back down.

From the entry, it's clear the living and dining rooms are empty. Officer Heinz notices the bags on the floor next to the powder room. "May I have a look?"

I shrug. "Sure."

He pulls out a couple cans of air freshener, two huge pails of odor neutralizer, and a bottle of deskunking spray. "I did notice you have a funky smell in your house. Something die in the walls?"

Another shrug from me. "Kinda smells like it."

When Officer Rombough opens the kitchen door, he takes a step back. "Whoa! That's enough to knock you out. I think whatever died is in the kitchen."

The five of us stand in the freshly painted kitchen/family room, eyes scanning the walls as though something might pop out. "Bad batch of paint, maybe," I suggest.

"Planning on a game of baseball?" Officer Rombough picks up the bat that is leaning against the kitchen wall.

"I was going to use it to defend myself," Mal explains.

His eyes flit from one to the other of us, and his mouth turns up in a smile. I can imagine what he's thinking.

Cute, sexy young chick with a baseball bat. Slave/master...

Officer Heinz continues through to the den. "Expecting a lot of guests?" He motions to the row of folding chairs along the wall.

"We host a support group on Saturday nights," Mallory says. "For people with marriage problems. We just started a couple of weeks ago."

"Either of you officers married? We've got room for more if you're interested?" I try to get their minds off the smell and onto their relationship problems.

It doesn't work. Officer Heinz heads over to the mudroom area. "Besides your cat, does anyone else live here? Or just the two of you?"

"Three." Mallory indicates her belly. "The baby."

I take the opportunity to direct Mallory back to the living room to sit down and rest for the baby's sake. "You need to get off your feet, hon. You've worked all day, and now this." I turn to the officers and explain she needs to get some sleep so she can deal with the kindergarten kids tomorrow, in hopes they'll get the hint and leave.

No such luck. They sit on the club chairs opposite Mal and ask if they can speak to her in private. Craig and I back away toward the kitchen, but I remain around the corner, listening.

"We'll let you get back to bed, Mrs. Shelton. But if you don't mind, can you explain what prompted you to dial 911 to report intruders in your home? You said it was a mistake. Can you clarify that?" Officer Heinz doesn't seem to understand the meaning of false alarm.

"Yes, once again, I apologize. I *thought* there were intruders, but it was just Jake and Craig. I was half asleep, and a noise woke me. When I got up to investigate, I heard whispering. Jake wasn't expected home till later, so I got scared and called 911, then grabbed Jake's bat. When I opened the kitchen door to take a swing at the intruders, I realized my mistake, but it was too late to cancel the call."

"You're not in danger, then?"

"No. Not with Jake and Craig home."

"You're sure?"

"Yes."

Officer Heinz reports an all-clear to dispatch. He seems satisfied and rises to leave. "We won't take any more of your time. Glad to see everything's fine. Good night, Mrs. Shelton." He opens the front door.

I escort Mal upstairs to bed and tuck her in. When I come back down, the entryway is empty. Thank God.

I hurry down the hall to the kitchen. "Craig? Where are you? We need to get rid of the…" I open the door and come face-to-face with Craig and the two officers.

"Get rid of what?" Officer Heinz asks.

"The smell. We need to use the air fresheners Mal bought and open up the windows. I thought you guys were leaving."

"We were, but I noticed we missed checking out a room." Officer Rombough points to the basement door.

"That's just the basement. We don't use it. My wife won't even go down there. It's old and musty."

"Actually, now that you mention it, I think the smell is coming from behind the door." He touches the doorknob, eases open the door and wrinkles his nose as the lingering stench wafts up the stairs. "What have you got down there? A dead body?" He chuckles.

Craig, who has been quiet this whole time, suddenly decides to speak, jumping in front of the stairs, blocking entry. "You don't want to go down there."

"Skunks." The high-pitched sound coming out of my mouth betrays me. Calm, cool, collected. With a dash of scared little girl. I need to pull it together. I swallow, take a deep breath, and try again. "We've been having a problem. With skunks. And rats. I think the rats won." I'm still squealing like a pig, despite my efforts to act nonchalant.

Craig backs me up. "It's a mess. Dead skunks, half-eaten. Rats the size of a small dog. Jake asked me over after work to help clean it up while Mallory sleeps. She'll move out if she finds out about the rats." His face is ashen, but his words are steady. As though he doesn't really believe they're going to find a body down there, but you just never know with Jake and Mallory.

"Yes. We'd better get to it, or we'll be up all night. Sorry to have taken so much of your time, Officers." Hint, hint. "But, if you're not busy, maybe you'd like to help with the skunk disposal." And maybe I can bluff my way out of this.

Officer Rombough folds. He closes the door halfway. "It's the end of our shift. I need to get home to my wife."

"We've got another fifteen minutes. We could give you a hand," Officer Heinz offers, calling my bluff.

I counter bluff. I've been playing poker long enough to know how this goes. "Sure. I'll need to grab shovels out of the garden shed. Some of the little buggers crawled into holes to die, and we'll have to dig them out. And we can whack the rats with the back of the shovels."

"Okay. We'll meet you in the basement." Officer Heinz, who knows a bluff when he hears one, opens the door again while Officer Rombough shrugs and takes the first step down.

Shit.

Maybe they won't look in the cistern.

The lights are still on in the main section of the basement. My miter box lies on the bench, the saw next to it. "I was cutting some trim before work. Must have forgotten to switch off the lights."

"I thought you said you don't use the basement," Officer Heinz reminds me.

"We don't. Except for my tools and storage. I've been doing the cutting down here to keep the sawdust from the new kitchen/family room we just paid a fortune to renovate. I'm doing some of the finishing touches myself to save money." My voice has lowered a couple of pitches. If I tell the truth, they'll turn around and leave. "And I check the sump pump and furnace now and then. The fuse panel is down here. Water heater, softener. But we don't use it as living space." I turn to lead the way up the steps, having given my tour of the basement.

"What's in there?" Officer Heinz points to the opening leading to the old foundation and the cistern.

"Nothing. Rubble."

"Skunks? Rats? Where are they? It looks pretty clean in here." His eyes scan the swept concrete floor, neatly stacked shelves.

Officer Heinz disappears through the opening to the older section of the basement. This is it. He's going to find the body. A dirt floor, a stack of rubble, an old cistern, and a dead body.

A body? No, Officer, I had no idea there was a body in the cistern.

Craig flashes me a look as we follow Officer Rombough into the cavern-like room. I interpret it as: There'd better not be a body in there, or you're on your own.

"It stinks in here." Officer Rombough searches the room for the source of the smell, swatting away flies.

"Like I said, dead skunks. They've burrowed into the rubble and the holes in the foundation to die."

"Where are those shovels you said you'd bring?" The young cop looks at his watch. "It's getting late."

"What's in there?" Officer Heinz points to the cistern.

"Nothing. It's dry. Used to collect rainwater." I turn toward the room opening to fetch the shovels. When you bluff, you can either fold, or keep bluffing and hope your opponents will fold.

Officer Heinz ups the ante, and I freeze. "How about we have a look?" He climbs the first two steps of the metal ladder along the side of the cistern.

Craig screams loud enough to wake the dead guy.

"You okay?" Officer Rombough asks.

"He's a bit squeamish," I explain.

"Aw, shit! That's disgusting!" Officer Heinz clamps his hand over his mouth.

Officer Rombough stands on his tiptoes to peer over the edge.

Craig eyes the doorway and contemplates making a run for it.

I take baby steps toward the cistern, hands behind my back, ready to be cuffed.

My bluff's been called. And I'm holding a losing hand.

Chapter Fifteen

I drag myself out of bed at seven, shutting off the alarm to allow Jake a few more hours of sleep. He came to bed late last night while I was sleeping, sometime after two, between my bathroom trips. I reset the alarm for ten and head for the shower.

Once I'm dressed for work, I grab a doughnut out of the box on the dresser and head downstairs to make a cup of tea. The house still smells enough to make me gag, but Jake has sprayed the rooms again and set out the odor neutralizers. While waiting for the kettle to boil, I throw the towels into the wash, add citrus-scented detergent, and leave the laundry door open to aid in dissipating the skunk smell. On my way out, I notice something sticking out beneath the back door. I unlock it and pick up the black rectangular piece of plastic, which I'm sure wasn't there last night when I scooted out the crickets.

Printed on the front is the River Grand Casino logo, with its roulette wheel; it's a VIP Platinum Member Card. Jake must have dropped it last night when he came in through the back.

I don't believe this. Jake promised he'd stay away from the casino. I watched him cut up his membership card nearly two months ago. Now he's right back at it.

The whistle from the kettle mimics me blowing my top. Red-hot anger flashes up my neck and face, steam rising from my head. How could he do this to me and our baby?

No time to wake Jake and confront him. I need to get to work. The first bite of doughnut sticks in my throat, and I pour a glass of orange juice and swallow several times, pushing it down. I won't let him spoil my day. I chew smaller bites and consider how best to deal with Jake. Nothing has helped wean him off his gambling habit before. Why did I think the near end of our marriage this summer, due to his overwhelming debt, would change things? What does it matter to Jake if we have a baby to think about now? How can counseling and the support group make a difference? Once an addict, always an addict. Jake's Mom knows. Both she and I have been enablers, lending him money when he pleaded with us.

That's over now, though. No more bailing him out. And if that weed doesn't disappear out of our cornfield by next weekend, Vicky and Craig's wedding might be closely followed by Jake and Mallory's divorce. I won't have my child raised like this.

The chamomile tea does little to calm me. With a fifteen-minute drive ahead, I need to stop seething, or I won't be fit to sit behind the wheel of a car. I won't argue with him. He'll just make excuses and promises. I'll threaten to withhold my money from him. He'll gamble away his grandfather's inheritance. I'll pack up and leave.

There has to be a better way.

Leaving the card on the counter next to the coffee maker, I grab my purse and sweater and head to the car. When he wakes, he'll find it and rack his brain trying to figure it out.

How did my card get here? Did Mal see it? Am I in deep shit?

I won't say anything. Let him worry. Listen to his lies. Watch as he digs a deeper hole.

With the car window down and the radio tuned to a classical music station, I try to get my mind off Jake's gambling and enjoy the beautiful morning. Sunlight filters through trees, the sky as clear as the country road leading to the town where my school is situated.

Sue, the kindergarten teacher I assist, greets me with her usual bubbly enthusiasm. "Hi, Mallory. What's new?"

My lying, gambling, drug-growing, secret-keeping husband is up to his old tricks, but that's not exactly new, is it?

"Not much. We've got a bit of a skunk problem around the house again.

66

Same old."

"Oh, that's too bad. Are you going to need to bring in the exterminators again?"

"Jake's trying to sort it out."

"Well, good luck to him. You don't need to be smelling that, especially with the baby."

We spend the quarter hour before bell time discussing this morning's plans, then the children stream through the hall. We welcome them outside the door as they enter the classroom to hang their jackets and backpacks and take their indoor shoes out of cubbies. Everyone meets at the carpet for circle time.

The carefree, expectant little faces beam at us as they sit cross-cross, applesauce. So cute. In a few years, little Jakey will be one of them.

The smile on my face fades as thoughts of Jakey being an only child with a single parent intrude into my head. Would we be better off without Jake? Maybe? But no, I won't let Jake break apart our family. I love him too much to give up on us. I'll fight to save my marriage. He fought for me when I was at my lowest, grieving and guilt-ridden over my parents' deaths, bringing more comfort than my therapy and the drugs ever could. Jake stuck with me when I hit rock bottom again this past summer, suffering a breakdown of epic proportions.

At lunchtime, we assist kids with opening their containers and pushing straws into juice boxes. I consider talking to Sue about my concerns, although I've never confided my personal problems to her before. It's a work friendship, not a wear-your-heart-on-your-sleeve type of relationship. But I need to let out some of this anger.

"Sue, do you have a few minutes to talk?"

"Sure, Mallory. But I've got yard duty. When I come in…"

"No, it's okay. You need to eat your own lunch and relax. It's nothing. I'll see if Brad's available."

"Catch up with me outside, if he's busy."

"Thanks."

Confiding in Brad seems like a betrayal of my own husband. My ex-boyfriend, though only in the loosest sense, isn't on Jake's buddy list.

On my way to the staff room, I encounter him heading there from the opposite end of the hall. "Brad, hi."

"Mallory."

"Do you have a minute?"

"Sure, for you, any time. My room?"

We walk side by side into his Grade 6 classroom, and he closes the door behind us. If people talk, let them. Everyone knows we dated before I met Jake. No reason why we can't continue to be friends. Except for Jake's jealousy.

Brad sits opposite me at the student worktable, his muscled arms resting on the surface, brown eyes set in an amiable face. "So, what's up?"

"He's gambling again."

"Oh, Mallory." He runs his hands through his combed-back black hair. "I'm sorry to hear that. I thought he was getting help."

"He is, but I guess it isn't working."

"These things take time. But you'd think he would have learned a lesson after...you know. What happened this summer." Brad shakes his head. "I can't believe he'd put you through that again. If he really cared about you... But, I don't know, I guess it's tough beating an addiction. What does he have to say for himself this time?"

"Nothing. I haven't talked to him about it."

Brad rubs his stubbled chin. "You should. Talk to him. But with a mediator. You don't want to lose your cool."

"I will. Maybe Craig can talk some sense into him."

"That's a good idea. And see if you can meet with the counselor more frequently. What about your support group?"

"They've got enough of their own problems." Don't get me started on Rod. Things could be worse than having Jake for a husband. Poor Janice.

Gazing across at Brad, I consider whether I would have been better off with him, a good friend, steady and reliable, rather than Jake with his magnetic pull and the physical attraction between us. Brad would have taken care of me, made a good husband. Jake, on the other hand, causes me

68

a lot of grief with his laid-back attitude toward life.

Chill out, Mal. Everything'll work out. You're gonna give yourself a heart attack worrying all the time.

But Jake's the one who rescued me from the darkness. He made me feel alive and *want* to keep living. He made me laugh. I can't give up on him. I can make him squirm for a while, though.

"Thanks."

"I didn't do anything." His eyes bore into mine. "But, you know I'm here if you need anything, right?"

I nod and rise. "We'd better eat before the kids come back in."

In the staff room, I sit on the sofa, feet up on the coffee table, and nibble my ham and cheese sandwich, washing down small bites with apple juice. My phone buzzes, and I check the message from my aunt, then forward it to Jake to remind him where his priorities lie.

And they better not be with the River Grand Casino.

Chapter Sixteen

I'm drowning in a dry well. Filled with rats. Smelling like skunks. Their teeth saw through the fingers on my handcuffed hands, spilling maggots among dead skunks lining the concrete. An alarm sounds. The sump pump can't keep up. Water floods the basement. The cops laugh. "Twenty years, Jakey."

I bolt out of bed, swatting in all directions.

Man, oh man, that was one hell of a nightmare.

In the shower, I let the spray wash away the memory of skunks, rats, maggots, and whatever else invaded my unconscious mind and run through what happened last night.

As the officers gazed into the cistern, I remained cool. Best to act shocked when they asked what a carpeted body was doing in my basement.

Just shut up, Jake. Keep quiet. Don't let on you know it's there.

"Is there a problem, Officers?" Squeaky girl voice again, not how I envisioned it in my head.

"I'd say so," Officer Rombough stated, turning toward me, eyebrows raised.

"I think we've found your problem, or part of it, anyway," Officer Heinz added.

"Really?" Nonchalant, keeping it casual. As if I hadn't a clue.

"Come here, have a look."

I sauntered over.

And I might have pulled it off, but my good old buddy Craig screamed, "No!" backing toward the door. "We don't know anything about that. We just found it," he blurted out. "No idea how it got here."

And he ended with, "I'm calling my fiancée. She's a lawyer."

"I don't know. You *might* be able to sue the people who sold you the house, if they didn't disclose this before you signed the paperwork," Officer Heinz said.

Sure, Officer. I'll sue my mom for the body in the basement. I don't know why she dumped it there and didn't tell me about it. Or why she covered it in Mal's new rug.

"But it might be cheaper to call in the exterminators," Officer Heinz continued.

"Exterminators?" To remove a dead body?

I hoisted my arms over the top of the cistern, bracing myself. "Aaaah!" I stumbled backwards. My screech made Craig seem like the tough guy.

"Not rats," Officer Heinz stated. "And I haven't seen any skunks yet."

"I...uh...I didn't know about...that." I pointed to the cistern.

"I don't think a couple of shovels are going to take care of this. But the experts should be able to handle the situation."

The evening ended on a sour note.

The whole thing put me off pizza last night. I don't think I have much of an appetite for breakfast, either. I spot the doughnut box on the dresser. Maybe I can handle a couple of those. I throw on some pants and carry the box downstairs, set it on the living room coffee table, and head to the kitchen to make coffee.

The smell still permeates the house, although the body has been removed. I open the patio doors and kitchen windows, then make my way around the rest of the lower level, allowing the morning breeze to flow through. When I return to the counter to pour my coffee, something grabs my attention.

A black casino VIP card stares up at me.

How did that get there?

A body in the cistern? A casino card on the counter? Maybe if I ignore it, it'll be gone by the time I get home from work.

I bring my coffee back to the living room, leaving the card where I found it. After a couple of doughnuts, I text Craig.

You up yet? We've got some digging and burying to do.

Chapter Seventeen

"You could have just knocked on the door," Craig mumbles, coming down the stairs and stumbling into the living room minutes later. "I didn't want to disturb your beauty sleep. Although, by the looks of it, a couple more hours wouldn't help anyway." I take in the bags under bug eyes, the mop of disheveled brown hair, and the creases in his face that weren't there before I involved him in the 'you'll never guess what's in Jake's basement' fiasco.

"This isn't funny."

"I didn't say it was."

He ambles to the kitchen to pour a cup of coffee and brings back the black VIP card. "What's this? I thought you swore you were done with gambling. You promised Mallory."

"I am done. It's not my card. I have no idea where it came from. It showed up there this morning."

"Like the body in your basement just showed up?"

"Yeah, like that."

"You know, you really had me going there for a while. And if it was April 1st, I might have expected this, but in September? A pre-Halloween prank?"

He's giving me way too much credit. Even I couldn't think up something this bizarre. But, as luck would have it, things seem to have worked out rather nicely. Now, it's just a matter of disposing of the bodies.

When the officers gazed down into my cistern, they *did* find a body, just not the one I was expecting. My shock was genuine, no academy award performance required.

"That's a possum, not a rat. And the rest of them…an infestation you need to get rid of. I'd hate to think how you guys would react if they actually were rats the size of dogs," Officer Heinz stated last night, looking down at me and Craig like we were a couple of sissies.

The squashed possum lay at the bottom of the cistern, surrounded by an enclave of mice munching on maggots, beetles, and assorted tidbits of flesh, flies swarming around the carcass. It smelled worse than you'd expect, but the sight of the rodents dining was enough to make a strong man upchuck his own meal. Good thing we hadn't got to the pizza yet.

"Like I said, call the exterminators. If there are this many critters in the cistern, Lord knows what else you've got hiding in that rubble. That should have been hauled out before you bought the place. A few shovels aren't going to clear out this mess." Officer Heinz pointed to the pile of debris along the back wall. "And you better ask the experts to check the basement for entry holes to find out where all the various vermin are coming from."

As the officers exited through the front door, the odor of freshly sprayed skunk hit our nostrils. "It's worse out here than inside. Glad I live in the city," commented Officer Rombough, screwing up his face under the porchlights.

The police car roared to life, and we waved to them as they backed out of the driveway, but not before a skunk raised his tail beside their front tire.

"Well, I don't think they'll be back anytime soon," I said, closing the door.

Despite the memory of what lies in the cistern, Craig now wolfs down a couple of doughnuts with his coffee. "I bet you weren't expecting the cops to be part of your little joke."

"Nope. Didn't expect cops to show up."

The rest of the morning and early afternoon are spent getting rid of the unsuspecting possum, who I'm sure was the victim of a dead body rolled up in a rug and thrown into the cistern, and the dead mice, murdered by Craig and me with the rat poison we threw in last night after the cops left, and the flies and related larvae and insects, which we sprayed the shit out of before heading to bed and having nightmares of epic proportions.

Ankle deep in dead mice, Craig holds the garbage bag while I shovel in bodies. The masks covering our faces don't improve the smell, and the old clothes and gloves we're wearing will need to be thrown out, but not having hazmat suits handy, it's the best I can do.

Fibers of chewed carpet lie interspersed with mice and insects. Scraping out the mess down to the bottom of the concrete floor, I uncover a round yellow and black token.

Craig notices it. "Is that what I think it is?" He picks up the clay casino chip and twirls it between gloved fingers. "What's going on, Jake?"

I feign ignorance, although I've got a pretty good idea of what's going on. Casino card, casino chip, dead dude in the carpet.

Craig climbs the ladder we had the sense to lower into the cistern before climbing in ourselves and removes the bag of bodies.

"Good thinking about the ladder, buddy," I say, complimenting him on his problem-solving. Left to my own devices, I'd probably be stuck down here hollering for Mallory to get me out when she got home from school. No guarantee she'd come to my rescue, either. "I'd hate to be trapped in here, trying to hoist myself out."

We drag the garbage bag and bury it across the road in the woods. "And that's that," I exclaim, brushing my hands together. "Thanks for your help. You're a real buddy."

In the mudroom, we remove our filthy clothing and stuff it into another garbage bag. I head for the ensuite shower while Craig de-contaminates in the shower off the mudroom. I bring down clean clothes for Craig to borrow. The towel won't be considered appropriate work attire, and his own clothes, which we didn't think to throw in the wash, still carry last night's basement aroma. We meet back in the living room.

"Lunch?" I raise my eyebrows, wondering how his stomach is holding up. "We've still got pizza."

"Sure."

We eat in front of the TV, Netflix tuned to a Clint Eastwood flick. Craig surprises me with a question. "What happened to the body?"

I gape at him, wide-mouthed, pizza not fully swallowed. I force it down. "What body?"

"I saw the carpet fibers. The poker chip. I smelled the dead smell. And I saw your reaction to the cops. You expected them to find something."

Bluff your way out, Jake.

The corners of my mouth turn up slightly. I chuckle. "Gotcha." And I roar like I've pulled the mother of all pranks.

Eyebrows raised, he remains serious, staring at me as though still expecting the punchline. Just great. When I told him there was a body, he didn't believe me. Now that there's no body, he thinks I'm lying. I can't win.

"Come on, Craig. How would a body get in my cistern?" At this point, it's best to leave him out of it.

"You tell me."

"Look at the time. We'd better hustle." There's still plenty of time before work, but I don't want to get into a discussion about bodies, Dom, and whatever the hell this shit is all about. "Thanks again. I'm going to stop in at the store to get a few dozen mouse traps. Want to come along?"

He surely won't discuss the body while we shop at my local hardware. Or at work. In a few days, he'll have forgotten all about it.

Especially with the wedding coming up.

Chapter Eighteen

She's pissed off about something again. It's been a rough couple of days, and I could use some lovin', but I've had nothing but the cold shoulder since Monday night. No sex, no kissing, no snuggling. Not even talking. It's not my fault the house stinks. And *I'm* not the one who called the cops. And when she texted to say her aunt and uncle were buying a crib for the baby, I texted back, saying that was great.

What did I do? Where did I go wrong?

Tomorrow is Friday, and I've still got work to do on the kitchen. Maybe that's what's bugging her.

I touch her shoulder. "Mal, is everything okay?"

"Mmhm. Just tired." Her tone indicates there's more to it as she moves to the very edge of the bed.

Communication. It's very important in a marriage, according to our counselor. Honesty and getting things out in the open. I'm not sure how that applies to dead bodies in the basement. With Mallory's delicate condition, it might be best to keep it to myself.

"Is it the kitchen? I'm almost done, hon. Just a few more pieces of trim. I'll get the taps in tomorrow and lights and blinds by the weekend. Then Craig and I can get the new furniture out of the garage, and we'll be all set. You can decorate it however you want. We'll go on a shopping trip..."

She mumbles into her pillow, stiffens when I stroke her back. "The carpet."

"The carpet?"

"Where is it?" She flicks on the night table lamp so she can watch my response.

"Oh, the carpet."

Think, Jake, think.

"I unrolled it to see how it would look in the new family room. I can't believe they sold it to you in that condition. Runs through the middle of the pattern, like a cougar used it for a scratch mat. I called the store and had them haul it away. The new one will be here in a few days." I'll order it first thing in the morning.

"Don't lie to me." She rolls over. Finally. "You sold it, didn't you? Did you sell the new furniture out of the garage, too?"

"What??"

"To finance your gambling."

"No. Of course, I didn't sell it. I'm not gambling, Mal."

And she becomes talkative all of a sudden. I move to my edge of the bed, my eardrums in danger of bursting. "You LIAR! No more secrets, you said. LIAR! You promised you wouldn't. How could you? You're right back at it, in the casino, involved with Dom again, throwing our money away. Did you blow your inheritance already? Now you're stealing my rug?"

"No, no, Mal. I'm not." I roll out of bed and back away. "Honest."

"Honest? You're a pathological liar."

"I swear I'm not gambling. On our baby's life."

That may have been the wrong thing to say.

"GET OUT!" She throws a pillow at me. "You can sleep in the guest room."

"But honey…"

"Don't. Or you'll be spending the night in the garage. I know it's an addiction, Jake, but the lying is the worst of it."

"But I'm not…"

"The garage. Or do you prefer the shed?"

I hold up both hands, in an attempt to shield myself from further flying objects and to indicate my surrender. "Okay, okay. I'll tell you the truth. You deserve that, Mal. I didn't want to upset you, with the baby…"

"Upset me? I'm not upset, Jake. I'm…" she blubbers. "I'm disappointed."

"Don't cry, honey. It's not what you think. Give me a chance to explain."

There's no way she's going to believe my story. But I tell her all of it. The body in the cistern, wrapped in her rug. My call to Dom. Telling Craig about it. The cops checking out the basement. The body disappearing. I leave out the possum and mice. I'm already in danger of having her leave me. The body is bad enough. No point in adding a rodent infestation.

I back closer to the door, ready to head to the shed after completing my explanation.

"A body in the cistern?" She rolls out of bed. My hand is on the doorknob. "You found a body in the basement?"

"I know it sounds crazy…"

"It is crazy. How would a body get into our basement?"

"Maybe Dom put it there? And he won't admit it."

"Dom?" She walks toward me.

"I'll just head to the shed, hon."

"And did Dom leave the VIP card in between the back doors?" She stares at me, mouth slightly open, brows drawn together.

Between the back doors? Not on the counter? "I found the card on the counter Tuesday morning, Mal. I wondered where it came from."

Mallory brings a hand up to her mouth. "I don't believe this."

"You have to believe me, Mal. It's the truth."

"I do believe you, Jake." Her voice is quiet now, scaring the shit out of me.

I stand still, waiting. For a slap. For a kick out the door. For a divorce threat. Instead, she says, "It's time for me to tell the truth, too."

Chapter Nineteen

"Friday night, I saw something fall out of the helicopter. But you didn't see it, and I didn't say anything in case I had imagined it. I didn't want you thinking I was losing my mind. A body dropped into our cornfield." I confess, hoping he won't suggest I visit Dr. Falcon to up the dose on my anti-anxiety meds. I've been cutting down, out of concern for the baby, although my doctor assured me the pills were safe as prescribed.

Jake's jaw drops, then he releases a huge sigh as though he was holding his breath, takes my hand, and guides me back to the bed. We sit side by side, his eyes not leaving mine. His brow creases as he tries to sort through what I've confided in him. "That makes two of us. Losing our minds."

"We can't both be imagining the same thing. Someone is dumping bodies onto our property. The question is, who?" I keep a small detail from Jake.

Jake runs one hand up and down my back, lays the other on my knee, and his Adam's apple bobs as he swallows. "Mal, honey. I'm pretty sure who's behind this. I just don't know why. But I do know it's my fault. I brought this upon us."

"Your fault? I don't understand."

"Like I said, it has to be Dom. Even though he claimed to know nothing about it. Who else could it be? I don't know anyone else who would dump bodies in my lap."

"Dom? I thought you paid your debt to him. Jake, please don't tell me you borrowed more." My eyes plead with him to tell me I'm wrong. I'll believe him this time.

"No, Mal. I swear I haven't borrowed any more from anyone. I don't owe Dom."

"So, what are we going to do if someone finds a body in our cornfield?"

"What we aren't going to do is involve the cops. The body in the basement is gone. And hopefully, the one in the cornfield has disappeared, too. As far as we're concerned, there are no bodies. End of story."

"What about Craig?"

"He thinks it's a big joke. We won't let on any different. Okay, hon?"

Something about Jake's solution to the problem seems off. Won't the police be looking for the dead people? Will Craig put two and two together? Will the police officers who were here Monday night be suspicious? Will more bodies turn up?

"Okay," I say, unable to think of any other course of action.

Jake heaves a big sigh and lies down, pulling me on top of him. "Now that we've got everything out in the open—no secrets, no lies—how about we ease some of that tension we've been carrying all week?"

"Thank you."

"For what?'

I pull myself up, so I'm straddling him and place my hands on his chest, my eyes locked on his. "For telling me the truth. About the body in the cistern. About Dom. But why didn't you tell me before now?"

"I didn't want to upset you."

"I'm a lot more upset by your lies, Jake."

"They weren't lies, Mal. It was just information I didn't think you needed to hear. I was thinking of the baby."

My fingers clasp his chin, and I force his eyes to remain on mine. "Not telling me things is the same as lying. I don't need to be protected from the truth. What I do need is to be able to trust you. And I can't do that if you keep secrets from me. We're a team."

He places his hands on mine. "You *can* trust me. You mean everything to me." Rolling me onto my back, his mouth claims mine, and I lose myself in the moment, pushing aside dead bodies in favor of my husband's live body. He cradles me in his arms afterwards, telling me everything will be fine if we stick together. As long as our stories line up, should anyone ask.

With a smile on my lips, I relax in the comfort of Jake's arms. Everything is fine, like he said. There are no bodies. It's just Dom's way of reminding Jake he could end up being one of the bodies should he get into debt again, unable to pay it back. Assuming Jake tows the line and stays out of the casino, Dom will leave us alone. While trying to convince myself of this scenario, something that's been niggling at the back of my brain comes to the forefront. Honesty is a two-way street. And so is trust.

"There's something else I didn't tell you."

"What, honey?" He props himself on one elbow, giving me his attention.

"I found a gun in the cornfield. I buried it in the woods."

Jake sits up, eyes darting back and forth, trying to process this information. I can almost see the wheels turn in his head. "You found a gun? And you buried it? When?"

"Sunday, while I was out for my walk. I used gloves and dug a hole in the woods down the road. No one will find it."

Jake buries his head in his hands. When he looks up, those cool pools of azure betray his feelings. The nonchalant, easy-going part of Jake is struggling with something darker. Shock? Anger? Terror? I'm not certain which side of my husband is winning this current battle. Just in case, I slide out of bed and back out of his reach.

"Let me get this straight, Mal." He enunciates each word. "You *thought* a body dropped out of the helicopter onto our property. You found a gun in that same field. A gun that was probably used on the body. And you buried the evidence? Why would you do that?"

His mouth gapes open, expressing shock rather than anger. That's a good sign.

"I...I don't know. I guess I thought maybe it wouldn't be good if a gun was found on our property and then a body showed up with it? What if someone found the gun and called the police? What if they found the marijuana? What if they kept looking and found a body?"

"Why didn't you tell me you found a gun?"

"Because I was afraid that maybe you were somehow involved in it." I blurt out my suspicions before I can consider the ramifications of admitting I considered my husband capable of murder, even if only for a moment. "You and Dom."

Hands covering his face again, he shakes his head. "You're the one always going on about being honest with each other. You should have told me you found a gun."

"Why didn't you tell me about the body in the basement?" He's a fine one to talk about honesty.

"Because...because...hell, Mal, there was a body in our basement." He rises and paces the room. "What was I supposed to say? Come up to bed after work and casually mention it? 'Oh, by the way, hon, there's a dead body in the cistern, rolled up in your new rug. Did you happen to put it there? I don't think that's the best spot for it. Why don't you come down and help me move it to a better location? Maybe bury it in the woods across the street?'"

The two sides of Jake move from one end of the room to the other, hands combing through his hair, eyes wild. He could be performing a comedy routine, except for the fact that he's about to blow his cool. I need to de-escalate this discussion. "Why don't we go downstairs, and I'll make you some coffee?" I tiptoe past him toward the door, fingers on the knob, when he places his hand over mine.

"Coffee?" His voice lowers an octave or two next to my ear. "Sure, hon, coffee will fix things right up. Maybe some cookies, too."

I need to distract him. Turning on the overhead lights, I face him head-on. "I'm sorry if I did the wrong thing with the gun. I was trying to protect you in case...But what were you and Craig going to do with the body in the cistern?"

Backing away, he flops onto the bed, lowering his head in his lap. And sobs.

Being a good wife, I reach out to him, my hand on his shoulder. "It's okay. We'll figure this out together. We're not guilty of anything. I'll dig up the gun tomorrow and throw it back in the cornfield where I found it, if that's what you want." He lifts his head, wipes the tears, and tilts his head, staring through me. "Now, let's go down, and I'll pour you a nightcap. Things will look better in the morning."

I lead him downstairs to the dining room, where I pour a half glass of the Jack Daniels we keep on hand for guests. He drinks it like ginger ale on a hot day. I pour another.

He deserves it. Having to deal with a crazy wife who buries evidence in a probable homicide.

Chapter Twenty

We can weather this. Our marriage has been through worse. Neither of us is perfect.

Jake's gambling problem started years before I met him. So did his debt accumulation. An objective observer of our marriage might conclude that he married me for the money I inherited when my parents died, taking advantage of my depression and loneliness. But the woman who knows Jake as well as I do will attest to the fact that he loves me.

When I first met Jake's mom, her warmth enveloped me as she welcomed me with an embrace. It was clear where Jake got his sweet side. She treated me like a long-lost daughter.

"I've never seen Jake so happy as he's been the last couple of weeks," Gloria said as she and I sat in the living room while Jake cleared the table and loaded the dishwasher. "When he talks about you—and he talks about you all the time—his eyes light up."

Gloria, that kindest and most loving, forgiving woman, became my second mom. Jake takes after her.

But then there's the other side of Jake. The part that is his father. Jake lives in constant fear that he will become like Steve—an abusive drunk who can't control himself. His fear of becoming a father stems from Steve, a man I only recently met. A man that Jake threatened to kill.

"Everyone deserves another chance. Everyone is worthy of forgiveness," Gloria said when she took Steve back after a long separation. "We all make mistakes. Steve wants to atone for his sins."

If Gloria were given the position of ruler of the world, there would be no wars. Only penance and apologies would be expected for transgressions, never retaliation.

Clinging to my edge of the bed, I fall asleep with these thoughts, Jake tossing and turning on the other side of the bed.

When the alarm buzzes, I ease out of bed so as not to disturb him, although the lack of snoring tells me he may not be sound asleep. Once I'm dressed for work, my hand on the doorknob, I steal a glance at my husband, curled up on his side of the bed in a fetal position. His eyes are wide open.

"Did you get any sleep?" I ask.

"Uh, yeah. Slept like a baby, hon. Just thought I'd get up early and get working on those finishing touches in the family room." Whether he's being facetious or dead serious, I can't be sure, but I'm not hanging around to find out and risk a replay of last night's discussion of the buried gun. "Okay, see you tonight."

When I arrive at school, Sue greets me in the classroom. "Good morning! How was your night?"

"Pretty quiet." If I can't confide in her about Jake's gambling, I certainly can't mention the bodies and the gun. "Jake's going to get the family room done this weekend, then we can concentrate on the nursery. My aunt and uncle have offered to buy a crib for the baby. I'm excited to start decorating."

"What colors are you thinking?"

We spend a few minutes discussing the decor for Baby Jakey, with Sue telling me they used traditional pink and blue for their kids, who are now five and three years of age and quite a handful.

"Two is good, but I've been thinking of trying for another," Sue says. "Jerry doesn't know if we can handle three, though. He says we'll be outnumbered." She chuckles, and I smile at the joke, thinking I've already got two—the one growing inside me and the big lug of a kid I call my husband. Maybe my thoughts of having three or four children need to be revisited.

The morning passes quickly as we move from one activity to another, observing groups of children and engaging with them. At lunchtime, I encounter Brad in the staff room. He joins me on the sofa, where I'm perched again with my feet up.

"Everything okay, Mallory?"

"Yes, all good. How about you?"

"I'm fine. You're looking a bit tired, though. Baby keeping you up?

"You could say so."

He waits for me to elaborate, but I remain quiet, and we eat side by side, him flipping through his phone and me staring at the clock. If I could turn back time...

What if I hadn't broken up with Brad? I could have *learned* to love him. He's steady, reliable, and he cares about me. We have lots in common, like our love of kids, our careers in education, our love of reading... But how well do I know him? How well did I know Jake when he proposed? Maybe Jake and I shouldn't have gotten married so soon after meeting. Do you ever really know anyone, even after years of being together? If I could turn back that clock...

Would I still choose Jake over Brad?

"Of course, I would."

"Would what?"

Shoot, did I say that aloud? What else have I said that I shouldn't?

"Sorry, just thinking about the baby's crib. My aunt asked if I would like to go shopping with her and get an idea of what I want for the nursery. My mind's elsewhere. What's new in your life?" Now that I've got the crib in my head, I can't help but think it should have been my parents who helped me pick it out. But they can't do that from their graves. As always, the image of them burning in their beds and the related guilt I've held onto for five years for being miles away when they died, assails me.

"Nothing much."

What is he talking about?

"Oh, okay." Not knowing what else to say, that seems like a safe bet.

"And Jake? How's everything going?"

"Good, yes, everything's good." *Liar, liar, pants on fire.*

When the bell rings, we head to our separate classrooms, meeting up again near the end of the day when his Grade 6 students partner up with our kindergarten kids and read to them.

"Try to get some sleep tonight, Mallory," he says as the three of us stand in the center of the room, overseeing the interaction between the kids. The older students are so good with the little ones, taking them under their wing like young adults. It's amazing how mature kids can be when given a position of responsibility. I hope I will remember that as a parent. If only it worked as well on husbands. The more responsibility Jake is given, the more of a goofball he becomes. Maybe this problem with the bodies will make him step up and be a man.

"Yes, take care of yourself," Sue adds. "Don't strain yourself. Stress isn't good for the baby. Go to bed early."

I promise to get right to bed after supper.

I'm tired enough to do exactly that when I get home. If only I had the energy to make supper. The house smells better now, but it's going to continue to need airing and sprays of freshener. With only one week to go until the wedding, I don't need the embarrassment of a smelly house as guests parade through our home on their way to the bathrooms.

Nellie follows me to the kitchen, where I remove a tin of cat food and scoop some into her bowl, then stare into the fridge, hoping supper jumps out at me. Nothing. I close the door, and my fuzzy reflection confronts me like a ghost. Startled, I consider whether I should have chosen white appliances instead of stainless steel. And grey cupboards. Granite counters instead of butcher block. Pregnancy may not be the best time to make major decisions about one's kitchen.

Something seems different. I scan the room. The trim is up around the patio doors and the bay window. That's good. Jake must have started to work on it immediately after I left this morning.

The sink. That's it. A curved metal spout stands above the stainless steel sink on the large island. I pull on the lever, and voila—flowing water! My eyes glance upward, but the space where the lights should be hanging is still empty, as are the holes with capped wiring above the counters along the walls.

Still, he's ahead of schedule. By the end of the weekend, it'll be perfect. He should be rewarded. I'll make a nice dinner on Sunday to celebrate the new family room/kitchen. Right now, though, I don't have enough energy to drive to town to pick up pizza, so I call for delivery.

By the time the pizza arrives, I'm in pajamas and my robe, with Netflix tuned to a romantic comedy. I curl up on the sofa, pizza and ginger ale, Nellie and the movie for company.

A nice, quiet night in.

Chapter Twenty-One

I t was too much to hope for. No sooner do I put the rest of the pizza in the fridge than the phone rings. The silence on the other end of the line prompts me to hang up, thinking it's another computerized telemarketing call. When the distinct sound of crying startles my ears, I wait, then ask, "Hello. Who is this?"

"Beth. I...I need to talk...to someone..."

"Beth? Is everything okay?" I pull the phone away from my ear as she blows her nose. Why is she calling *me*? I barely know her, having first met a couple of weeks ago at Group.

"It's Jason. He hasn't come home."

"Isn't he still at work?" Jason and Jake work the same shift at The Auto Supply Warehouse. Of course, he wouldn't be home.

"He hasn't been..." Sniffles interrupt her flow of words. "I haven't heard from him since Friday. A week now."

"Oh my. I'm so sorry, Beth." Still, I'm not sure why she's chosen to talk to *me* about her marital problems. Group is tomorrow night. Surely, she could wait till then to vent their issues.

"I know you and Jake had some problems this summer."

The way she says it makes it sound like an accusation or a threat. Like 'I know what you did this summer.' But of course, she couldn't. We didn't disclose the particulars of what happened to anyone.

"I'm not sure how I can help, Beth."

"I thought maybe..." She seems to be struggling with what to say. "Maybe if you're not busy, I could come over and talk. Since, you know...Since Jake and Jason share a problem."

I sit up straight. She has my attention. What problem? Something to do with the bodies on our property? How is Jason involved?

"Um, yes, of course."

Although it's still early in the evening, I don't feel like getting dressed again. Whatever Beth has to say, she'll surely understand I'm exhausted after a full day with the kids.

Within twenty minutes, the doorbell rings. Beth's pale, haunted face is visible under the security lights as dusk settles over the front yard, the maple trees transforming from colorful welcomers to dark intimidators. Her red eyes and puffy lids surround a vacant stare; chin wrinkles run from her downturned mouth. I know this look—I sported it when Jake went missing in the summer. The ghost of Beth, so unlike the pretty brunette I met recently, looks right through me, boring a hole between my eyes.

I take her hand and lead her to the sofa. "I'll put the tea on. Be back in a minute, and we'll talk."

When I return to the living room and set down the two cups of herbal tea, she is standing at the window overlooking the darkening yard and the woods across the road.

"Do you ever get scared?" she asks.

"All the time. This place is so isolated. It's not bad during the day, but at night, when I'm alone, it's creepy. With Jake working nights, I'm always on edge. Every strange sound or movement makes me jump."

"No, that's not what I meant."

"Oh?"

"Do you get scared Jake might leave you and never come back? That something might happen to him?"

The memory of those nightmarish days of this past summer has been relegated to the dark recesses of my mind, and I don't want them pushing their way to the forefront. "All the time," I confess. "I suffer from anxiety disorder. I worry about everything."

Without being specific, I hope to empathize with Beth. She must be frantic with Jason missing for a week.

90

"I keep wondering if I could have handled things differently. Did I nag too much about the gambling? I know it's an illness, but I couldn't ignore it and act like everything was fine. How do you cope with Jake's addiction?"

I'm beginning to see why she came to me with her worries. Only another wife of a compulsive gambler could understand. Beth joins me on the sofa, and waits for an answer, as though I might be able to pinpoint where exactly Jason has gone.

"I don't cope well," I say with a sigh.

"What happened to Jake this summer? When he was gone?"

"He just needed some time to himself."

"Where did he go?"

"A cabin retreat." I hate to lie to her, but the truth won't help find Jason.

"And he didn't tell you he was going away for a while?"

"No. Do you think that's what Jason might be doing? Taking a time out?" I suggest that possibility to give her hope that he'll be back soon.

A tear rolls down her cheek. "Why hasn't he called?"

"I don't know. Have you notified the police he's missing?"

"I did. They said if he has a history of taking off for a couple days, it's possible that's all this is, but they're keeping an eye out for him."

A shudder goes through me like a sudden draft, chilling my flesh. Does Jason's disappearance have anything to do with what Jake and I found on our property?

"I'm sure he'll turn up."

After seeing Beth to the door, no wiser about what may have happened to Jason and certainly no less upset, I settle back onto the sofa for another movie to get my mind off Beth's troubles and the bodies on our property. Poor Beth. I hope he shows up soon. There's nothing worse than not knowing where your husband is.

Unless it's a missing child. My hand protectively covers my stomach. Yes, that would be worse.

Chapter Twenty-Two

Rain pelts the window, waking me. I dozed off before the movie ended, Nellie curled up on my chest. Time to drag myself upstairs and go to bed.

A text comes through on my phone.

Out with Craig tonight. Don't wait up, hon.

Craig, again? He spends more time with him than me. Is anything ever going to change? We're going to be parents. Craig's getting married. And they're still going out to bars like single guys. When will they grow up? I'm so sick and tired of this. *I* should be Jake's priority.

Maybe it's hormones, but the more I think about it, the more I fume. How is Jake going to be in shape to get up in the morning and finish the kitchen if he's out half the night drinking? He didn't get much sleep last night. Which means he'll sleep away the whole Saturday.

Is Vicky okay with Craig's behavior so close to the wedding?

Needing to vent to someone who will understand, I text to see if she's awake. At least I'm not the only woman without a husband tonight. Beth, Vicky...Maybe all husbands are the same.

When she responds right away, I call to commiserate about our deadbeat husbands.

"Craig's not out with Jake, Mallory. He's right here with me."

"Oh." My jaw drops. "I...I guess I misunderstood. Sorry, Vicky."

"Text me when he gets home so we're not worrying."

If Jake's not with Craig, who is he with? Another woman? Why is he lying?

I brew another cup of chamomile tea to calm myself. I'm sure there's a reasonable explanation. Maybe he's got a surprise for me. Something to do with the new kitchen. Although what that could be after eleven o'clock on a Friday night, I can't imagine. I text Jake to tell him I miss him and to hurry home.

While the kettle boils, I use the toilet off the mudroom. After flushing, water trickles into the tank. When the toilet doesn't stop running, I flip the lever. The flapper must be stuck again. A few more flicks of the handle, and the water continues to gurgle into the tank. Not only is it wasting water, it's annoying.

I can fix this.

I've seen Jake do it. He lifts the lid off the tank, makes sure the chain is attached to the flapper so it will close, checks the float is rising, then replaces the lid. Problem solved. I don't need to wait for him to come home to take care of a running toilet. I'm not some helpless woman who needs a man to do everything for her.

With my hands on either side of the lid, I lift up and...

Crash!

The lid, heavier than I expected it to be, lies in pieces on the floor and on the toilet seat, which now has a gouge in it. My eyes take in the four or five pieces of cracked white porcelain, and for a moment, I stare in disbelief, wondering why the lid is no longer on the toilet, nor is it in my hands.

Following a moment of suspended animation, my mouth flies open, and I consider how to put the pieces back together. Glue? Seconds later, my brain fully registers that the lid is broken, it can't be fixed, and it's my fault. It's bad enough I put the roll on the toilet paper holder the wrong way, now this. Jake won't be happy when he comes home to find the toilet broken.

I remove the phone from my robe pocket to see whether I missed Jake's text or call. No response. Is he too drunk to answer? Is the bar too loud?

Who is he with?

Staring into the watery abyss of the toilet tank, I fumble with the keyboard as I type in another message, asking where he is. I need him. I can't deal with this toilet thing.

The phone slips out of my fingers and plops into the bowl, sliding halfway down the hole, blue water covering it.

The crying seems almost forced at first as I think about how I'm going to tell Jake and how he is going to react to this. Another thing that needs fixing. A phone that needs replacing. More expenses. I pull my cell out and wrap it in Kleenex, then take it to the kitchen, where I dry it with paper towels and place it into a bowl filled with rice. I've heard that can fix phones that fall into toilets.

Tears well in my eyes as I whimper, walking with my head bent in shame back to the sofa, where I curl up and ball my fists in frustration. The crying builds to a crescendo when I remember the upcoming wedding and think of guests gazing inside my disgusting rust-lined toilet tank and asking what happened.

Nellie comes to investigate the source of the disturbance on the sofa as I convulse and blubber, having difficulty catching my breath. She nuzzles me, asking what's wrong.

Deep breaths, Mal. In and out. Calm down.

It's just a toilet tank lid and a seat. We can probably buy another one.

I blow my nose several times, putting a stop to the sniveling. Except, it doesn't stop. I choke on my sobs, trying to inhale air.

You'd think someone had died.

After a while, I quit mourning my toilet. Stare into space. Concentrate on breathing. Accept that the tank lid is gone for good.

Maybe if I close and lock the bathroom door, Jake won't notice. The wedding guests will think someone else is using the toilet and go in search of another bathroom. After the wedding, I'll unlock the door and Jake will think one of the guests did it. He'll be so relieved they aren't suing us for getting cut or squashed by the toilet lid that the cost of a new one, maybe the whole toilet, won't seem so bad. Maybe he'll think it's funny. The thought of a wedding guest breaking the toilet and being too embarrassed to say anything.

A few more sniffles and snorts, another deep breath, and I'm okay. I go back to the kitchen, put the kettle back on, and finish making tea. I return to the scene of the crime, careful not to cut myself, and touch the lever. The toilet stops running after the first flip and fills normally.

Fixed. All good.

I turn the lock on the door and pull it closed behind me.

Back on the sofa, I sip my tea and take calming breaths in between swallows. Nellie climbs onto my lap, as if knowing I still need consoling. My hand runs through silky fur; her purring helps me settle down.

I pick up the novel on the coffee table and try to immerse myself in the world of the protagonist, who I suspect is being gaslighted by her husband. The rain batters the front door, the wind now shrieking through the cracks, the draft creeping into the hall. I pull the throw over myself, and Nellie resituates herself, kneading her claws into the plush fabric.

As I turn the page to find out who is stalking the heroine during her evening stroll through town, everything goes black. Nellie reacts to my startled jump and yelp by leaping off my lap, leaving me alone in the dark. I feel my way to the hall closet and pull a flashlight from the top shelf.

The power must be out because of the storm. I do a quick tour of the house to make sure everything is secure before heading upstairs to bed. I sweep the yellow beam into the dining room across the hall, then tread toward the kitchen, one hand holding the flashlight, the other allowing the wall to guide me. Nellie sits on the window seat in the family room, guarding the back of the house as rain streams down the glass panes.

"Good girl, Nellie. You keep a lookout."

My eyes follow the rays as I direct them into the den, then head to the mudroom. The back door is locked. I venture into the laundry room and peek out the window, almost expecting to see something out of place after the helicopter last week, but only the dark cornfield, stalks bending, stares back. Stretching its arms toward me. Beckoning me to join the body lying in the midst of it.

My shoulders shudder, and though I know it's irrational, I just want to get out of there. Fast. On my way past the basement door, an image of another body lying in the cistern intrudes into my brain. I tell myself it's no longer there. Neither is the one in the cornfield, I suspect. Whoever left them there has picked them up. As though they were placed on layaway for a while, kept in storage till payment could be arranged. To threaten Jake? Because he racked up more debt that he isn't paying?

Before climbing to the safety of our bedroom, I double-check the front door. Locked up tight, in spite of the wind's attempts to break and enter. Pointing the beam down, holding the railing, placing one foot next to the other as I climb, I retreat to our upstairs haven.

With the bedroom door left open for Nellie and in order to hear Jake when he comes home, I remove my robe and make another bathroom stop before settling in bed, keeping my hands off the toilet lid this time. The flashlight, set on the vanity, brings some relief in the dark room.

I turn on my iPad for both light and company, snuggle under the covers with Nellie joining me, and listen to my audiobook. I'll wait up for Jake. See what he has to say for himself.

The battery-operated security light filters through the curtains. He's home. I wait for him to turn the key in the knob, stumble into the entry, flip the switch, and swear when he realizes the power is out. He'll trip on his way up the stairs, swear some more, then fall into bed, expecting me to be asleep.

Nothing happens.

I rise and peer through the curtains onto the partially-lit front lawn. I don't have a view of the front porch from here, and I can't see whether there's a vehicle sitting on the driveway on the other side of my Toyota.

What's he doing?

The yard darkens, still no sound coming from below.

Grabbing the flashlight off the night table, I slip down the hall to the guest room and gaze out on the back yard, the solar-powered garden posts doing little to brighten the night. The lawn spreads out to the shed in the far corner, with trees and flower beds filling in some of the stretch of grass. At the back and to the left, corn surrounds the landscaped grounds. On a cloudy night, nothing is visible except as a dark shadow of its true self.

Movement to the left of the house catches my eye. A shadow that doesn't belong.

I scream as the shape of a man makes its way toward the back door. Who would be skulking around our yard at midnight? The person who put the bodies on our property? One of Dom's people? Nick? Adam? Are they here to bring another body?

I hurry back to our room, the yellow stream guiding my way, and grab Jake's bat out of the closet, just in case they come into the house. With the bedroom door closed, I slip under the covers and wait. What will happen first? Either Jake will come home and scare off whoever is out there, or the intruder will break through the door and come up the stairs for me.

The front security bulbs flick on.

Bang! Bang! Bang!

The pounding travels up the stairs while I cower in bed.

Bang! Bang! Bang!

Then silence. I rise and peek through the curtains. The security lights extinguish, bringing darkness to the lawn, shadows looming across the road, haunted woods seemingly closer than during the daytime.

A car horn blasts through the night rain. And again. Again. Impatient.

Jake?

Did he forget his key? Why doesn't he ring the doorbell?

Bat firmly in my right hand, I grip the flashlight and railing with my left as I descend to the entryway. In the dining room, I gaze through the window to get a better view of the driveway. A figure runs through the rain, setting off the security lights again.

It isn't Jake.

I fling open the front door as he reaches it.

"Brad? What are you doing out here this time of night?"

"Why didn't you let me in? I've been ringing the doorbells, pounding on the door, and honking the horn. I saw your car in the driveway, and I knew you were home. Why are you standing here in the dark?" He flips the switch in the hall.

The house remains pitch black, except for a single beam of light.

"The power is out," I explain. "I didn't hear the doorbell. And I thought someone was trying to break in when I heard the pounding."

"Oh. I guess the doorbell won't be working with the power out."

We sit in the living room, and I set the flashlight on the coffee table, illuminating our faces.

"Were you crying, Mallory? What happened?"

"No. I mean, I was. But it's nothing. Just hormones. I've been weepy lately. With the baby."

He studies my face for signs of a lie. Does he think Jake and I had a fight? That Jake walked out on me? Because his car isn't in the driveway?

"Why are you here? Is everything okay?" I ask.

"Yes, everything's fine. Except...I was worried when you didn't answer your phone. So, I thought I'd better check on you."

There must be more to it than that. For all he knew, I could have been sound asleep. Or Jake and I might have been busy making love. It *is* Friday night. No work tomorrow.

"What is that smell?" Brad sniffs the air.

"We had some trouble with skunks."

I light a couple of scented candles, then join him back on the sofa. "Why were you so worried you drove out here in the middle of the night?"

"It's Jake. I saw him tonight."

I'm afraid of what he's going to say. "Saw him where? He was at work, then he texted me to say he was going to be late. He and Craig were going out." I don't need Brad knowing that's not the whole truth.

"He wasn't with Craig, Mallory. He was with someone else."

Another woman? He wouldn't.

"I went out with some friends after work today. For a few drinks. I decided to call it an early night. As I was walking out of the bar at the River Grand, I saw Jake heading into the casino with those guys, Nick and Adam."

My worst fears are realized. He *is* back at it. And lying about it.

"I tried to text you, then called, but you didn't answer. I wanted you to know, to be prepared when he came home late, smelling of booze and lying about where he was. And I wanted to know you'd be okay, that you'd be safe." Brad puts an arm around my shoulder. "You know how much I care about you."

I'll kill him. After he promised. On our baby's life.

98

CHAPTER TWENTY-TWO

"You deserve so much better, Mallory. He's no good. You know that."

I do know that. Why do I keep defending Jake and giving him the benefit of the doubt? Is it because I know he loves me? Because I truly believe he's trying to change? Because I don't think I can live without him?

Maybe I'm a fool. But for every time Jake has upset me, he has more than made up for it. The small, sweet gestures of affection show his true colors. Jake senses what I need, and he goes out of his way to make me happy.

When we got engaged, Gloria offered up her childhood home for the two of us to make our own. Jake left the decision up to me. "We don't have to live here," he said, showing me around the old red brick farmhouse. "We'll get our own place. Jake and Mallory's place."

But I had already fallen in love with the property, still decorated to his grandparents' tastes. "This is Jake and Mallory's place," I said. "Our home."

From the beginning, Jake has been attuned to what makes me smile. The beach honeymoon he surprised me with. "You said you'd never been to the ocean," he said, his turquoise eyes twinkling as the waves rippled against our bodies. "I want to give you everything, Mallory. This is just the start."

The flower beds he dug up. The roses he planted.

The windchimes he hooked up on the back deck. "The sun, the moon, and the stars, Mallory. For you. I'd give you the world if I could."

The birdbath/feeder he set up on the front lawn. "I noticed you watching the birds. I think this will attract them. You can watch them from the front porch."

The window seat he built so I could read while enjoying my gardens and the sunshine.

The office he gave up to make way for a nursery. The renovations to keep me happy.

Jake professes his love and makes love in a way that leaves no doubt in my mind that he means it. But it's those little things he does that prove it a hundred times over. The things other people don't see. My sweet Jake.

A sweet little boy who wants to please but needs to grow up.

I don't feel like discussing my marriage and why I put up with Jake's nonsense right now, especially with my ex-boyfriend's arm around me, sitting in the dark. I change the topic. "Did you come to check on me because the power is out?"

"No, I didn't know it was out. Like I said, I came so you'd know what to expect when Jake came home, you know, in case he's drunk and in a bad mood after losing. I was worried you'd have a fight, and things might get out of control," he says. "The power must be out because of the downed lines on the sixth concession. I came across an accident on the way over."

"Accident?" My hands fly to my mouth, and I jump out of Brad's reach. "Oh, no! That's the way he'd be coming home. Let me use your phone."

Brad hands it over, and I enter Jake's number. After several tries, I fall back onto the couch, allowing Brad to place his arm around me again.

What happened to Jake?

He's not answering his phone.

Chapter Twenty-Three

The end of another long workday, another week in. And now home to Mallory. Friday night, and I'm ready for some quality time with my wife. She's bound to be in a better mood with the work I put in on the new room this morning and all our secrets out in the open.

Everyone's eager to escape tonight, rushing to the employee exit door. I stride along with them, whistling as I pass through the wide warehouse aisle, work shoes slapping the concrete. I throw my safety gear into my locker, slip into sneakers, and push open the metal door to freedom just after eleven o'clock.

Yellow and red pierce the night in the parking lot as vehicles roar to life, some already ripping down the country road to the main highway. Light from lampposts along the edge of the parking lot and from the signage shimmers in puddles. I jog through the rain toward my new Honda, keys in hand. I pop open the lock with my key fob and get into the driver's seat, sensing something's off the minute my butt slides across the leather.

Someone waits in the passenger side. I turn my head toward the intruder.

"Jake." Nick, tall, dark, and a man of few words, greets me as though he was expected.

And I *should* have been ready for a response after the message I left on Dom's voicemail this morning. As he wouldn't take my calls, I made demands.

What the hell is going on? Someone dropped in on my cornfield Friday night. Now I've got a missing person situation in my cistern. I want answers.

"What's going on?" I look over my shoulder, sensing that someone else is watching me, but the back seat is empty. When I turn to the left, the hefty muscle man outside my window confirms that Nick has brought a date.

"Dom wants to see you."

"I didn't know I had an appointment. I've made other plans for the evening. With my wife. Maybe we could reschedule."

Nick gives me his expressionless look. "Let's go."

Adam thumps the hood of my car as he walks to the dark sedan parked in front of me and pulls out of the lot, expecting me to follow.

"Can I at least text my wife to let her know I'll be late? So, she doesn't call the police to send out a search party?"

Nick shrugs. "Make it quick."

Ten minutes later, I'm escorted toward the River Grand Casino entrance, like some high roller bigshot with a bodyguard on either side. They lead me to Dom's private office in the back where I'm deposited and locked in.

Dom remains seated behind his massive mahogany desk. "Sit," he orders without looking up from his computer screen.

I do as I'm told and wait.

After a few minutes, he lifts his head and gives me his full attention. In his early forties, Dom is what most women would call a hunk, at least that's what Mallory said. 'Too bad he's a thug,' she added. I explained he's a family man, just looking out for their interests. Tall, with abundant black hair, a touch of grey, strong facial features, and a body he maintains well, Dom puts up with no shit.

I first met Dom when I reneged on the loan payment owed for the funds extended to me by one of his staff in the parking lot, courtesy of the casino. At the ripe old age of twenty-one, my finances didn't allow for the kind of fun the River Grand offered. I didn't see the harm in accepting a bit of cash I was bound to win back. Compound daily interest and payment for services rendered weren't terms I understood. I'm not a bloody accountant.

Over the next few years, I found myself escorted to Dom's office on many occasions, each one more pleasant than the last. Dom kept me in line with frequent reminders to accept my responsibilities and obligations like a man. No longer having a father figure to guide me with his slaps, Dom took it upon himself to smack sense into me. Not personally. Through his henchmen.

The first time I called him Dad, I thought I was a goner.

"Yesserie, Dad. I'll get right on that." I joked, my right hand flying up to my forehead in a mock salute.

The ensuing silence gave me time to reflect that Mom would never know what became of me as my body decayed at the bottom of the river. "I'm sorry, Dom. I don't know where that came from."

He sat back and drummed his fingers on the desk, glaring at me as if trying to decide on a punishment worthy of my disrespect. While he considered my future or the absence of it, I took the opportunity to tell him about my drunken, abusive father and how I kicked him out of the family home.

Dom pushed himself out of his chair, leaned forward, and raised his hand to me. I closed my eyes and braced myself. The brisk slap on the back was followed by Dom's first terms of endearment towards me.

"Jakey, my boy, I'm sorry to hear you had a tough upbringing. No kid deserves that kind of shit. But do not call me Dad ever again. I'm nowhere near old enough. Think of me as a big brother, watching out for you. A mentor, of sorts. You're lucky I like you. Now get out of my office."

"So, what can I do for you?" Dom asks now, as if I were one of his important clients.

Having been given permission to speak, I spew out the whole nasty situation about the cistern, leaving out the police visit and the gun my wife buried in the woods. "And now, the body is gone. That's quite the vanishing act you pulled. Did your mom buy you a magic kit when you were a kid?"

He chuckles. "I'm no magician, Jakey, but I do know how to make unpleasant things disappear. You're welcome."

"Excuse me?"

"You called me with a problem. A body taking up your personal space where it didn't belong. I took care of it. However, there is the issue of payment for services rendered." Dom sits back in his chair. "Body removal doesn't come cheap. Added to that, the cost of carpet disposal has skyrocketed. It's getting tougher to find places that accept that kind of stuff. Environmental concerns. And don't get me started on inflation. Damn politicians."

"Body removal?" Holy shit! He's dumping bodies on my property, then charging me to get rid of them. "You took it away?"

"I assumed you didn't want to keep it."

"No. No, I didn't."

"Well then, problem solved. Generally, I'd charge a hundred grand for this type of service, but since we're family, I'll give you a break. Fifty grand, and we'll call it even."

"Fifty grand? Is that per body?"

The corners of his mouth turn up. "You've got more? I can give you a two-for-one discount this time, but there's no free ride in this business, Jakey, my boy. The overhead is high. My employees don't work cheap. So, if more bodies happen to show up on your property, I'm going to have to charge the full disposal fee."

He's messing with me. Just another way for him to extort money from me now that I'm done with gambling and borrowing at his exorbitant rates.

"Come on, Don. You and I both know you arranged for those bodies to be dumped on my property. I'm not paying to get rid of something you did. It's got nothing to do with me. We had an agreement. I held up my end. Paid you off in full for my debts and stayed the hell out of your casino. You're just lucky I didn't call the cops."

Dom's reaction makes me regret my bravery. He stands and towers over me, his voice low and sinister. "I gave you a break, Jake. Because I like you. And that pretty little wife of yours with the baby on the way. But, don't think for one minute that you can take advantage of my kindness by coming in here and making accusations and threats."

He lowers himself into his chair and folds his hands on the desk. "Now, do you want to write a check, arrange for a bank transfer, or would you prefer to apply for a personal loan?"

"Neither."

He raises his eyebrows. "I won't ask again. Adam and Nick will be more than happy to persuade you to fulfill your financial obligations if we can't come to a mutual agreement."

"We're doing renovations to the house, and we've got the baby's future to think of. I don't have extra cash sitting around to pay for disposing of bodies you drop out of helicopters or drop into cisterns. Find another dumping ground and another chump." I'm well aware my attitude is about to be adjusted by his goons, but I promised Mallory my association with Dom was over.

Instead of calling for Nick and Adam to drive me to a quiet place to reconsider my response, Dom rubs the dark scruff on his chin and leans forward. "Tell me more about this helicopter. You saw a body dropped out of it?"

Not sure honesty is the best policy in this case, but I repeat what Mal told me about Friday night. "I didn't see anything. But Mallory saw something drop out of a copter into our cornfield, and she thought it could have been a body. I don't know. She has a crazy wild imagination, blows things out of proportion, gets a bit paranoid, if you know what I mean. It might have been nothing." Or it might have been a gun. But I sure as hell don't need to be charged for two bodies. "And the one in the basement, who knows? Maybe the furnace guy came to check things out and fell into the cistern. I'm not blaming you, Dom, and I appreciate the help with cleaning up the mess, but I don't want to involve my family in this. So, if we can come up with a solution that prevents any more bodies landing in my vicinity and avoid disposal fees, I'd be really grateful." Best to stay on his good side.

Dom nods. "Like I said, Jake, I like you. I see great potential in you. You don't strike me as the kind of guy who wants to spend his life working in a warehouse, struggling to put food on the table. Family comes first with you. I admire that. You've got a lucrative future ahead of you." He rises again and escorts me to the door, giving me a friendly slap on the back. "Why don't we call this one a gift from your buddy Dom, and you can owe me one. An advance on future earnings, maybe."

Nick and Adam escort me outside. Wind and rain batter my face as I run to my Honda. I settle into the driver's seat, lock the doors, knowing that won't keep them out should they decide to follow me, and text Mal that I'm on my way home. Wipers swishing to keep up with the deluge, I focus on the road, considering whether I might have been better off to accept the fifty grand loan at hourly compound interest rather than 'owe one' to my buddy Dom.

Mallory doesn't respond to my text. She's probably pissed off about something again.

Partway down the expressway out of the city, I take the next turnoff and head back to the casino, wondering what the hell Dom meant. Owe him one? No way am I leaving things like this. I'll try to reason with him one more time. If that doesn't work, I *will* call the police. He's the criminal here, not me. If I don't put a stop to this crap, he'll keep dragging me in deeper. And Mallory isn't going to put up with me 'owing one' to Dom and being part of whatever the hell he's involved in.

The casino hotel doors slide open to welcome me back, and I stride through with a purpose, winking at security as I pass through to the gaming floor. "Back again. At Dom's request."

For a minute, the hand on my shoulder tells me I'm about to be bounced back out on my ass. So, I add, "I owe him something. I'm here to pay up."

That works. And surprisingly, no one else stops me.

I stop myself. The high-limit room beckons me to enter as I saunter past. *Keep walking, Jake. That's what got you into trouble in the first place.*

I won't gamble. I'll simply watch for a while. No harm in that. A quick flash of the VIP card that I found on the counter at home gets me in, no questions asked. They know me well enough here, borrowed ID aside, and must assume my privileges have been reinstated.

Or, maybe, they *have* been reinstated. Is that what Dom meant by 'you owe me one'? Is he trying to lure me back into gambling and borrowing money from him? Well, it's not going to work. My family is more important than...

The blackjack table catches my attention. I can do this. This is my game. A couple of hands, easy money. One last time.

But, out of the corner of my eye, I notice Dom at the bar, engaged in a conversation with some bald-headed dude. Well-dressed, important looking, obviously a high roller. Seeing Dom reminds me why I'm here. And it's not to play the cards.

The barstool fits me perfectly as I sidle up within earshot of Dom and his friend, waiting for an audience. He's too engrossed in what the guy's saying to notice me.

"I'm really looking forward to doing business with you, Dom. When I see everything you've created here, I know it's going to be a lucrative deal for both of us. A new casino for you. A great investment opportunity for me."

"So, everything's good to go? When can I expect the building to start?" Dom asks.

"Soon. It takes time to clear that huge of a site. I'm sure you understand. Patience, my friend." The dude holds up his lowball glass in a toast. "Here's to the new Island Casino and our partnership."

As the glasses clink together, the dude asks, "Have you given any more thought to me running the place for you?"

"I appreciate the offer, Marco, but like I told you, I've got it covered."

"It's a long drive to Kingston. And I live minutes from the new casino. Why bring in someone else? I'd be happy to take care of things for you, have a more hands-on approach, rather than sit back as a silent partner."

"Thanks, but I have one of my own guys in mind to oversee the place. You remember the guy I told you I was grooming for a management position? He's actually right here now, over to your left."

I turn around looking for this guy Dom's talking about. Nobody sits to our left. My eyes scan the area for the mystery person Dom has great plans for, but he must have slipped off to the john or something.

As I turn back to face them, Dom acknowledges my presence. "Jake."

Shit. He's known all along that I'm sitting here, listening in on his conversation.

"Sorry, Dom. I'll be on my way." My ass peels itself off the stool in a hurry, but before I move away, he tells me to join them, motioning to the stool on the other side of him.

"Marco Ricco. Jake Shelton." He introduces us, and I get a good look at the dude when he stands to shake my hand.

Whoever this guy is, I've seen him at the tables before. Too rich for my tastes. Bets more in one hand than I do in an entire month. I also saw him in Dom's office a few weeks ago when I personally delivered my last interest check and signed off on the loan, ending my nine-year indebtedness to Dom. We had just concluded our meeting when this guy knocked and walked in. The cut of his clothes and the confidence in his walk told me he was important. Moreover, the fact that he entered Dom's private domain without an escort added to his air of authority.

"Marco, have a seat." The guy was an obvious bigwig. He made himself right at home in the leather chair next to me.

I excused myself and headed for the door. "I'll leave you gentlemen to your business."

But Dom caught up with me in the hall, closing his office door. "Hold on, Jake."

At first, I thought Dom would say there was still a matter of interest charges accumulated on the interest since I signed the papers two minutes ago, but he had something else in mind.

Dom held out his hand. In shock, I stood and stared at it for a while. What kind of a deal would I be shaking on?

"I just want you to know, Jake, that I admire your tenacity in seeing through your debt repayment, with continuous interest being accrued. You remind me of myself when I was younger. A lot younger than you."

"Uh, thanks." I shook his hand.

"I see a bright future ahead for you, Jake. As luck would have it, an opportunity is about to arise in my organization. I think you might be just the man for it. Why don't you step back into my office, and we'll discuss it?"

"Thanks for thinking of me, Dom. But Mallory's waiting for me, and I see you've got an important appointment as well."

"Don't worry about that." Dom indicated the door. "He can wait. I'd rather play 'let's make a deal' with you. You're much more trustworthy."

"Just the same, I'd better get going. And as much as I appreciate a potential opportunity, I'm afraid I'm out. I need to cut my ties with the casino. For the sake of my marriage."

"I understand. I'll give you some time to think it over. I think you'll find it's in your best interest." Dom turned and headed back to his office, leaving me to wonder what the hell he was talking about.

The last time I saw this Marco dude was a week ago after I said goodbye to my buddy, Terry, at the casino bar.

I have no idea why he'd remember me. I'm no one important. Just another loser.

But as we shake hands, he says, "We've seen each other around, but it's nice to formally meet you, Jake. I've heard a lot about you. How long have you and Dom been working together?"

Working together? As in, I borrow money from Dom, and when I don't pay up in time, I get the crap beaten out of me?

"Uh, actually…"

Dom interrupts me by saying we've been associates for many years. "Jake's been part of the River Grand Casino for a long time. He has a promising career here."

Not unless I want my wife to kill me.

"Do you have a lot of experience in running a casino? You seem a little green," Marco says.

"Don't let his youth fool you," Dom laughs. "Jake's clocked a lot of hours at the casino. He knows his way around the business."

My smile and nod come from not knowing how to respond.

"Well, then. I look forward to seeing you in Kingston." Marco shakes my hand once more before leaving, as though I'm somebody important. "I'm heading back to the tables. Care to join me?"

I politely decline, saying I have business to attend to, meaning my wife, Mallory, who is going to have a fit if I don't get my butt home soon.

Dom has other plans for me. "In my office. Now."

Behind closed doors, Dom tells me exactly what I'm going to do to repay the 'one' that I owe him. "Like I said before, I'll give you some time to think it over. But not too long."

As Nick escorts me back to the parking lot, I consider what Dom has asked of me.

Gambling is one thing. Borrowing money from a mobster is another. Letting people grow weed in my cornfield is also another.

But this? This is a whole new ball game for me.

When I pull into my driveway, I recognize the car parked beside Mal's Toyota. It's the work husband. What the hell is he doing here at this hour?

I march up to my front door and shove it open. The house is dark except for a dim light in the living room. The sight of the two of them on the sofa, his arm around her, romantic candles lit, sends me through the roof.

"What the hell is going on here? I can't leave you alone for two seconds."

Brad rises from the sofa, outweighing me in muscle, and tells me I don't deserve my wife. My fist flies up and meets his jaw, knocking him backwards. Mallory screams.

I don't remember the rest.

Chapter Twenty-Four

My eyes open. I'm on the living room floor, a bag of frozen corn spread across my ice-cold face. All the lights are on. Mal and Brad are gone. I ease myself off the hardwood, pick up the corn, and holler up the stairs.

"Mal!"

No answer.

I open the front door, find Brad's car gone, and lock up. One problem dealt with. Mallory must be asleep. After checking the main level of the house and turning off lights, I climb to our room, find her on the edge of the bed, back facing me. So, we're back to the cold shoulder. Which makes no sense, because she was the one entertaining her old boyfriend while I was at work, and I'm the one who got knocked out for being upset about it. What am I missing?

"Honey, are you awake? I'm sorry if I did something wrong. Are you mad?"

She rolls over. "No, honey. What possible reason could I have for being mad?"

None that I can think of. But her swollen red eyes tell me she's been crying. She rolls back to the edge of the bed. Too tired to 'communicate' right now, I strip down and fall onto my side of the bed, returning her cold shoulder.

When I wake in the morning, she's already up, eating cereal at the kitchen table.

"Hi honey," I say, testing the waters.

She glares at me, and I put on the coffee, grab a bowl out of the cupboard and prepare my own granola breakfast, assuming it would be a bad idea to ask for bacon and eggs.

"I'll get those lights put in this morning and blinds in the afternoon." Maybe she'll warm up if I get these renovations done.

Still no response.

"Thanks for the first aid last night." I assume Brad was the one who delivered the sucker punch that knocked me out, and Mal placed the corn on my face, not the other way around. But I could be wrong. "It's still sore."

I don't get any sympathy from her. She shovels in spoonfuls of milk and cereal, chews, and continues to glare at me. I wolf down my breakfast, lay out the plastic sheeting to protect our new floors, and head to the basement to shut off the kitchen breaker and get my hand tools.

Mallory puts the breakfast dishes in the dishwasher and wipes down the table and counter while I bring the ladder from the laundry room and set it in front of the new kitchen island, then go back to fetch the box of hanging lights Mal picked out.

I climb up a couple of steps and inspect one of the holes with capped wires hanging from it. Black, white, copper. Attach like-colored wires. Duh. I don't need to check out Electricity for Dummies to install new lighting.

"Are you sure you know what you're doing?" Mallory stands off to the side, observing. "Maybe we should get the electrician back in."

Finally. She's talking.

"No need to pay for that. It's just a matter of connecting this black wire... Fuck!" The jolt throws me off the ladder, and I grab the edge of the island to break my fall.

Mallory screams, runs to me, and asks if she should call 911.

"I'm okay, hon. Just accidentally grazed my finger across the wire for a sec. Got a bit of a tingle. But I'm fine." I flash her a smile as I straighten myself to a standing position. "I'll live. No need to plan my funeral."

She insists I should see a doctor, but I assure her it's not necessary. I do agree to lie on the couch till the tingling subsides and to put ointment on my fingers.

"Call an electrician," Mal says. "I'm not letting you try that again."

"You *do* care. I wasn't sure, after finding you with Brad last night."

"You idiot."

And those are the last words she says to me for hours. After I call my buddy, Ian, who takes care of electrical issues at the warehouse, I get comfortable with the remote control and my Zombie series. A little low-voltage zap should be good for a day off.

Ian shows up around one o'clock, and I show him to the kitchen, indicating the job to be done. He's happy to earn a little extra on his Saturday off.

"None of my business, but what happened to your face?" he asks.

"Ran into a door."

"Huh. I'm guessing the door won. Where's the breaker panel?"

"Basement. But I already turned off the power to the kitchen."

Ian climbs the ladder with a voltage detector. "No, you didn't."

"I guess I should have used one of those," I say, pointing to the tester in his hand. "Could have saved myself a zap."

Together, we check out the circuit breaker. The one labelled 'kitchen' is shut off. Ian runs his finger down the labels next to each breaker. He taps the one labelled 'new kitchen island'.

"There's your problem. You shut off the wrong one." He shakes his head. "You're lucky it wasn't worse. Always use a voltage tester when you're working with electricity. That stuff can be lethal. By the way, something smells kind of funky down here."

Back in the kitchen, Mallory joins us from the den, where she's been reclining on the couch reading—some romance novel, judging by the cover. She greets Ian and thanks him for coming on such short notice, opens the fridge, takes out a bottle of water, a pack of cheese, an apple, and a yogurt, then grabs a banana and crackers, piling it all on a plate. When I ask what I'm supposed to have for lunch, she brandishes the knife she picked up from the block, pretends she didn't hear me, and closes the door to the den behind her.

Ian raises his eyebrows and nods his head in that direction. "Problems with the Missus?"

"Hormones. You know how it is."

"Yeah, I get ya."

While Ian installs Mal's lighting, I head into town to order lunch. After placing my order for a burger and fries, I slip into the FoodMart and blow a few bucks on a wrapped bouquet of carnations and a box of chocolates.

Before sitting down to my gourmet meal, I carry my peace offering to Mal, passing Ian on the ladder. I open the den door, walk toward the couch, cough to get her attention, and hold out the gifts.

She glances at the chocolate box in one hand and the flowers in the other. "I'm glad you're not dead."

Well, that's something. She goes back to her reading. I leave my carefully chosen gifts on the end table next to her. Now that everything's smoothed over, I can enjoy my burger and fries in front of the TV. I grab a couple of beers on my way back to the living room couch.

With a full stomach, I close my eyelids.

Zombie grunting and growling awakens me, and I bolt to a sitting position. Using the remote, I check to see how many episodes I've missed and need to rewatch. Better check on Mallory first. And grab another beer while I'm at it.

The kitchen is empty. I flip the switch and illuminate the counters and the island. All done. In the family room area, the woodgrain farmhouse ceiling fan with lights complements the flooring. Mal should be pleased with the job I've done. The wildflowers in the glass vase on the counter have been replaced with carnations, and the chocolate box has been half demolished. I grab a handful before they're all gone and go in search of Mallory.

She's not in the den. Nor anywhere else in the house. A peek out the front door tells me she's taken her car. Where the hell did she go?

I get my answer fifteen minutes later when she rings the doorbell, hands full, and thrusts a tray at me. "Take this to the kitchen. Veggies for tonight. It's our turn to bring snacks. And don't eat them. I'm going back to the car to get the cheese tray."

An hour later, our support group members start showing up, with Rod and Janice first, followed by Sid and Gail, Mom and Steve pulling up the rear.

"Sorry we're late," Mom says. "We got a bit sidetracked."

The red flush of her cheeks and the smug look on Steve's face tells me more than I need to know. I'm tempted to wipe the grin off him, but what Mom does with my good-for-nothing father is her own business.

"No problem. We can all set up together," Mal says.

Noses twitch, and eyes roam the room for the source of the smell as the eight of us sit and wait to see whether Beth will show up. Jason hasn't been to work all week. When it's obvious she's not coming, I turn to my right and ask Rod how his week went.

"Same old. Only now she's not talking to me." Rod throws his hands up in the air.

"Did you put to use any of our suggestions from last week?" Mom asks. "Steve cleaned the house today." Her blush deepens.

"If I waited around for Rod to clean the house, I'd suffocate under a foot of dust," Janice says, shooting her husband a look that makes me glad the steak knives are safely tucked in the kitchen.

"I cleaned the house *and* did the laundry today," Sid joins in. "Gail and her mom sat in the back yard with a couple bottles of wine. I'm not complaining. But, when your mother-in-law passes out on the picnic table, the neighbors are bound to talk. She'll probably still be there when we get home."

Gail looks like she's not far from passing out herself. She hiccoughs in response to Sid's words, her face a rosy red, a likely match to the wine she consumed before Group.

And the bickering between the two couples starts in earnest, while the rest of us sit and listen. Thank God Mallory and I don't have problems. I'm embarrassed for these two guys, their wives nagging and making a scene like this. I need to put a stop to it before one of them murders her husband.

"Wow, time sure flies. How about we take a break ?" I need one, whether they do or not. "Mal's got some great snacks for us, doncha, hon?"

"Yes, I do, hon."

She leaves the den, and we follow…Mom to help her out and the rest of us to the living room. I glance out the window and comment on the nice weather. Seems like a safe topic.

Dad picks up the ball. "Great for September. Except for the few storms we've had. Guess it's kind of like marriage—you have to take the bad with the good."

I continue the weather conversation, stating how the sump pump kept up nicely with last night's rainfall. The guys join in, discussing pumps and drainage, eavestroughs, and the like. Mal comes to the rescue with food trays on the dining room table, and Mom's got the coffee and tea ready. There's peace and quiet for the next fifteen minutes while everyone stuffs their face.

Gail leaves the room and returns with a puzzled expression. She uses her finger to count the number of people in the room. "Seven, counting me. And Janice is in the powder room. So, who's in the...?"

Mallory ushers her out of the room and toward the stairs. "You can use the upstairs bathroom."

Back at Group, things fall apart again. I squeeze Mal's hand, indicating I could use some help.

Let's show them what a successful marriage looks like, hon.

She's quiet.

I guess she wants me to start. "Mal and I have had a good week. I've been working on finishing touches to the new room. We had a picnic at the lake on Sunday. Mal's aunt and uncle have generously offered to buy a crib for the baby. We had a bit of a skunk problem earlier in the week, but it's all taken care of."

I turn to Mallory to see if she wants to add anything, encouraging her to speak up with a smile on my face and a hand on her back.

"I don't think the skunk problem has been resolved yet," she says.

"Oh...I think it's all good, Mal. It just takes a while for that smell to be completely gone."

"You're the foulest skunk around here, Jake."

"Mal?"

"All that talk about honesty and trust. That's all it was. Just talk. I thought we were done with the secrets and lies."

"We are, hon."

CHAPTER TWENTY-FOUR

But she's not done. She lets it rip.

"You promised you weren't going to gamble anymore. You lied to me. When I found that casino card, you swore it wasn't yours. And last night, you said you were out with Craig. Liar! Brad saw you. Going into the casino."

"I can explain, honey. It's not the way it looks."

"Not the way it looks? I tried calling you, and you didn't answer. Because gambling means more to you than me and the baby. *That's* the way it looks, Jake. I thought maybe you'd been in an accident when I couldn't get in touch with you. I thought maybe you were dead. Again. Just like you've let me think so many times. But you didn't consider me, did you? All you cared about was betting. And then you came home and punched Brad for no reason. He was worried about me and came to check I was okay. But your jealousy won't allow me to have friends. You expect me to sit out here in the middle of nowhere, by myself while you're out drinking, gambling, wasting our money, and…sleeping with other women. Is this what it's going to be like when the baby comes? Because I don't want to raise my baby like this. I'd rather be on my own."

My mouth flies open in protest, but I can't get a word in edgewise. Mom runs over to put her arms around Mallory to console her and to lambaste me.

"How could you, Jake? Mallory deserves so much better than you. Gambling, drinking, lying. Ignoring Mal and letting her worry. And other women? What is the matter with you?"

"I guess that explains the bruise on your face," Sid comments.

"I'm innocent, I swear. On the baby's…on my life. I can explain, Mal, honest, I can."

"We're all waiting to hear it, Jake." Good old Dad adds his two cents worth.

All eyes on me, I whimper, "Honest, Mal. You have to believe me. Trust me. It's not the way it looks. Can we talk about this in private?" I'm very conscious of six pairs of eyes taking it all in, Jake and Mallory's perfect married life that isn't so perfect after all.

"Honest? Trust? You don't know the meaning of the words."

I open my mouth to say she hasn't exactly been honest with me more than a few times, then I clamp it shut. The whole world doesn't need to know every shitty detail we sweep under the rug.

Mal leaves the room, Mom following. Dad shakes his head. The other two couples are silent. At least I've made them forget their own marriage problems for a while. I start folding chairs, indicating the meeting is adjourned.

That went well, Jake.

At the front entrance, Rod turns on the outside lights, opens the door, and comments, "I didn't know you had a dog."

Nellie slinks around my legs, notices the Russell Terrier running circles in our front lawn, and hunches her back, hair standing on end. Mal scoops her up and locks her in the laundry room.

As I kick everybody out the door, Paul saunters along, on cue, huffing and puffing. He dodders up our lawn, sets his hands on his knees, about to collapse as he tries to catch his breath. The dog's lead hangs from one hand. "Russ…there you…are…come…to…Daddy…boy."

I pull out my phone in case the old guy needs emergency assistance.

Russ scoots back and forth between Paul and our guests, dodging attempts to contain him. Something hangs from his mouth. A plastic grocery bag weighed down with its contents.

"Your dog steal your groceries?" I ask.

Paul takes a few deep breaths. "No. He found…something. Russ…likes to…dig."

Our guests circle Russ so Paul can leash him, but Russ is having a great old time playing 'Catch me if you can.' He darts back and forth amongst us.

Paul, who isn't in danger of having a heart attack after all, regains his normal breathing and speech. "We were out in the woods. Russ likes to go for a run on the trail. And he's a digger. Always digging up some great gem. I don't know what he found today, but he took off like a shot and made a beeline for your place."

Rats. I mean, mice. And a possum. Covered in maggots, flies, and other goodies.

This is all I need. What if there's some DNA in that bag? From Dead Guy? From me and Craig? But hold on. Something's not right. We used green garbage bags, not white grocery bags. Russ didn't dig up what was in the cistern. The bag probably holds somebody's garbage, out on a stroll through the woods, too lazy to take it home and dispose of it in an environmentally friendly way. I realize I've been holding my breath and let it out in a whoosh.

"Probably somebody's garbage. Lazy buggers can't be bothered to get rid of it properly." Paul echoes my thoughts.

"People throw stuff out of their car all the time," Sid adds. "Disgusting."

"To be fair," Rod says, "sometimes there's nowhere else to throw it."

"This wasn't near the street," Paul explains. "I took Russ down the road for a long walk, and we followed the trail deep into the woods. Russ ran way ahead—he's a fast little—anyway, he got away from me, and the next thing I knew, he was digging up something. When I tried to take it from him, he took off like a bat out of hell."

Russ makes a few more rounds from one to the other of us, manages to sneak through the circle completely, then back in again. When he finally stops zooming around like a crazed lunatic, he drops the bag and barks.

By the glow of the streetlamp and the house lights, Mallory's face is visible as she stands staring down at the bag and the dog, her mouth open, eyes wide.

Russ picks up the bag and delivers his treasure to Mallory, ripping open the bag. He sits back on his haunches, panting, his tongue hanging out, expecting to be petted.

Eight of us stare at Mallory, the dog, and the object on the ground. I'm no expert, but I've seen these before in Dom's goons' possession.

A black Glock lies on my front lawn, exposed for all the world to see. It's only a matter of time till someone calls the cops. There damn well better not be any more bodies on my property.

This won't end well.

Chapter Twenty-Five

The gun, it turns out, is not my biggest concern of the evening.

As our eyes flick back and forth to see who's quickest on the draw to pull out their phone and summon the cops, the buzz in my back pocket alerts me to a call. Checking the caller ID, I excuse myself. "Uh, I'll be right back. I'd better take this. Stay where you are. Nobody do anything stupid."

I retreat to the front porch, where I can speak in private while keeping an eye on the gang assembled on the edge of our lawn. My best friend from high school, Terry Cox, is on the line. The last time I saw him was a week Friday, the night the helicopter showed up above our cornfield.

I've got a bad feeling about this.

"Hey, Jake, buddy. You won't believe this."

Try me. I just might.

"What's up, Terry?"

"A body, Jake. That's what's up."

No. No, no, no. This can't be good.

"I don't know if there was anything about it in your local news tonight..." Terry begins.

"About what? A body?"

"My construction crew and I were breaking ground on a new building site on one of the islands this afternoon when we uncovered something. A dead guy. I called the cops, but I had a good look at him first. They're not releasing details yet, you know the drill—proper procedure, contact next of kin, ID the body. But this guy was at Dom's place Friday night. I recognized the flashy ring on his finger."

"You're sure it's the same guy? Other people wear rings."

"I could be wrong. But he was wearing those Jimmy Choos I wanted for my birthday. Becky bought me knockoffs. Said food on the table was a priority."

"Jimmy Chews?" Sounds like a dog treat.

"Shoes. Designer shoes. He wore them at the casino, and he wore them two feet under. Somebody didn't bother to hide him well, if you know what I mean."

"There must be other people with the same shoes. And what would he be doing five hours away, in Kingston? Did you get a good look at his face?"

"What was left of it, with the decomp and the bullet hole in his head. Maybe you're right. Could be some other poor schmuck. Same ring, same shoes, bullet through the brain. Anyway, I thought I'd warn you in case the police start asking questions over your way. I'm keeping quiet about it. Minding my own business. I'd strongly suggest you do the same."

"Okay, good. That's probably for the best. Thanks for the heads up, Terry. But I'm sure it must be someone else."

"You haven't heard, then?"

"Heard what?"

"Dom's setting up a new casino here, in the 1000 Island tourist trap."

Dom. Casino. Gun on my property. Body in cornfield. Body in cistern. And now, a body in Kingston. Put the clues together, Jake.

The phone slips from my hand, landing on the porch swing.

"You still there, Jake?"

"Yeah," I scramble to pick up my cell. "Thanks again, Terry, for the newsflash. But I'm not sure what it has to do with me or you."

"We're on the same wavelength, then."

After ending the call, I hurry back to the evidence bag and all the witnesses. Their circle protects the Glock from any stray passersby, as unlikely as they'd be to wander by on our stretch of road, especially after dusk.

"So, I think we can all agree we don't want to spend the night being interrogated by the cops. What do you say we bag it up and rebury that sucker deep in the woods?" I offer the only reasonable solution to the problem at hand.

Rod and Sid bob their heads up and down. Paul comments he'd just as soon not be involved, which I take to mean as agreement. Dad says he's not going back to prison. It looks like we're good to go. Pack up the gun and return it to its grave.

"Who wants to do the honors?" I motion toward the gun. "Paul? Your dog dug it up. What do you say you put it back?"

He shakes his head. "I think that's tampering with evidence or something. Isn't that illegal?"

"Maybe we should vote on this," Sid suggests. "It seems important, don't you think? What if it was used in a crime?"

"A crime? Out here? Naw. It's probably a hunting rifle," I say.

"Doesn't look like a hunting rifle to me."

"I want a vote." Paul speaks up again. "Russ and I found it, but I don't want trouble. Whatever everyone else decides, I'll go along with it. I vote neutral."

"Okay, good." I ask for a show of hands. "Who wants to bury the gun and forget about it?"

Four hands shoot up. Rod, Sid, Dad, me.

"And who wants to call the cops and answer a bunch of questions?"

Janice, Gail, and Mom raise their hands.

"Well, there you go. Four against three wins."

"What about Mallory?" Mom asks.

Mallory has been standing still, white as a ghost, since the gun was deposited at her feet.

"I think Mal's still in shock, Mom. Why don't we just leave her out of it?"

"I vote for the police," Paul says.

"You're neutral," I remind him.

"I changed my mind. I'm too old to do time for burying evidence."

I try to convince him it's in his best interest to pretend there is no gun. The other guys back me up. Meanwhile, Janice has called 911 to report a crime.

"What have you done?" I pace back and forth, trying to figure out my next step.

"We can't lie," Janice defends her actions. "If the truth comes out, we'll all get charged."

If the truth comes out...

The truth will set you free. Not likely.

Chapter Twenty-Six

Keep it cool, Jake. Casual.

K eep it cool, Jake. Casual. The cops arrive on the scene quicker than I can lose a grand at the craps table. Not the same guys who were here earlier in the week, thank God. One older male, the other a cute young chick.

Best to meet this head-on. "Good evening, Officers. Thanks for coming out so quickly. There's no real emergency here. My neighbor, Paul…" I point him out. "Well, he's got a bit of a problem. His dog dug up a gun in the woods. He wasn't sure what to do with it, so we decided to let you guys handle it."

They flash a heavy-duty flashlight on the Glock, then scan the crowd on my lawn.

"Mrs. Shelton," the woman officer turns her attention to Mallory. "Is everything okay? This is the second 911 call this week."

Mallory has composed herself enough to speak. "Yes, Officer Chen. Thank you for coming out. It's like my husband said. Russ dug up a gun. Is it *real?*"

The gloved male officer picks it up by the trigger guard and examines it. "It's real, all right. Did anyone touch it? Besides the dog?"

"No, Officer Glencoe. We called you right away."

Since when does my wife know the entire police force by name?

"Were you having a party, Mrs. Shelton?"

"A party?"

He indicates the people assembled on the lawn and the cars in the driveway. "It's just the two of you who live here, right?" His eyes move from Mal to me. "The rest are visiting?"

"Sorry, do we know each other?" I try to ascertain how he knows about Mal and me.

"Officer Chen and I were here this summer, when you were presumed dead."

"Well, as you can see, I'm alive."

"We were glad to hear things worked out for you. Too bad about the other guy, though."

"Yeah, thanks." Somebody's got to be the victim. "It's too bad."

Officer Glencoe places the gun in an evidence bag, and scoops up the plastic grocery bag, as well. He turns to Paul. "I take it the gun was wrapped in this?"

"Yes. I didn't know what it was until Russ dropped it here and ripped it open." Paul shrugs his shoulders and gestures toward Russ.

The officers want to speak to each of us in private. "Would it be okay if we come inside?" Officer Glencoe asks.

"Sure, no problem." I gesture toward the front door. We've got nothing to hide. Now that the bodies have been relocated.

He takes Paul into the den for questioning. The rest of us split up into the living and dining areas under Officer Chen's watchful eye as she stands in the entry hall between the two rooms. Nobody speaks.

It's my turn to be questioned next. Officer Glencoe tells me to take a seat opposite him on one of two folding chairs he's set up. A coiled notebook is open on his lap. When he asks for my account of how the gun ended up on my property, I tell the truth.

Dog ran down the road past his house to mine. Saw a bunch of people. Dropped a bag in front of us. Ripped it open. It was a gun. We called the police.

He asks some questions about Paul, then about the party we were having. A few minutes later, it's Mal's turn to talk. I give her an encouraging smile as she leaves the living room, hoping she reads my mind.

Don't tell them you found it in the cornfield and buried it in the woods. And, for God's sake, don't say anything about the bodies.

Mom catches on to the fact that something's off and asks Officer Chen if it's okay to make a fresh pot of coffee since everyone's staying longer than expected.

When Officer Chen hesitates, Mom adds, "It's been a long day. And the stress of what's happened must be getting to everyone. Especially Mallory. She's pregnant. I'm sure she'd appreciate a nice cup of herbal tea when she comes back out."

When Mom is given the okay to go to the kitchen, she asks if I can give her a hand. Officer Chen gives me permission to leave the room, which is really nice of her considering it's my house and my kitchen. And my den that's being used as an interrogation room.

"What's going on?" Mom whispers as she prepares the coffee, and I plug in the kettle for tea. "Do you know something about this?"

"No, of course not," I whisper back, shaking my head. Then I place my ear against the door and listen to what Mal has to say to Officer Glencoe.

Sounds like she's sticking to the story. Neighbor's dog. Found something in the woods. Bag. Gun. Still in shock. Someone called the police.

When she opens the door, I catch myself before I fall into the room. "Hey, Mal. We were just making coffee and tea. I wanted to ask if you'd like chamomile or peppermint. How about you, Officer? How do you take your coffee?"

Dad gets summoned next. Everyone continues to sit and wait, only now the sound of cups on saucers and sipping of hot liquid fills the space. The cute cop in the hall holds her teacup, eyes continuing to examine us for silent clues.

When they finally leave, our guests follow suit. Mal trudges up the steps, Nellie following, as I check the house to make sure everything's locked up. All's good, except for the mudroom bath, which is locked. Someone must have accidentally turned the button, and it latched behind them. I head downstairs and grab a screwdriver off the pegboard.

My head turns to the door leading to the cistern. The odor of what used to be there still lingers. It wouldn't hurt to check in case another body happened to drop in. Armed with the screwdriver pointing straight ahead, I walk through the door and scan the dirt floor.

CHAPTER TWENTY-SIX

Shit!

Several mouse traps hold carcasses. It might just be necessary to call the exterminators. Don't want any little critters scurrying up ladies' gowns next weekend. Mal would have a fit. In the kitchen, I pull a plastic grocery bag out of the drawer, cut up some cheese, and head back to dispose of the vermin and reset the traps. I'll call someone in the morning before it gets out of hand.

I'm halfway up the stairs with the dead mice when it occurs to me that I forgot to look in the cistern. The bag set on the kitchen floor, I return to the old section of basement and peer inside the concrete structure. A blood-curdling scream knocks me off the ladder.

Not taking the time to brush off the dirt, I run up the stairs to the source of the yelling. In the kitchen, a white-faced Mal stands backed up against the island.

"Honey, are you okay?"

She points to the bag of rodents.

"I'm sorry, Mal. I didn't know you were coming back in here. I was downstairs getting a screwdriver when I noticed we've got a few mice. Nothing to worry about."

"Get…rid…of…them."

"Sure, hon. Why don't you go back to bed? Let me finish up. I won't be long."

She walks out of the room without another word.

Things could be worse. At least the cistern is free of bodies.

Once the dead mice are taken out to the bin in the garage, I wash up and go back to what I was doing. With the head of the screwdriver inside the hole of the doorknob, I push and twist until it unlocks. The door swings open.

What the…?

Pieces of toilet tank lid lie on the floor. The toilet seat is closed, a gouge out of it, with a piece of cracked porcelain on it. Where the lid should be is a gaping hole showing off the rust inside, even though it's only a few years old.

What the hell happened here? Does Mal know about this? No, I would have heard about it. She'd have a meltdown with this happening so close to the wedding. The nerve of some people. Using our facilities and leaving them in a disgusting condition. It's going to take more than a toilet brush and air freshener to clean up this mess.

It's late, and I want some time with Mallory to make up after our little tiff this evening. Once I explain where I was last night, she'll understand. I'll promise to finish up the family room tomorrow. That'll put her in a better mood.

She's on her side again, clinging to the edge of the bed. I touch her shoulder, and she pulls away.

"Honey? I think we should talk." Communication is important.

She ignores me. Maybe I should start.

"Don't worry about the gun, hon. They can't trace it back to you."

No response.

"I'm going to call the exterminators tomorrow. Just in case there's another mouse or two down there."

Silence.

"I think Group went well, don't you? We dealt with a lot of issues tonight. Communicated really good."

Nothing.

"I'm sorry about Brad. I shouldn't have hit him. You've got every right to have your male friends over in the middle of the night when I'm not home. I overreacted. I just love you so much, and you're so beautiful. I get jealous sometimes."

Maybe she's asleep.

"Did you happen to know who used the back bathroom last? They had an altercation with the toilet. The toilet lost. Don't go in there till I take care of the problem."

I'm not sure whether the snorts into her pillow are the result of crying or laughing, but it's a reaction, so I keep going. "Looks like a bomb went off. Pieces everywhere. You'd think someone would have mentioned they'd had a problem instead of leaving it in that condition."

Mallory rolls over. She's bawling, tears streaming down her face, but laughing hysterically at the same time. "It was...me. I'm...sorry."

"Oh. Okay. What happened, hon? Did you and the toilet have a disagreement?"

Laughter overtakes the crying. I join her. Better to have a hysterically amused wife than a hysterical one.

She takes a deep breath, snorts a few more times, then tells me what happened. "I wasn't going to say anything. I thought you'd be mad if the toilet was broken."

"You didn't think I'd notice?" I'm still chuckling.

"I hoped you'd think someone else did it. I know how upset you get when things are a bit out of place. And that...seemed out of place." She snorts again. "I'm sorry."

"It's just a toilet, Mal. I'll head into the city tomorrow and pick up a new one. This one's already a couple of years old. Time for a replacement anyway."

I can replace the toilet, but Mallory is irreplaceable.

"You're sure you're not mad?"

"No, hon. Craig and I will put in the new toilet tomorrow afternoon. And get the blinds up, too. The new carpet should be in any day, and we'll set up the furniture. All set for the big weekend."

"You and Craig? Are you sure you know how to put a toilet in? Maybe you should call a plumber. I know it will cost more, but..."

"How hard can it be to put a toilet in?"

She reminds me of the kitchen lights I tried to install this morning. And she adds, "The kitchen taps work great."

"See. I'm not totally incompetent."

"But shouldn't the cold water be on the right and the hot on the left, not the other way around?"

We convulse with laughter again. Since she's in a good mood, I move in for some snuggling, maybe more. I luck out. She *is* in the mood.

Afterwards, she lies in my arms; a big sigh escapes her. "I didn't want to lie to you about the toilet. Or the gun. Or the body falling from the helicopter.

129

And…I know I haven't always been honest myself. Sometimes, it's better to keep things to yourself to keep the peace."

Yep. Like what you did this summer. Like sleeping with my best friend. Let's just pretend none of it happened.

"But you should tell me if you're still tempted to gamble," she continues. "You shouldn't have lied about being with Craig instead of the casino. We need to face your problems—I mean, *our* problems—together. No more secrets, no more lies, right, Jake?"

"No, Mal. No more. You can trust me."

"I do. I trust you more than I don't trust you. More than I trust anyone else."

"Me too. I trust you with my life."

Her blue eyes, deep as the ocean, hold mine. "I *do* love you. It's just that there's a lot of work to be done in the trust department."

Maybe marriage isn't all fun and games. Work? I kiss Mal's forehead and her cute little nose, brush my lips against hers, and whisper into her ear as I hold her in my arms. "You're everything to me. You and our baby. Our family. I'm willing to spend the next sixty years to life working on us."

And I tell her where I was when I lied about being with Craig, and exactly what happened. Last night and the Friday night before that. And Terry's phone call.

We're in this together. As deep as it gets.

Chapter Twenty-Seven

L ast Friday night is when all this began. Terry, back in town to visit his parents, had invited me out for a drink to celebrate his thirtieth birthday. When I explained my weekends were tied up with renos and getting ready for Craig's big day, we agreed to meet after my Friday evening shift.

I could hardly turn him down. We'd grown up together, were best buds right through high school and college, and even when he and Becky moved to Kingston, we stayed in touch. But when he mentioned meeting at the River Grand Casino, I balked.

"Sorry, Terry. I'm done with the casino. I promised Mallory I'd stay away from there. No more gambling." I had told Mal I was going out for drinks, not to the River Grand.

"Sure, I understand, Jake. Gotta keep the wife happy. I know all about that. But I'm meeting a couple other old buds from high school there. What do you say we have a couple of drinks at the bar, catch up a bit, and you can be on your way?"

I didn't see the harm in that.

Not much had changed since I kept my promise to stay out of the casino. I parked in the well-lit lot and strode past the cascading fountains into the casino resort. Sliding doors sporting the River Grand logo welcomed me into the stone and wood lobby, vegetation and rock waterfalls creating an outdoorsy setting. I continued to the left, down the wide hall, past boutiques, toward the neon casino sign. No sooner had I set foot past the entrance than a couple of goons stopped me.

"Hey, I'm legal. I'll show you my ID."

One of the goons smirked. "Anybody can see that. That's not the issue. You've been barred. Dom's orders. No entry without an appointment."

Shit!

I'd forgotten that. Not exactly, but I figured he'd have other things to do besides monitor my activities.

"I'm just here to meet a friend for a birthday drink, that's all. No gambling for me. No siree."

"You're on the 'do not admit' list."

"There's a list?"

"Complete with license plate and facial recognition," said the other goon. "And you're a match."

"I'm sure Dom won't mind if I spend a few bucks on drinks for my pal's thirtieth birthday."

The first guy spoke into his microphone, indicating my request to Dom, who granted me a temporary pass. Terry and his friends were already working their way through a pitcher of beer and a bowl of nachos as I was escorted to their table.

"Jake! Glad you could make it," Terry greeted me. "You remember Todd and Chris from high school?"

I scrutinized their faces. "Hey, haven't seen you guys for ages." They were older, but still sported the same mischievous look about them. We'd had a blast partying through our last couple of years of school together.

As the midnight hour came and went, we reminisced about our youth and caught up on our lives, toasting Terry for joining the thirty-year club. Every now and then, my eyes wandered to the gaming floor, taking in the colorful slot machines, their musical jingling competing for my attention.

Like a midway. Like fireworks. A Christmas parade. It's like being a kid in a room full of candy when you're diabetic. I want...I can't have.

I was trying, and failing, to keep my eyes and ears off the machines when some guy placed his hand on my shoulder. "Jake, isn't it?"

Turning around, I took in the familiar face but couldn't put a name to him. Faking it, I plastered on my charming smile. "Hey, good to see you. How's it going?"

"Haven't seen you for a while. Where've you been?"

"Oh, here and there. Keeping my nose clean."

"No more high rolling?"

That's where I knew him from. He was one of those rich guys (richer than me, anyway) I lost to during the few times I was stupid enough to play in the high-limit room. Great place to make connections and a perfect place to lose your cash. Not to mention your furniture, car, investments, and house.

And your wife.

"No more gambling, period," I responded. "Just having a drink with a few friends."

"Well, it was nice seeing you." He nodded to the other three guys at the table. "Enjoy the rest of your night."

Which reminded me, I needed to get home if I wanted to enjoy any quality time with Mallory. "Guys, it's been great getting together, but I need to head home."

"Sure you don't want to play a few hands first?" asked Terry.

"Yeah, I'm sure. Gotta get home to my wife." As I pushed back my chair, I bumped into someone.

"Hey, Jake. Leaving already?"

I turned around and came face to face with Jason Bartlett. Our first Group session apparently had done nothing to keep him from pursuing his addiction. Guess some guys just don't have willpower. "Yep. So should you, Jase. Or we'll both be facing the wrath of our wives."

"One more night out won't hurt. I need to win back some of the money I've lost. Then, I'll quit cold turkey."

I nodded toward Terry, Todd, and Chris. "These guys are heading off to the card tables, if you want to join them."

I shook Terry's hand. "Happy birthday, bud. See you again soon." He gave me a pat on the back, and I waved goodbye to the gang, proud of myself for not giving in to temptation.

As I walked away, my eyes took in the gaming floor, lit up like a carnival, enticing me to go for a ride, but what really attracted me was the casino pit.

The magnetic pull of chips, cards, dice, and the wheel held me prisoner as the croupiers and dealers distributed cards and took bets.

Just one bet. One win. Then I'll go home.

As I stopped outside the high-limit poker room, considering whether to go in, a guy I recognized brushed past, opened the door, and held it for me. "Haven't seen you at the tables lately. Joining us tonight?"

"Good evening, Mr. Ricco." The doorman greeted the bald-headed man. "Your usual table?"

Inside the room, several of the regulars concentrated on their cards. I stepped foot inside and told myself one game wouldn't hurt as I scanned the room, Mallory's voice in my head arguing with me.

I didn't get the chance to make a decision. The two goons showed up, told me I'd overstayed my welcome, and walked me to my car.

"Dom wishes to extend his greetings to your lovely wife."

Large drops plopped onto my hood as I thanked them for the personal service and slid into the driver's seat. I waved through my window as I turned the key in the ignition. Hopefully, Mal would still be awake reading or watching a movie.

Rivulets flowed down the gravel when I turned into our driveway. A nice, cozy bed with my loving wife awaited me. Under the glow of security lights, I unlocked the front door and stepped into the house, removing my wet shoes. At the top of the stairs, the nightlight shone, beckoning me.

Mal had left the bedroom door partially open. A good sign.

"Hi, hon, I'm home."

"Just after one o'clock. Not bad. Did you have a good time with Terry?" She closed the cover to her iPad and set it on the night table.

"Yep. Caught up with a couple other friends from high school, too."

"That's nice."

"Not as nice as coming home to you."

I peeled off my damp clothes, hung them on the edge of the hamper, and slid in next to Mallory, pulling her on top of me. Turned out she was more fun than a room full of slots.

Hours later, Mallory woke me complaining about the wind. As if there was something I could do about it. If she wasn't so paranoid about every little noise, we would never have seen the helicopter. What if Mal hadn't found the gun? Would I be blamed for something if someone else found it?

Chapter Twenty-Eight

J ake is trying. Telling me the truth about the casino and how he was tempted is a positive step in our marriage. I'm not sure what Dom is up to and how Jake fits into his scheme, but Dom won't destroy us. I won't allow it.

I fall asleep in Jake's arms, the steady beat of his heart reassuring me that we *will* survive whatever hurdles are thrown in our path.

When I wake, the room is brightening, indicating a pleasant Sunday ahead. Jake is gone. I roll onto his side, taking in the indentations from his body, his smell, his warmth, the part of him he left behind. The comfort of knowing he's downstairs while I inhale his essence lulls me back to sleep.

By the time I'm ready to begin the day and head downstairs, no trace of darkness remains. In the kitchen, the smell of coffee lingers, although Jake has cleared his breakfast dishes. No sound comes from the mudroom area.

Where is Jake?

The back door, still locked, indicates he isn't in the back yard. He was supposed to be working on the bathroom. Is he behind the closed door? Awfully quiet. No whistling, humming. I turn the knob to find it latched.

I pull the new doorknob on the freshly painted basement door and call down the stairs. No answer.

Nellie slinks out of the laundry room, stretches, and meows around my legs, asking why breakfast is late. On the fridge, I find a note attached with a magnet.

Gone to city to pick up new toilet. Noticed you need a new phone, too.

Nellie and I eat together, her bowl of pate on the floor next to my chair, cereal and tea on the table for me.

After breakfast, I gather a load of laundry and deposit it into the washing machine. Reaching for the detergent on the shelf, my hand grazes something hard. A screwdriver slides to the edge and stops at the trim. Jake probably thought he'd need it today, so he didn't bother to put it back on the tool bench pegboard.

I pick it up and turn it over in my hand, examining the point on the end. I've seen him use this tool before. When I locked myself in the ensuite bathroom with his wallet and keys so he couldn't go to the variety store to buy lottery tickets. This is how he got into the bathroom and found the broken tank lid last night.

So, why is the door locked now if he unlocked it?

With the pointed tip in the small hole of the doorknob, I push, then turn. It pops the lock, and I swing open the door to find the toilet lid pieces lying on the floor in a neat pile, smooth surface to the floor, lip facing up, and a few slivers swept toward the wall. Jake started to clean up, then left it sitting there.

What made him leave it like this?

My eyes scan the porcelain on the floor, and I bend over the pieces, furrowing my brow.

A sound at the front entryway makes me jump. Footsteps creep down the hall toward the kitchen. My fist tightens around the screwdriver, pointed end straight ahead. A shape comes through the doorway of the mudroom.

"So. You found it."

Chapter Twenty-Nine

"Found what?"

Jake tilts his head and narrows his eyes. "The money." He brushes me aside, kneels, and sorts through the pieces of broken porcelain.

"What money, Jake?"

"Where'd you hide it, hon?"

"I don't know what you're talking about."

"Don't mess with me, Mal." He looks up, his iridescent eyes turned a steely teal. "Where is it?"

Jake searches through the mess again, pulls towels off the towel rack, rummages through vanity drawers, and dumps the contents onto the mudroom floor. He opens the shower door and scans the niches. "What have you done?"

"Jake? You're scaring me." I back away toward the kitchen.

He stands in the mudroom, facing me, and speaks in a low voice. "This morning, when I came down to clean up the mess you made, there was a wad of cash in a plastic baggie, taped to the underside of the toilet tank lid."

He's doing it again. Jake's been hiding money, keeping it from me to finance his gambling. Same old Jake. Promises mean nothing to him. "No more secrets, you said. And you're still hiding money. Still going to the casino. Lies, Jake. That's all you're good for." My hands instinctively cover my belly, protecting our unborn child from his father.

"It's not mine, Mal. I didn't put it there."

"Of course, you didn't. It just magically appeared and disappeared."

"I'm telling the truth, honey." He slides down the side of the wall, sits on

138

the floor, knees bent, hands covering his face. "Please, I *need* you to believe me. I need you on my side."

"I am so sick and tired of these games, Jake. How many times do we have to do this? If you're telling the truth, then why didn't you say something? Why lock the door and keep it secret?"

His hands slide down, and he meets my eyes. "I didn't want to disturb your sleep. That's why I left it where I found it, taped to the inside of one of the large broken pieces, and went to the city to pick up a replacement toilet. I was going to talk to you about it. I thought maybe you had put it there."

"Why would I put money down the toilet? That's something you would do, not me. Why can't you take responsibility for your own stupidity?"

Jake shakes his head. "You're right. I haven't got a good track record for being responsible or smart. But I swear, Mal, I'm doing my best to change."

"Maybe your best isn't good enough."

"Maybe it's not. But I know I saw that money this morning. And if you or I didn't put it there, or take it away, then who did?"

"Do you think...?" The doorbell rings, cutting off my question.

Jake eases himself to his feet and walks past me to answer the door. "Not a word about this to anyone."

Great. Another secret.

Vicky's voice travels through the hall. "Hey, Jake. You look white as a ghost. Are you feeling okay? Where's Mallory?"

"I'm in here," I call from the kitchen. "I'm making another pot of coffee. Be right there."

Vicky glides into the kitchen with a box of bakeshop pastries, removes mugs from the cupboard, and sets them on the counter, along with the sugar bowl and milk pitcher. Dressed in designer jeans and a skin-tight sweater, her makeup and hair perfect, Vicky notices my pajamas. "Did you just get up?"

"I slept in. The baby—"

"Of course, you need to get your rest. Let me start the coffee. Why don't you sit down?"

The aroma of freshly brewed coffee fills the room as Jake and Craig lug in a box, which I assume is our new toilet, with its tank lid intact and no cash on the underside.

"Just leave it here," Jake says, meaning to the side of the kitchen doorway leading to the mudroom. "We have to haul out the old one first. I'll go down and get my tools. You can check online for instructions on how to install a toilet."

"You mean you don't know how to do it?" Craig raises his eyebrows.

"I'll figure it out. Won't hurt you to learn a few things about toilet repair, too. When your wife smashes the toilet to pieces, you'll be able to replace it lickety split."

"O...kay."

Everyone's eyes are on me, waiting for an explanation.

"I tried to fix the toilet. It was running. The lid was heavy." Enough said.

"It must have been a shock when it fell and broke," Vicky says. "As long as you didn't get hurt, that's the main thing."

"No, I'm fine. It just took me by surprise, that's all."

Craig researches on his phone while Jake assembles tools in the mudroom. Before getting to work, we sit down at the table for a mid-morning snack.

"I don't know about this. It looks complicated." Craig looks down at his phone. "Maybe you should call a plumber."

"And waste good money? We've got enough expenses running this house and doing all these renos. And there's the baby to think of. Babies are expensive. Mallory will be off work for a year, and we'll have to manage on one salary. Not that I'm complaining. But we do have to watch the money." Jake spills the details of our financial situation but doesn't mention we'll be fine with the inheritance from my parents and his grandfather, as long as he doesn't gamble it all away. I guess he wants to show he's the provider in our family.

"Okay, if you're sure. I've never done anything like this." Craig looks dubious, eyes going from his screen to the mudroom where the toilet job waits.

"You'll get used to it. Once you're married."

Warm yellow rays stream through the windows onto the new hardwood, and Jake suggests Vicky and I spend the day outside while the men work, and he'll barbecue later. The weather is deceptive this time of year. Cool air greets us as we open the back door. I grab a couple of sweaters from the back closet, and we head for the rattan sofa, which now sits on the lawn until the deck can be rebuilt.

"I can't believe that in less than a week, I'll be married to Craig," Vicky says, pulling the throw over our legs. "It all happened so fast. A whirlwind romance."

Not exactly. They've known each other for as long as Jake and I have been married, which is over three years now. Just because they couldn't get their act together and kept breaking up doesn't make it a quick courtship. If anyone had a whirlwind romance, it was Jake and me. We were married six months after we started dating just weeks after he and Vicky broke up.

"Well, when you know it's right, there's no point in waiting." And the sooner she marries Craig, the less of a threat she'll be to my own marriage.

"Let's just hope Saturday's weather is as nice as today's."

"The long-term forecast looks good. And even if it rains, we'll mostly be in the tent, anyway." I point to the expanse of lawn in front of us. "If they set it up over there, it won't be too far from the house."

"So, they're setting it up Thursday?"

"It's all scheduled. Tent, lighting, heat, and furniture. The landscapers will be here Wednesday. Then, Thursday, the cleaning crew is giving the house a thorough scrub. The potted flowers are going to be brought into the tent early Saturday morning, along with all the decorations, and the DJ is setting up then, too. How is everything on your end?"

Jake and I had promised to take care of all the major details as we're hosting the big event (at Vicky and Craig's expense, of course—it *is* their wedding).

"All set. Caterers. Liquor permit. Cake. Photographer."

"Officiant?" I joke, knowing she's taken care of this.

Vicky laughs, tossing back her straight auburn hair. "That was the first thing I booked. And we've got the license. I want to be sure it's all official."

We bask in the sun, eyes closed, enjoying the September late morning.

Memories of my own wedding flash through my mind, and I smile. A beautiful June day, the best of my life.

"Mallory?" Vicky interrupts thoughts of Jake waiting for me, smile wide and eyes twinkling as I walked down the aisle. "Is there someone in your cornfield?"

My eyes fly open, and I sit up straight. "Not that I know of. Who would be out here?"

"I thought I saw movement among the stalks."

"Probably just the coyotes." I stand, ready to yell, and wave my arms in the air.

"Coyotes?" Vicky bolts off the sofa toward the house. Seconds later, she runs back out. "Mallory! Do you have any more towels? The bathroom's flooded."

She wrings out a couple of towels on the lawn as I run inside to find water seeping out of the bathroom into the mudroom and toward my family room hardwood. Throwing the basket of folded towels in the laundry room onto the ground to save my new flooring, I yell at Jake.

"What did you do? Didn't I tell you to call a plumber?"

"It's Craig's fault," he shouts back.

Not waiting to hear Craig's response, I hurry up the stairs to grab more towels out of the linen closet. By the time I return to the flood, Jake and Craig are sitting in a puddle on the mudroom floor. Craig has his phone up to his ear. Jake is swearing up a storm. Vicky is carrying another load of sopping wet towels out the door. Nellie, her paws and tail wet, shakes off excess water into Jake's face.

"The plumber's on her way. She charges double for emergency calls on a Sunday," Craig informs Jake.

"Why the hell didn't you remind me to shut off the water valve first?" Jake glares at his best friend.

"I figured you'd already done that. How was I supposed to know you didn't? I told you I'm not a home reno expert. Like you."

This cracks Jake up. "Like me?" He roars with laughter, and Craig and I observe him closely for signs he's about to blow.

But he takes a deep breath and asks, "Did Mal tell you about the lights yesterday? And have you tried the kitchen taps yet? Did you get a good look at those perfect angles on the trim? I'm an expert do-it-yourselfer, all right. Can't wait to come over to your new house and help you out; return the favor."

"Did anyone turn off the water yet?" I ask, mopping up the floor as Vicky removes the wet towels and replaces them with wrung-out ones.

"Of course, we shut it off. What do you take us for, idiots?" Jake deadpans as Craig jumps to his feet to check the valve.

Craig stands in the bathroom doorway, hand rubbing his forehead. "It's off. Now."

"I think you'd better call in the professionals when we do our renos," Vicky says.

"Renos? I thought the house looked in good shape the way it is."

"We'll want to add our own touches to the place. It *is* our first home together. I've got some ideas already for the great room and the master bedroom."

Jake chuckles. "And wait till the kids start coming. The nursery, the family room, another bathroom. It's never-ending."

"Kids?" Craig blanches.

"Yep, kids, renos. Welcome to the club."

Craig gazes at Vicky standing by the back door, then glances over at me, blocking the way to the front exit. If he had a clear path, I'm sure he'd make a run for it and never look back. But the doorbell rings, bringing out a sigh from deep within him, and he says, "I think your plumber is here."

The middle-aged woman greets me with a curt nod when I answer the door. "Hi, I'm Lou. I hear you have a problem that needs to be taken care of."

"Yes. A couple of husbands who think they can install a toilet because they're men."

"Tell me about it. I wouldn't have half the business without guys like that."

I escort Lou to our flooded back area, where my husband sits in a pool of his own stupidity. "This is Jake, my expert handyman husband who doesn't like to spend money if he can do it himself. And this is Craig, his partner in home destruction who didn't think it was necessary to read the first instruction for toilet installation because Jake is too smart to be told the water needs to be shut off. And Vicky, his wife-to-be, who has great home renos of her own to look forward to."

I've learned a thing or two about not taking things seriously from Jake.

We leave the plumber to it, Jake and Craig changing in the basement into the fresh pants and t-shirts I throw down the stairs at them, and Vicky and I head upstairs to exchange our damp clothing for dry.

Vicky looks pensive. "You're happy, right? Being married? Renovating the house? The baby on the way? Watching your money? Tied to one man? Forever. Till death do you part?"

I assure her I'm very happy, and she will be, too.

Don't tell me they're both *thinking of backing out.*

It'll be fine. Everyone has second thoughts just before the wedding. I nearly voice this out loud, but I don't need to give her any ideas. The worst thing that could happen next Saturday is that instead of saying 'I do,' Craig will say he's changed his mind. Or that Vicky will not show up at all.

"Jake's problems make it a struggle sometimes," I say instead. No point in pretending with Vicky. She knows Jake. "But he makes me happy. I love him. And I don't want to live without him."

Vicky smiles. "Craig makes me happy. I guess I'm just worried I'll turn into a boring housewife and mother, and he'll get tired of me."

A boring wife and mother? Like me? Is that what she means?

"But when I see you and Jake together, I want what you have." Vicky surprises me with her assessment of my marriage. "Anyone can see you're meant for each other. And Jake is committed to you, despite his issues."

"Craig is committed to you, too. And he doesn't come with 'issues' like Jake," I joke, using my fingers as parentheses around the word. "Being married to Craig will be a fairytale come true. He's just a bit squeamish about marriage because of his own parents' unhappy lives."

At least Vicky has some understanding of why a woman would be attracted to Jake. I'm sure many others see me as weak, putting up with his nonsense.

There are many faces to my husband. He's a lot more complex than most people know.

His acquaintances see the easy-going, happy-go-lucky jokester who thinks he can't lose and who can be a bit of a jerk at the expense of others. That's the facade, the makeup covering the scars. Even Jake doesn't recognize that as his most superficial self. Jake's friends know about his addictive personality—the gambling, drinking, jealousy, obsessive-compulsive drive, short fuse. Those who love Jake see the abused little boy who grew into a teenager who saved his family by threatening to kill his own father if he didn't leave. Only Jake knew the part of him that struggled with the fear of becoming his own father. And only his mother and I know the true Jake. The boy within a man's body who wants nothing more than to be loved.

Having reassured each other and ourselves that we have chosen correctly in marrying the man we love, Vicky and I share a moment of genuine sisterhood, hands clasped in a bond I thought we had lost after high school.

"They don't deserve us," Vicky laughs. "What do you say we ditch them and go on that honeymoon together, you and I?"

"Sounds like a plan. But I don't think we should leave them to housesit. There might be nothing to come home to."

We giggle, breaking into a roar as we descend to the entry where Jake and Craig are hauling out the old toilet.

While the plumber fixes their toilet mess, Jake and Craig barbecue steaks and baked potatoes, and Vicky and I fix a green salad. On his way to the fridge to get barbecue sauce, Jake motions for me to join him in the dining room.

"We've got a big problem," he says.

"I know. The bathroom."

"I mean the money."

"What money?"

"The money somebody hid in the toilet. When they come back for it and find it missing, they're going to be really pissed off."

Chapter Thirty

My phone rings in the middle of the morning during activity time. I check the caller ID, motion to Sue to let her know I need a minute, then slip into the hall, closing the classroom door.

On the other end of the line, Beth sobs, unable to speak. All I can do is listen and wait for the inevitable. I know what she's likely to say, having heard from Jake about the body found on Dom's construction site two days ago. They must have made an identification.

"Beth?" I do need to get back to work.

"Sorry." She blows her nose several times. "I…"

"It's okay, take your time." I peer through the classroom window, checking the kids and the clock.

"He…he's gone."

"I'm so sorry, Beth."

"The police came…"

I know that feeling all too well. The police at my door when Mom and Dad died in the fire, when Jake went missing, when they thought he was dead. Poor Beth.

"…and they posted a notice."

"A notice?" A death notice in the paper?

"I don't have anywhere…no family nearby."

"Oh, Beth. I can't imagine." I can, but I won't burden her with the trauma I experienced. "You're not alone. We're here for you. Whatever you need."

"I don't think Jason is coming back."

No, I wouldn't think he is.

"I don't have anywhere…to go. I'm on my own." Beth starts up another round of convulsions.

What choice do I have but to be a shoulder to cry on? "I should be home by four-thirty at the latest. Come to our place. You're welcome to stay as long as you need."

When I return to the classroom, I whisper to Sue. "A friend of ours—her husband died."

"Oh, Mallory. I'm so sorry," she says. "How awful."

I nod, not explaining his death was neither the result of illness nor an accident. Bodies found in construction sites tend to be murder victims. At least, that's what I've learned from reading hundreds of mystery novels.

When I see Brad at lunch, he asks about Jake.

"He's fine," I say, referring to his bruised face as well as his ego. "And he apologizes. To me and to you."

Brad accepts that, but he reminds me to call whenever I need him.

Knowing Beth is going to need *me*, I hurry home at the end of the day. Cloud cover forms a white blanket over the sky, and the chill of autumn invades my bones as I scurry to my front door. I should have worn a jacket today. You never know what to expect from the weather in southern Ontario. One day, you need a snowsuit, and a few days later, it's a swimsuit. Or vice versa.

Before changing into comfortable loungewear, I turn on the furnace and light candles in the living room and kitchen to create a warm atmosphere and to take the dampness out of yesterday's wet floor tiles. At least my new hardwood was spared.

Nellie insists it's suppertime, so I take care of that and peer into the freezer looking for inspiration. What do I offer to a guest who has just lost her husband? She won't be hungry, but she needs to eat something. And I'm starving, with the baby needing sustenance, but I'm too tired to fuss.

Chicken. I take out a package of chicken breasts and set them in cold water to thaw, chop onion and garlic, then prepare a romaine and tomato salad and set the bowl in the fridge. Add rice, broth, and spices to the chicken, and I'll have a one-dish meal in the oven while I focus on consoling Beth.

I tune the radio to a soft pop station on low volume as a distraction and to set a calm mood, and lie on the sofa, picking up my book. Before long, the sound of a vehicle prompts me to open the front door. Beth exits her car, pulling out a small suitcase from the passenger side.

"Thanks so much, Mallory. You have no idea what this means to me." She deposits her bag and purse in the entryway.

"Of course, Beth. You shouldn't feel alone at a time like this. Come in and make yourself comfortable."

Her face shows evidence of the trauma she's suffering, pale with hollow eyes, but Beth seems to have reined in her emotions temporarily, if only for the short drive to get here. She seems to be taking her husband's death with stoicism. A bit older than me, somewhere in her thirties, Beth has long suffered from the effects of her husband's gambling addiction.

"He's left me. With nothing."

At risk of repeating 'I'm sorry' again, I set my hand on hers and sit quietly.

"I don't know what to do now," she continues.

"Have you thought about making arrangements for…things?" I can't bear to say the word 'funeral'. And I have no idea how it works when the deceased is a murder victim.

"I don't know where to start. All I have left is my car, and it's not paid for. And my job."

Beth is a makeup consultant at a boutique in the city. With no children and not being a homeowner, I suppose her job consumes all her attention. And now that Jason's gone, what else can she cling to?

"It's important to keep busy. Work is good," I say.

"It's not a husband," she states.

"No."

"Our savings are gone. Most of the furniture, too."

"What about insurance?" Early in our marriage, Jake made sure we'd be covered if anything should happen to one of us.

"Property insurance?" Wrinkles form on Beth's brow. "I thought that was just if stuff was stolen or ruined or something. Not if your husband sold it on you."

"Oh." I'm not sure what she's talking about. I meant life insurance, so I tilt my head and raise my eyebrows, encouraging her to elaborate.

"Jason has been selling off the furniture to pay for his gambling. We were saving for a house, but he blew it all. I didn't even know until recently. Jason takes care of..." Tears roll, and she chokes up. "...the bills and everything. But now he's gone, and the police put up an eviction notice on the door of our condo today. Jason hasn't been paying rent for months, and the landlord threatened to kick us out, but I didn't think he would actually do it."

"Oh, my." I realize she's in a position I could so easily have been in myself had I not put my foot down when it came to Jake and his gambling.

"Do you think he's with another woman?" Tears stream down Beth's cheeks.

She doesn't know he's dead yet. How can that be? Wouldn't the police have notified her that his body was found? Unless...he's not dead?

"Have you heard anything from him? Or about him? From the police, maybe?"

"No, the police said they'd let me know if they had any news, but there's been nothing. And I haven't heard from Jason since he left last Friday."

"Do you know where he was going?"

"Out for drinks with the guys, he said. But I know he lied. He was at the casino."

Beth is a mirror image of me. We're interchangeable. Two women who are victims of their husband's addictions. Why don't we simply leave them? That would be the smart choice. No more financial woes, no wondering whether he got so drunk he ended up in bed with someone else, no worrying he's lying dead somewhere.

I pat her hand again, but it seems too little to do for the poor woman, so I put my arms around her and tell her I understand what she's going through, and she needs to have faith that it will all work out.

"I hope you can manage to eat something. I'm making chicken and rice for supper."

"Oh...I...thank you. I haven't been eating well the past week."

"Come into the kitchen, and I'll make you a cup of coffee or tea while I get the food into the oven."

We sip our tea, the comforting aroma of supper cooking mixed with the scented candles, and I confide in Beth, telling her what happened to Jake and me this past summer. Not everything, but enough to let her know I went through a similar experience.

"And he came back. It was a rough road for both of us, but we worked through it." I want to give her hope, although I have serious doubts her story will end up as happily as mine did.

Beth excuses herself to use the bathroom. When she comes back through the mudroom, she asks, "Is that a new toilet?"

"Yes, we got it yesterday. The old one broke."

"Oh. What happened?"

I tell her the whole sordid tale, making it sound funny, to get her mind off Jason. "Jake doesn't like to spend money on things he can do himself, so he tried to install the new toilet. It didn't go well."

"So, he had to pay double in the end?" Beth chuckles in spite of her situation.

"Yes, and he wouldn't let the plumber take the old one away. Said he wasn't paying extra for disposal fees, even when she said it was included in the price. I don't think he believed her."

"What did he do with the broken toilet?"

"He and Craig hauled it to the garage. He'll take it to the dump with the other junk we've piled up during the renos. It will probably cost him more than whatever the plumber was going to charge to take it away." I laugh, once again attempting to instill some levity into a grim reality.

"I'm pregnant," Beth says out of the blue, placing a hand on her belly. "I need Jason."

Definite deja vu. Beth is a reflection of me. I stare into her brown eyes and nod. We understand each other well. Although Beth and I only recently met, we are kindred spirits. Both soulmates to men who can't control their urges. Gambling, drinking. Jake has other issues I don't share with Beth, and I'm sure she must have secrets as well. But the addictions are something we have in common. And that creates a bond between us.

We eat our supper on trays in front of the television. A historical drama series, one neither of us has watched before, to distract us. When Jake comes home, I explain that Beth is staying with us for a while, until things get sorted out. I show her to the guest room.

Later, Jake and I sit at the kitchen table while he eats leftover chicken and rice and washes it down with a beer. "How long is she staying?" he asks.

"I don't know. Till Jason comes back, I guess. Or the police find him."

"Well, it probably won't be that long then, will it?"

"Do you think he's coming back?"

Jake stops eating and sets his fork down. He covers his face with his hands and shakes his head. "I think that's unlikely."

Chapter Thirty-One

The rug arrived early this morning. After Mal and Beth left for work. Just as well that they weren't here when the delivery guys carried the rolled-up carpet into the garage and dumped it on the cement floor. My breakfast nearly landed next to it as a vision of Dead Guy wrapped in the rug, thrown into our cistern, flashed through my head. But I managed to swallow down the bit of cereal stuck in my throat and flushed it with a beer. The real breakfast of champions.

Today's goal is to get the blinds up. Tomorrow and Thursday, the house is going to be teeming with people, getting it shipshape for the wedding. Barring any unforeseen disasters, Craig and Vicky will have a perfect day. As long as no more bodies, guns, or bags of money show up. Or toilets break. We must have exhausted all the possible things that could go wrong in organizing the venue for a wedding.

The money. I had wondered for a fraction of a second whether that was Dom's way of assuring my cooperation. A pre-payment for doing what I was told. But that's not Dom's style. Hiding money in a toilet. And why would he take it away? Then, I considered whether our toilet was a conduit for a drug operation. Bags of drugs exchanged for bags of money. We'd never noticed because nobody broke the toilet lid before.

Which reminds me of another loose end I need to tie up. It lies in the cornfield.

Out back, the corn rustles in the breeze. Whatever evidence remains in the field will be cleaned up in a few days. My eyes search the crop, my ears stand at attention, but nothing pops. No clues about what's happening deep in the middle of the corn. Good.

Back to the blinds. First step—check the instructions. After watching a couple of YouTube videos, I'm an expert on window treatments. Seems idiot proof. Measure, mark, drill, screw, hang. I gather my tools out of the basement and haul the blinds from the garage. Halfway out the double roll-up door, I'm accosted by a yapping terrier.

"Hey, Russ, old buddy. Dig up any more guns?" I lay down the blinds and rub his ears.

Paul waves as he approaches from the end of the driveway. "Hi, Jake. What's new?"

"Not much. Same old. How about you?"

"All good." His head turns in all directions, as if expecting someone to sneak up on him any minute. "Listen, I just wanted to let you know the police have been asking questions."

"Police? Questions?"

"You know, about the gun."

"I guess they would. It's not every day a dog digs up a Glock."

"Well, I withheld a few things from them." He does another quick check of the surrounding area, which is deserted as usual.

"Oh?"

"I didn't say anything."

"About?"

"You know…" He nods toward the cornfield.

What the hell does he mean?

"They asked questions…" he whispers, "…about you."

"Me? Why me?"

"I figure it's because the police have been out to your place a handful of times the last couple of months. Makes them suspicious. But don't worry. Your secrets are all safe with me." He winks like we're co-conspirators. "I didn't mention the crop in your field."

"The corn? It got hit by that high wind last Friday night."

"Not the corn. The other stuff."

"Other stuff?" Best to play dumb. See what he actually knows.

"Yeah." He pretends to puff a reefer. "Russ likes to go for runs. He finds some real gems, like I said."

"I see. Well, I appreciate you letting me know about the police, but I'm not sure what else we can tell them about the gun. It *was* Russ who found it. And thanks for letting me know something's going on in our cornfield. I'll have to look into that."

"Like I said, I'm not saying anything. Good neighbors look out for each other. How are those renos coming along?" He points to the blinds.

"Great. Almost done. Blinds today, the carpet and furniture in place tomorrow."

"Speaking of carpet, I noticed you had another one delivered today."

"Uh huh, yeah. The other one was flawed, so I had them replace it."

"You've got to be careful with these flooring places. They'll try to fleece you every chance they get. Subpar materials. High markups."

"Well, I'd better get back to work, or Mallory won't be too happy when she gets home." I pick up the blinds to signal the end of our conversation. "And thanks again. It's great to have good neighbors watching our back. Maybe we can return the favor someday."

The blinds go as well as can be expected, considering my hands are shaking. One set goes up. Two more to go. Then, the vertical blinds on the patio doors. I take a break, grab a beer, and head out to the cornfield, making my way inward, calling out, "Hey, anybody here?"

The stalks part and my harvester friends appear.

"Jake, what's up?"

"Wanna come over for a beer? Take a break?" Get on their good side.

"Sure." The big guy, muscles straining to get out of his sweaty t-shirt, speaks for all three. I'm not on a name basis with these dudes, but he's the one who approached me about renting my field for cash, so I guess he's kinda employed by me in a roundabout way.

We sit on the rattan furniture, none too cozy in the cool breeze, but we're tough guys. Not bothered by a bit of chill in the air, we chug our beers. I ask how the harvest is coming along.

"Good. Should be done by the weekend," says Muscle Man.

"Great. Any chance we could get this stuff out of here any sooner? I've got the landscapers coming tomorrow and cleaners on Thursday. It's going to be busy, so you'll need to keep a low profile. Can you possibly bring in some more manpower and finish the job quicker?"

"That's gonna cost, man."

"I've been really generous, allowing you the privilege of borrowing my field. Surely you can expedite the flow of product by a couple of days."

"The deal was to be out by Friday night."

"I need this shit out of here ASAP. The police are sniffing around. Which reminds me. You didn't happen to find anything out of the ordinary in the field this past week, did you?"

He shakes his head. "Nope. Nothing."

"Good. So, can I depend on you guys to clear this area by, oh, let's say tomorrow night?"

He sniggers. "Two days ahead of schedule? Yeah, that's no problem. We'll just head down to the employment office and hire some temp workers. Get them off the government dole for a couple of days."

"Mmhm. Yeah, well, I don't know the logistics of hiring in your profession but, like I said, I really need this shit out of here before the cops find it." And my wife divorces me.

"We'll see what can be done. Thanks for the beer, Jake." He signals to the other two that it's time to get back to work.

The rest of the blind installation goes smoothly, probably because the windows are new and professionally installed, which makes things nice and level. After polishing off the rest of last night's leftovers, I shower and get dressed for work. On my way out the door, lunchpail in hand, my phone rings.

"Hello?"

"Jake."

Dom. What does he want now?

"I heard we may have a bit of a problem," he says.

No idea what that might be. "Oh?"

"You need some crop cleared out in a hurry."

How does he know about that? "I have no idea what you're talking about. You must have me confused with another client. Anyway, I can't chat now. On my way to work."

"Don't hang up on me." His voice sends ice cubes down my spine.

"No. Of course. I wouldn't do that, Dom."

"Your little staff shortage has been taken care of. The job will be done by the end of tomorrow, as requested. We'll have to shave some off the rent, of course, to cover wages."

"I don't understand. I rent my fields to corn farmers. They hire their staff directly. Nothing to do with me."

"I'll make it clearer, then. You may own the land. But I run the operation on that land. *I* hire the staff. *I* pay the rent. *I* protect you from the cops. So, when it comes down to it, Jakey, if it wasn't already clear, I own *you*. By the way, have you given any more thought to my offer?"

Chapter Thirty-Two

Dom is behind the weed growing op? Why would he involve himself in something so trivial as growing marijuana in my field? Well, apart from the obvious. He must have a distribution system. Still, I would have thought there'd be more money in hard drugs. This seems like small change for a guy like Dom.

I pull into the parking lot, making it just in time, passing the day shift, scurrying like rats, looking for a way out. This 3 to 11 grind cuts into my life. There's gotta be a better way to make a living. Another 35 years of the same old crap? Dom's right. I'm too smart for this.

Lots of action as one shift replaces the other. I climb the steps to my glassed-in office and watch the ants begin the evening round of receiving and shipping auto parts, then turn on my computer and check inventory levels. Before supper, I take a stroll down the straight aisles, blue shelving from concrete floor to ceiling, checking on incoming product. Craig works in receiving.

"Did we get the right quantity on those premium batteries that were back ordered?"

"Yes, it's all good," Craig answers. He adds, "Can I join you for supper in your office?"

"Sure, see you later." I continue my supervision of auto parts coming in and going out, employees loading, unloading. Going around in circles.

The LED lights are bringing on a headache. Or maybe it's all the other shit going on in my life. I dodge a forklift on my way to check on one of the new hires. Kid out of high school. Poor schmuck. A lifelong career of warehouse shipping. The only thing that got me into a supervisory role was a couple years of college.

Halfway through the evening, Craig joins me in my office for supper. Ham and cheese for me. Leftover lasagna, reheated in the staff cafeteria, for him. It smells familiar. I ask if he wants to switch.

"No chance. Vicky borrowed Mallory's recipe, made a huge pan last night."

"You should have brought some for me. Especially since it's my wife's recipe." I watch him bite into it, gooey cheese stringing from his mouth. Wait till he's married for a while. It'll be cold sandwiches if he's lucky. Or slap together your own meal if he's unlucky.

"Maybe next time. Did you happen to hear about the body they found on that construction sight in Kingston?"

"No. They found a body?"

"Yes. They haven't identified it yet, or aren't releasing the name, anyway. But they did say it looked like a targeted murder, and there's little danger to the public."

"Huh. I guess things like that happen all the time."

Craig swallows, stops to watch my expression, and his eyes go wide. "You mean bodies turning up in strange places?"

I shrug.

"If you have connections to the mob, I guess it might be commonplace." He continues staring as if he expects me to confess, then resumes eating.

"Did you hear anything more about this body in Kingston?"

"No. Did you find any more possums in the cistern?"

"None." Watching him devour my wife's lasagna reminds me how cozy he and Mal have become the last few months.

"Kingston. Isn't that where your friend Terry lives? A bit of a coincidence, isn't it?"

"Yeah. That's what it is."

"Are you happy, Jake?" He scrapes up the last of his lasagna.

"Happy about what?"

"Being married. Your life."

"Of course, I'm happy. What kind of stupid question is that? I've got the woman of my dreams. I'm king of my own castle. What more could I want?"

"Are you looking forward to being a dad? Vicky's talking about kids."

"Mal's baby. Yeah. Can't wait."

"Your baby." His eyes meet mine, then he lowers them.

"Yeah. *My* baby. Like I said, what more could I want? Why? Are you having second thoughts about getting tied down?"

"No. Maybe. I don't know. I love Vicky. But it's a big change."

"A good change."

He nods. "It's just…are we really suited for each other? Vicky's so glamorous, and I'm just an average guy. She's a hotshot lawyer, and I'm a warehouse receiver. Vicky makes four times what I do. I'd never be able to afford the house we're buying. She's got all these highbrow friends. And I've got…well, I've got my drinking buddies from work, and I've got… you."

"Thanks. For not equating me with the highbrow friends."

He laughs, closing up his Tupperware and reaching for a bakeshop chocolate croissant. I pull a couple of store-bought cookies from my lunch pail. Mal used to fix better lunches for me when we first got married, but now I make do with whatever I can get.

"Mallory doesn't outearn me, but she doesn't let me forget who holds the purse strings," I commiserate. "Rubbing in her inheritance. But, now I've got my granddad's money, too. So, we're more evenly matched in the financial department. You can't let money decide who you love. Marriage is a partnership. Mal and I are a team. You and Vicky will be, too."

If he backs out of this wedding, it's not going to do my marriage any good.

"I know. You're right. You don't miss dating other women?"

"I've got Mallory. She's all I need."

He lets out a big sigh. "Yes, you have Mallory. You're one lucky guy. She puts up with a lot. Do you ever worry about losing her?

If he's thinking of stealing Mallory from me, I'll…

"Because I worry all the time. Why would Vicky choose to spend the rest of her life with me? She can have any guy she wants. I'm nobody special. I've got nothing to offer her. What if she figures that out and dumps me? Again. I don't think I could handle it."

So, my best buddy's bachelorhood hasn't been about playing the field. It's more a fear of being put out to pasture. Who knew? "She won't. She's already figured it out. And she keeps coming back to you. This time, she's making it permanent. Because she loves you. Consider yourself lucky. She *could* have any guy, but she chose you."

His mouth spreads wide. "Yeah, you're right. Vicky loves me, and I love her. She's all *I* need."

Now that we've got all that sorted out, it's time to get back to work. But first, I ask, "Do you ever consider getting into a more lucrative line of work?"

"Like what?"

I raise my eyebrows. "There are a lot of opportunities out there. I've made a ton by grabbing onto one of them when it came my way, if you know what I mean."

He knows exactly what I mean. No need to spell it out.

"You've been lucky, Jake. But luck can run out. This is good, honest work."

Craig gets back to his receiving, and I survey my kingdom of auto parts. Maybe someday I'll be the warehouse manager.

I wonder what kind of future Dom envisions for me and whether I should drag my best friend into it.

Chapter Thirty-Three

Beth twists the band on her right hand. It looks familiar.

"That's an interesting ring."

"Jason gave it to me when we were dating. It's his fraternity ring. We met at a party at his frat house." Beth extends her hand to show me the crest and inscription.

"That's romantic, him giving away his school ring."

"He didn't exactly give it away. He bought one like his, sized for me. Said we'd always be connected with them. When I touch my ring, I think of Jason touching his own. It makes me feel closer to him."

The lump in my throat closes off any further words.

Earlier this evening, Beth made arrangements with the landlord to remove her belongings from the condo. The movers will be taking what's left of Jason and Beth's lives and placing it in a storage facility until Jason returns. I offered to take care of those expenses, as Jason had emptied their bank accounts and maxed out credit cards. After supper, we settled in front of the television to watch someone else's drama while we consumed half a tub of ice cream.

Beth switches to her wedding band and engagement ring and gives them a twirl. "I didn't realize Jason had a problem until after we were married. He hid it well."

I'm all too familiar with what it's like having a husband who keeps things hidden. There are only two choices when you marry an addict. You accept they have a problem and help them to seek counseling, or you leave. The last option may seem like the easiest, but it's not necessarily the best one. It takes a lot of strength to support someone you love through a sickness. But if you give up on them, what's to stop them from total self-destruction?

"Maybe I should have left him when I found out," Beth continues. "But I wasn't strong enough to walk out, so I stayed and put up with it. I don't know how I'd survive without him."

I hope I'm wrong about Jason being in Kingston. Once I regain my voice, I change the topic to the upcoming wedding. "There's going to be a lot of excitement around here this week. My best friend is marrying Jake's best friend right here on our property on Saturday."

"Is he a gambler, too?"

"Craig? No, he's..." I stop and consider what to say.

"A drinker?"

"No."

"Drugs?"

"Craig doesn't really have any vices." I've never voiced this before, but Craig and Jake don't have much in common. Craig does everything in moderation.

"So, he's the perfect guy, then?"

"Not perfect. But, yes, he's a really nice guy."

"Well, I envy your friend then. She'll never have to wonder where her husband is or what he's doing." Beth sighs and moves her fraternity ring up and down her finger, as though considering casting it off.

"Why would Jason do this to me? Make me worry about what's happened?

I put an arm around her shoulder and tell her I don't have answers, but hopefully, she will soon know. "Try to be strong, for the baby's sake."

Tears draw liquid lines down her face. "I told him I was pregnant, and he was happy. Less than a week later, he left, and I haven't heard from him. He's just gone. And I think he could be in serious trouble."

Chapter Thirty-Four

Where the hell is she? And why isn't she answering her phone? Is she okay?

Her car isn't in the driveway. Beth's is. So, they must be together, wherever they are. It's nearly 11:30. They can't have gone far this time of night. She would have texted or left a note if she planned to be gone for long. And it's a school night. She should be in bed.

I exit my Honda and set off the security lights as I head to the front door. It's locked. Inserting my key, I turn the knob and shove open the door, flipping on the switch to illuminate the entry.

"Mallory? Beth?" I call out just in case one of them is here. "There you are, sweetie."

Nellie rubs against my legs. "Where's Mommy?" If she knows, she isn't talking.

I roam from room to room, searching for a note or some clue as to where they could be. Did we run out of milk or something?

Nope. Inside the fridge is a nearly full carton. Bread in the bread box. Maybe she had a craving for something. Some of that red licorice she's been inhaling lately. That's it. She's probably at the variety store in town, picking up a bag of Twizzlers. She'll be back any minute.

Although why it takes two women to buy a pack of candy, I don't understand. But you never know with women. Especially when they're pregnant.

The main level of the house is quiet. Way too quiet. Kinda spooky, with the bay window overlooking the dark yard. I open the basement door, flip the switch, and holler down, knowing there's no way Mallory's down there unless someone dragged her kicking and screaming. No sign of anyone, just the tool bench and shelving and a bit of a smell that lingers. I shut the door, turn off the lights, and...

A noise snaps my head to the patio door. Scuffing? Scraping? Scratching? At a high speed. Someone trying to get in.

Holy shit!

Something's glowing outside the glass door. On the wooden step. Tapping on the glass.

I run down the hall and up the stairs to our bedroom, retrieve the baseball bat from the closet, and scurry back down. Whoever's out there, they better get the hell off my property.

I leave the kitchen in darkness and tiptoe to the mudroom to illuminate the back yard, a flick of the switch spreading soft light past the corner to the side of the house where who or whatever wants in keeps up its rhythmic rubbing on the door.

My sigh of relief resounds through the kitchen when I see Nellie scratching on the inside of the patio glass. All this time, it's been the dang cat and her shadow creeping me out. It's a good thing Mallory and Beth aren't here. I'd look like a complete sissy, afraid of my own cat in the dark.

"Hey, baby. You scared the crap out of Daddy."

I crouch down to pet her black and white fur. "Good girl. No, you can't go out. Let's go up to...Jesus Christ!"

A set of green eyes glare at me through the clear door, and I catapult backwards, knocked right off my feet, my ass hitting the hardwood.

What the...?

Nellie scrapes the door with her claws, meowing. I sit still and watch. Then I slide across the floor toward Nellie to get a closer look at who the hell is out there.

As my eyes adjust and the exterior fixtures shed light on the subject, I feel like a complete moron. It's that blasted stray cat that's been hanging around, trying to get in the house. No intruder. No murderer. No alien. Just a black cat.

Mal says Nellie and the stray are friends. She wants to take it in. I put my foot down and said one cat in the house was enough. I should have let Mal bring Nellie's little buddy inside. It's my own damn fault the stray cat's out there giving me a heart attack.

"Come on, Nellie. Bedtime." I make smoochy noises with my mouth to get her attention. When that doesn't work, I get out the treat bag.

Upstairs, I do a quick tour of the rooms, text Mallory again, and crawl into bed to wait for her. It's midnight.

Where the hell is my wife?

Chapter Thirty-Five

I'm at a loss. For words. For what to do to help her get through this. So, I make a stupid suggestion. "Why don't we go to the casino and find out if anyone knows anything? If that was the last place he went, someone must have seen him."

Beth stares at me, draws her brows together, and says, "But wouldn't the police already have checked there?"

"Some people don't like to talk to the police." People like Dom. "I know the owner of the casino. Maybe he'll talk to me."

Beth agrees it's worth a try. We change out of the pajamas we put on after supper and leave for the city. Stars twinkle as we walk to my car, shedding hope over a dark situation.

The casino is lit up when we drive into the lot, as though the only way to attract customers is with its bright facade. But Beth and I know the outward beauty is a misrepresentation, disguising the ugliness within.

"I've never been here," Beth says. Funny coming from the wife of a gambler.

"I've only been once. And I didn't come voluntarily."

We follow the steady stream of people through the main doors of the complex, taking note of the signs that indicate the location of the casino. The grandeur of the hotel lobby gives the impression of prosperity for all who pass through, but again, looks are deceiving. Once we enter the casino, the fever of its patrons consumes the vast space. Elderly people seated at the slots, pulling levers, rings and bells sounding from colorful machines, catch my attention. An arcade for adults. It seems a lonely way to spend an evening.

Beth and I scan the area.

"Is there an information booth, or something?" she asks. "When you were here, where did you go?"

"Not in the main part of the casino." I don't elaborate. I want to put that experience behind me." As we continue walking, I note a row of booths, labelled 'Cashier'. "Maybe we can ask here."

Or not. When I ask the woman behind the counter if Dom is available, she shakes her head and says her job is to hand out chips and cash. "Do you want some chips, or not?"

"Um, yes." I hand her a twenty dollar bill, all I have in my wallet.

"We came here to find out if anyone saw Jason, not to gamble." Beth places her hand on my arm to indicate I should put my money away.

"We'll mingle," I suggest. "Move around the tables. Talk to people as we go."

"Okay. Where do you want to start? At the spinny wheel?"

We watch the Roulette game as people place bets, and the chips come and go on the table. Once we have the hang of it, I exchange two of my chips for roulette tokens, and Beth and I each place a bet, hers on even and mine on odd.

The croupier calls, "No more bets."

Beth and I watch the wheel, mesmerized by the white ball. It lands on 19, and we end up with the same number of chips we started with. I look for an opportunity to speak with the croupier, but there's no break in the action, and the excitement in the air precludes questioning strangers about whether they know Jason.

We move on to observe various games and their clientele. Playing cards are laid out at some of the tables. I recognize this game. Jake taught me how to play Blackjack when we were dating. It was fun for a while, but when he kept winning, I said it was all a matter of luck. Jake explained there was more to it and showed me his strategies, including card counting. When I started to beat him at his own game, he lost interest.

I slide into an empty seat while Beth stands and observes. The first hand I'm dealt totals nine, and I double down when the dealer shows a three, beating him with a count of nineteen when he goes bust. In the next hand, I split my bet when I'm dealt a four and a four, and ask the dealer to hit me, which results in total counts of nineteen and twenty, beating the dealer again. All along I keep a close eye on the other hands and use Jake's system for counting the cards laid on the table.

After several rounds of wins and a few losses, Beth nudges me and says we need to move on. "We're here to ask about Jason, remember?"

"Just a few more hands." I glance at the pile of chips in front of me. Why stop when I'm on a winning streak?

But Beth is right. We're not here to gamble.

"Excuse me," I say, my voice loud enough to startle myself. "Do you happen to know Jason Bartlett?"

The dealer stops, shrugs his shoulders, and asks if I'm in or out.

"Is Dom around? Maybe I could talk to him?"

He says I need an appointment to see Dom and continues dealing cards, leaving me out.

I place a stack of chips on the betting circle next round and keep counting cards as the dealer lays them out. When the seat next to me is vacated, Beth joins the game, losing the first hand when she stays at fifteen.

"You should draw again when you have a soft hand," I say, eliciting a blank stare from Beth.

I give her advice during the next few hands, and once she has her own pile of tokens piled in front of her, Beth gets lost in the fever of the game. I suggest we move to another table if we hope to find anyone who knows Jason.

We agree that Blackjack is our game. At the next table, we sit together as soon as two adjoining seats are available. I ask about Jason when I set my chips down and receive a similar response as before, except this time the dealer tells us all about her boyfriend, named Jason, and how they broke up last week. I'm in absolute awe of how well she can do her job and chit-chat about her personal life at the same time, and I lose track of the running card count in my head. Playing Beth's hand as well as my own and listening to the dealer distracts me enough that we lose a few rounds.

Beth and I gather our remaining chips and look for a third table. No sooner do we sit down than a hand touches my shoulder.

"Mrs. Shelton, I'll need you and your friend to come with me."

I recognize the face when I turn around. Nick. One of the men who works for Dom. Under normal circumstances, I'd be frightened. Here, in the middle of a busy casino, his presence is less intimidating. And if I want to talk to Dom, he's my ticket in.

"Actually, we're not here to play. I was hoping to speak with Dom."

He tilts his head toward the back, and we are escorted into an office. Dom rises when we enter.

"What a pleasure to see you again, Mrs. Shelton. We've been keeping an eye on you from above."

Of course, cameras.

Now that I'm face to face with him, I can't find my tongue. He motions for us to sit in the leather seats facing him.

"What can I do for you lovely ladies?" Dom sits and dismisses Nick with a wave of his hand. "If you're here to see me about Jake, I can assure you he's held up his end of our deal."

"No, not Jake. It's about Jason, Beth's husband." I motion to her. "He's missing. The last time she saw him was last Friday. Jason told Beth he was going to the casino, but he hasn't come home since." I spit the words out in spite of my shaky voice.

Dom turns to Beth. "I'm sorry to hear that. Did you expect him to still be here?"

Beth shakes her head, and I'm not sure if she's silent because she's frightened by the authoritarian attitude that emanates from him or awed by his charisma and good looks. As charming as he appears to be, I don't doubt for one second that he would sell both of us into the sex trade if we displeased him.

"Um, actually, I suggested we come here to see if you might know something about where Jason is." I put on my best doe-eyed expression to show I'm not suggesting the possibility he may have something to do with Jason's disappearance.

"Jason, who?"

"Bartlett?" Beth whispers, then states it louder as though she wasn't quite sure of his last name. "He comes here a lot."

Dom smiles. "So do a lot of people."

"Maybe," I address Beth, "if you had a photo, it might help?"

Beth searches her phone and turns it toward Dom. "This was the most recent picture taken a couple of weeks ago."

Dom studies it. "Jason, yes, of course. Yes, he's a frequent player."

"Was he here last Friday night?" I ask.

Leaning back in his chair and steepling his hands, Dom says, "I'm always happy to help out a couple of beautiful ladies. Let me check the surveillance videos."

He calls Nick back into the room and tells him to check on video from Friday night. "Find out exactly what Jason Bartlett was up to."

Nick leaves without a word.

"Is there anything else I can do for you ladies?"

"No, that's good." I'm not sure what our next move is. Should we stay or go?

Dom strides over to an oak cabinet and opens a door, revealing a bar fridge. "In that case, why don't we have a drink while we wait."

"Oh, no, I can't. We can't." I motion to my belly to remind him I'm pregnant.

"Of course. A soda?" He removes a couple cans of ginger ale and pours them into glasses and a whiskey for himself.

Raising his glass, he makes a toast. "To Jake and his new path in life. And to Jason, who will hopefully be found soon."

We sip our sodas under Dom's intent scrutiny.

"Apparently, you've played cards before," he states, speaking to me. "But, if you don't mind, I'd like to give you a piece of advice."

I nod, the rest of my body trembling as Dom leans forward.

Elbow on the table, hand supporting his chin, he whispers, "If you're going to count cards, try to be a little more discreet. It's sort of frowned upon by casinos."

CHAPTER THIRTY-FIVE

"Oh. I didn't know."

"Jake teach you to play?"

I nod again.

"Did you enjoy yourself tonight?"

My head bobs.

"I'd suggest you stick to playing at home." Dom drains his glass, sets it down, and leans back again. "I'd hate to see a pretty young girl like you get herself in over her head. Especially now that your husband is showing some backbone and trying to get his act together."

Hearing that directly from Dom sends a tinge of guilt through me. Jake has been trying. Have I? Beth fidgets next to me, a reminder of our purpose here. I need to learn more about Jason's association with Dom, if any.

"Did, um, Jason owe you money?"

He brushes his hand across his chin stubble. "No."

A knock on the door stops me from asking further questions. Nick enters and says he's found the information Dom requested. Dom raises his eyebrows and gives Nick an almost imperceptible nod.

"Jason Bartlett came through the main entrance at 11:20 pm last Friday and spent time in the pit before moving to the high-limit room half past midnight." Nick glances toward me. "With some guys Jake introduced him to."

"And when did he leave?" Dom asks.

"The same time everyone left. There was an altercation later in the evening. Someone accused someone else of cheating and not paying up. Things got out of hand, and the noise level escalated. So, for everyone's safety, we shut down the games and evacuated the room at 1:45."

"Oh my God! Was he hurt?" Beth gasps, covering her nose and mouth, her eyes wide.

"Our video surveillance shows he was fine when he was ushered through the back door."

"Who was he with?" I ask.

"According to the dealer at his table, he left with his new buddies, Terry Cox and company. None too happy to be kicked out. His losing streak was just starting to turn around."

Dom rises and tells us as much as he has enjoyed our company, he needs to get back to work. "So now you know Jason left here in one piece."

Dom instructs Nick to escort us out. "Give these lovely ladies a few hundred worth of chips, courtesy of the house." He directs his next comment to me. "And no more card counting."

Nick leaves us in the middle of the casino pit with a bucket of chips.

"As long as we're here, we may as well spend these," I say.

"We need to talk to Jake about his friend, Terry." Beth urges me out of the gaming area.

"We'll talk to him when we get home. Do you want to play the spinning wheel again?"

"No, I don't...well, maybe once or twice." Her eyes fixate on the white ball.

We lose ourselves in the moment, winning, then losing. I suggest we try cards again. The bucket empties, fills, empties. When it's nearly full again, I check my phone.

"Oh! It's late! Jake has been texting and calling me. He must wonder where on earth we are." I'd completely lost track of the time. "And we have work in the morning."

After cashing in the chips, we hurry toward my car. Beth says, "Jake knows how worried I am about Jason. Why didn't he tell me he saw Jason Friday night?"

Chapter Thirty-Six

"What was that?"

Something's not right. I can't put my finger on it, but something's bugging me. "Did you...?" I roll over to find Mallory sound asleep, curled up facing me, cute little snorts coming from her open mouth. She's exhausted, and her alarm is set for 7:30. Six hours of sleep, if she's lucky. That's what she gets for going to the casino in the middle of the night.

That's what it is. That's what's wrong. Usually, I'm the one passed out from being out too late and she's the one who wakes me, not the other way around. So, what woke me? A noise. No, the security lights. Yellow lines border the edge of the curtains. Something is out there. Probably the stray.

I couldn't believe it when Mallory told me what she and Beth were doing at the casino. Talking to Dom. About Jason. What was she thinking?

She didn't get any answers for all her trouble. Mal and Beth know Jason was at the casino Friday night. I could have told them that. Of course, he was there. Where else would he be on a Friday night? He was there; he left. It's what happened afterward that's the mystery. To everyone except Terry and me.

"I think he saw something he shouldn't have behind Dom's place. If he got caught..." Terry left the rest unspoken when I called to ask if he knew what happened after leaving Jason with him Friday night.

The lights go off. Cat gone, I huddle underneath the covers next to Mallory.

Rrrrr...rrrr.... Screech. Clunk.

Shit! Is that the garage door? Someone breaking in to steal the new furniture? Not happening. Not on my watch. I grab my phone and baseball bat and ease my way through the dimly lit hall and down the stairs, taking care not to wake Mallory.

The front door is locked. That's a good sign. If someone managed to get into the garage and found the emergency key, they'd have access to our home. Not much chance of that, with the key well hidden, but I'd better have a thorough look. Especially with all the shit that's been showing up in this house lately.

Who would know our access code to the garage? Besides Craig. And Mom, of course.

Or have the key to the back garage door? Did someone break into one of our cars and use the remote opener? Or steal our car keys?

Best to leave the exterior lights off, catch them by surprise. I step out onto the porch, pulling the door closed behind me, and inch toward the wooden stairs, setting off the motion-activated security light.

Shit! So much for approaching the intruder unawares. Might as well make a run for it now, try to catch them before they take off. I've got the advantage, being on home turf. Baseball bat in the air, phone in my pocket, I rush along the edge of the porch, toward the garage and trigger the garage security light, illuminating the closed door.

Closed? I was sure the garage opening was the source of the sound I heard. Maybe I dreamt the whole thing. This damn business with the body and the gun has frayed my nerves. I'm almost as paranoid as Mallory. I'd better get some sleep.

I march back to the front door, turn the knob, and...

You have got to be kidding me.

It's locked.

Good thing we keep that spare key in the garage. I enter our anniversary date into the keypad, and the door creaks open. As it does, I raise my bat, just in case, then realize how ineffective my weapon is. What if the guy in there has a gun?

Too late to do anything about that. It's just me and my bat. If Mallory wasn't so adamantly against hunting, I'd still have my granddad's rifle.

The security light falls on the boxes of new furniture that take up a good portion of the garage. On one side, next to my mechanics tool chest, is a shelving unit for wiper fluid, oil, and stuff. We keep the key behind it for times like this. I reach in the dark to grab it and realize I'm not alone.

Something scuffs in a corner of the garage. Crunching, smacking, slurping. Behind one of the boxes, eyes watch me. Glowing in the dark. That dang stray again. How did he get in here? I flip the switch and bring to light pointy ears and a long snout. Not the stray.

What the hell?

The compost bucket lies on its side, contents strewn on the concrete. A raccoon munches on a rotten apple. Cute little masked bandit, with its whiskers and paws. And razor-sharp teeth. Might as well let him finish his meal before I kick him out.

My eyes take in the rest of the garage. Somebody has been busy. Stuff is knocked over on shelves, and next to the old toilet, the garbage has been ripped open and the heap of junk rooted through. Thankfully, the unopened boxes of furniture seem to be untouched.

"How did you get in here?" I edge closer as beady eyes dare me to steal his food. More sounds come from behind the box. Bat raised, I slink past and peer between the cardboard. The raccoon has brought little ones along. Just great.

"What did you do? Bring the whole *famn damily*? Sorry, but the free room and board's about to end."

I head toward the back of the garage to retrieve a push broom off the wall when I notice the back door is open. Did I do that? When was the last time I was in the garage? When I talked to Paul this morning? He must have distracted me enough that I left the damn door open. Anyone could have been in here. Not just the raccoons.

The wooden door, which swings in from the back yard, sits against the back of the left wall, inviting everybody and their uncle to come on in. For all I know, another body has been dumped right here. Bat in the air, I wander across the back of the house, looking for any sign of an intruder still lurking on my property. Guided by the flashlight app on my phone, I check out the far back of the yard, peek into the shed, then stride along the evergreens, past the garage, and back to the driveway. The road out front is dark and quiet, the dang streetlight out of commission again, but the front security lights flash on as I check the property along the cornfield side.

Finding no sign of anyone outside, I head through the back garage door to scoot the little critters out and lock up. The snarling reaches my ears before I set foot inside. What's got her all rattled? She run out of food scraps?

"Listen, dude, or should I say, ma'am…" I stop in my tracks.

Holy crap!

At the entrance to the roll-up doors, another creature with pointy ears and a long snout stands, peering in. Mama raccoon continues snarling and hissing, teeth bared, as the coyote advances, measuring her up.

Swinging my bat, I say, "I got your back, Mama."

As if she understands, Mama raccoon takes a flying leap at the coyote, chasing him off all the way across the road and into the woods, me following, swinging and hollering.

"That'll show him. You've got balls." Lesson learned. Never mess with a mother and her kits.

The raccoon scurries back to the shelter of the garage and her family. I grab the house key, and close up the garage after propping the back door open a crack to allow them an easy way out.

"You've earned a free night." I leave them to feed. There are worse things to have on your property than raccoons. I'll clean up the mess tomorrow and escort them out, if they're still here.

Once inside, I do a quick walkthrough of the main level of the house before heading back to bed. No one's lurking in the living room or dining room or hiding out in the powder room. The door to the kitchen is closed. That's strange. I turn the knob and push it open, a yelp escaping my throat when I detect a shadow moving in the near dark.

A scream pierces the air in response. I flip on the lights.

And catch Beth wandering around my kitchen.

"Beth, what are you doing?" I realize I'm gripping the bat with both hands, ready to hit a home run.

"Jake! You scared me. What are *you* doing?" She backs away, wide-eyed.

"It's my house."

"I mean, what are you doing with the baseball bat, sneaking up on me?" Beth grabs a knife out of the wooden block, eyes on the bat.

"I heard a noise outside, so I investigated."

"Did you find anyone?"

"Just some raccoons and a coyote. And you."

"Coyote?"

I didn't think she could get any paler, but there you go. "He's gone now. What are you doing up at this hour?"

"I couldn't sleep, so I came down to make tea." The kettle whistles to confirm her explanation.

"All right, then, I'll leave you to it." I head down the hall.

"Jake? Why didn't you tell me you saw Jason at the casino just before he went missing?"

The question brings me to a stop.

"You were one of the last people to see him." She says it like an accusation, as though I know what the hell happened to Jason, and I'm not talking.

I turn to face her. "I thought you already knew he was there Friday night. And besides, I barely saw him. I was with some friends of mine, having a few drinks. They stayed to play cards. Jason joined them. I went home."

"So, he was okay when you saw him?"

"Why wouldn't he be?"

"Because he didn't...come home." And she starts to blubber.

What is it with women and their emotions? It doesn't take anything to set them off.

"Look, I know you're worried. I wish I could tell you more, but he seemed his usual self. My friends invited him to play poker. I have no idea what he did after that. He's bound to turn up sooner or later." I'm surprised the police haven't contacted her yet. Connected the dots. Missing husband, last seen at Dom's. Body dug up at the location of Dom's new casino.

"He's never been gone...this long," she snivels.

What does she expect from me? "I'd better get back to bed."

When I slide in under the covers, Mallory stirs. "Is everything okay? Where were you?"

"Just fighting off a pack of hungry wolves. Everything's fine, hon. Go back to sleep."

"Okay." She sighs, rolls over, and goes back to dreamland.

But I've got a bad feeling the bodies that keep turning up are going to come back to haunt me.

Chapter Thirty-Seven

"Somebody have a party in here?" Craig plugs his nose as I open the double garage door to reveal compost and garbage flung around the floor.

"Yeah. Raccoon family. Help me look for them. They better be gone." I rattle a jar of screws to get the attention of any freeloaders. "Keep an eye out for skunks, possums, mice, black cats, and coyotes, while you're at it."

"Coyotes?" Craig raises his eyebrows and backs out of the garage.

"I think he's probably still in the woods, tail between his legs. Did you know raccoons make good guard animals?"

Craig glances over his shoulder toward the woods and decides to return to the safety of the garage. "The carpet okay? They didn't wreck it, did they?"

"They better not have. Mallory will have a meltdown if another one's ruined."

I get Craig to straighten up the shelves while I shovel the compost and garbage back where it belongs. We turn over the rug, rolled up in plastic, and seeing no obvious problems, haul it out of the garage. The landscaping truck sits on the road with several cars behind it, where I asked them to park to avoid any obstructions with Craig, Beth, Mal, and me pulling in and out at different times.

Early this morning, they woke all three of us with their arrival. Their equipment made enough racket to raise the dead (or wives who stay out late at the casino). We'll do our best to stay out of their way, bringing the furniture through the front door as quickly as possible.

Once the carpet is in the family room, we unroll it and inspect it for damage. Phew! Looking good. Now to bring in the rest.

Sectional sofa, recliner/rocker, coffee table, lamps, television stand, new sixty-inch Smart TV. The basics. I'm leaving it to Mallory to add the finishing details, but that will have to wait till next week. A big shopping trip for decor items. She'll love it. And I'll tolerate it because I love her.

Now that everything's in the house, I need to remember where Mallory said it should go. Sofa first. "Help me move it over to the window."

"The window? Mallory won't want it there. It'll block the window seat and the view." Craig thinks he knows my wife better than I do.

I give it further thought. "You're right. That's not where it goes."

"Put it here, perpendicular to the window, making a room divider between the family room and kitchen and dining nook. TV along the wall."

"Perpendicular?"

"Yeah. Like this." He motions with his hands.

"I know what it means." Not only has he become an interior decorator, he's a math whiz all of a sudden. "I'm just trying to remember if that's what Mal said."

While we're arguing about how to arrange the furniture, the doorbell rings.

"Expecting company?" Craig asks.

"Not that I know."

Officers Chen and Glencoe stand on my front porch, watching the riding mower come around the corner. Please don't let them be here to deliver bad news to Beth. Although…how would they even know she's moved in with us?

"Good morning, Officers. What can I do for you?" I flash them my most charming smile. "Is there a problem?"

Then a thought goes through my head, and my face falls. Are they here for me, not Beth? "Is it Mallory? Has something happened?" Has she had an accident on her way to work, not getting enough sleep last night? My knees buckle.

Craig comes up behind me, his hand on my shoulder. "Mallory? Is she all right?" The tremble in his voice scares me. Mallory is dead.

"No, no, it's nothing like that," Officer Chen assures me, shaking her head.

"We have some questions for you," Officer Glencoe says. "About the gun found on your property."

I exhale the breath I didn't realize I was holding and feel Craig do the same. "It wasn't found on my property. Russ dug it up in the woods. Nothing to do with us."

"Actually, it has everything to do with you."

What is he talking about? Did Mal leave fingerprints on it?

"The plastic bag we took as evidence Saturday night. The one we were told held the gun." Officer Glencoe takes his time getting to the point. "There was something else in it."

"Something else?"

"A receipt," Officer Chen explains. "For groceries. From your local FoodMart."

What are they getting at?

"Really? Is that unusual? It *is* a grocery bag."

"The thing is…it's your receipt. Or, your wife's, to be exact."

No. No, no, no. Mallory did *not* leave a receipt in the bag she used to bury the gun. She's too smart for that.

"My wife's? How do you know it's hers? A lot of people shop at the FoodMart. It's a busy place. It could be anyone's receipt."

"There are credit card digits on receipts."

"And you have a warrant to check my wife's credit cards, I assume?" I'm no fool. They can't just access her private information. Can they?

"We spoke with the clerks at the FoodMart. One of them verified that Mallory Shelton bought a pack of red Twizzlers, a package of chamomile tea, and a romantic suspense paperback on the 12th of September at approximately 4:30 p.m."

I shrug, holding my palms up. "And? She can't be the only one who did that."

"The bag was found on your property, with the gun next to it." Officer Glencoe reminds me. "How do you explain that?"

"Well...I..."

"Someone broke in and stole the grocery bag," Craig interjects, speaking for the second time since I opened the door to find the two uniformed officers on the porch.

"Someone broke in and stole the grocery bag," Officer Chen echoes.

"I just finished helping Jake clean up the mess in his garage. Stuff all over the floor, garbage and compost dumped out. Someone was rooting around in there. It's happened a lot lately, right Jake? Someone messing around on your property?" Craig's voice is high-pitched, but these officers don't know him. They'll assume he always talks like this.

"Yes. Someone's been rooting around, all right." I need to agree to whatever Craig says. We have to have our story straight.

"And they stole a grocery bag?" Officer Chen repeats as though she didn't hear correctly.

"Yes, among other things," I elaborate.

"Such as..."

"An apple."

A loud sigh of exasperation comes from Officer Glencoe, his arms crossed. "A grocery bag and an apple. That's what they stole?"

"And some money."

"From the garage?"

"No, we don't keep money in the garage. That's just asking to be robbed. It went missing from the toilet."

"Money went missing from the toilet?" Officer Chen parrots.

"Jake has a gambling problem. He hides money from his wife all the time," Craig cuts in.

"Can you show us the toilet where the money was stored?" Officer Chen asks, looking over my shoulder, expecting to be invited in.

"Sure, it's in the garage," I say.

"The toilet is in the garage?" Officer Chen, for all her good looks, isn't the quickest to catch on.

"With the rest of the garbage and the compost." I open the door wider and step outside, motioning for them to follow me.

"I notice you're doing some major work on your yard," Officer Glencoe states, looking out at the vehicles parked on the road. "Doing some digging?"

"We're having a wedding here Saturday. Want to get the place looking good. My buddy, Craig here, is the lucky groom."

In the garage, I tell the cops about hearing the garage door open in the middle of the night and discovering the place had been ransacked. "And it's not the first time this has happened. You wouldn't believe how much crime there is out here in the country. Break and enters every other day. No matter how tightly you lock up."

"This the toilet where the money was hidden?" Officer Chen points to the broken pieces in the corner, next to the rest of the garbage created from the renos.

"Yes. It was under the tank lid."

"And someone smashed it to get to it?"

"No. My wife…"

"Mallory got mad when she found out Jake was hiding money in there, and even madder when he told her someone stole it, so she threw the lid on the floor," Craig intervenes again.

"Yeah, you know how wives can get about that sort of thing." I appeal to Officer Glencoe for empathy.

"No, I don't know. I'm not married," he smirks as his eyes examine the garbage pile for clues. "Getting back to the grocery bag. Why would someone steal that? The money, I understand. An apple? Maybe the thief got hungry and grabbed a snack. But why a grocery bag?"

"Because…because…" I try to come up with something logical.

"It's obvious," Craig says. "Someone is framing Jake. For murder."

Chapter Thirty-Eight

"**M**urder? Whose murder?" Officer Chen asks, her brown eyes flitting between Craig and me. "Is someone dead?"

"I don't know. You're the cops. You tell me." She's having a rough time following. Of course, somebody's dead. Missing person. Buried gun. Body found on construction site. If it swims like a duck and quacks like a duck... "I guess Craig was just figuring if someone buried a gun, there must be a good reason. And for it to turn up on a property nearby, in a bag stolen from my garage, means someone is pointing the finger at me for something, or else it's all just a big coincidence."

"Uh-huh. A coincidence. Thing is, I don't believe in coincidences. Not in my line of work," Officer Glencoe says, eyes finally moving off the garbage pile to study my reaction.

"In that case, I'd suggest you get busy looking for whoever's steering you in my direction. Because that gun has nothing to do with me, and neither does the body."

"The body?" Officer Chen's eyes bore into mine, her brow raised. "What body, Mr. Shelton?"

Did I say 'body' out loud? "No body. But if the gun was used on someone, there's a good chance there's a body somewhere out there. And if my neighbor's dog happens to dig one up, I'll be sure to give you a call."

"You do that. And let us know if you have any more break-ins," Officer Glencoe says.

As they head toward their cruiser, Russ runs along the driveway, yapping. Paul jogs along behind him. How hard is it to keep a leash on a mutt?

The cops watch the dog run across to the woods where he paces and sniffs the ground, then get in their vehicle and pull out of the driveway. I wave them off, and motion to Paul, who joins me and Craig.

"Hey, Paul. How's it going?"

"It's going. How about you? I see you've got the cops around again."

"Yeah. Somebody broke into my garage last night."

"Broke in?" Paul crinkles up his face, showing more lines than usual. "We've never had any problem in all the years we've been here. And we don't even lock the doors half the time. Someone looking for something in particular?"

"Naw. Just made a bit of a mess. Vandals, likely. Young kids, maybe."

Paul nods. "Kids have it too easy these days. Nothing to do. When I was young, I worked two jobs and kept up my grades."

"Well, I guess we'd better get back to arranging that furniture. Mallory wants it done today. Cleaners are coming tomorrow."

"I see you've pulled out all the stops, getting the yard manicured."

"Yep. Big day, Saturday. The end of Craig's freedom."

"I feel for you." Paul turns to Craig. "They reel you in, and next thing you know, you're floundering in a net."

Craig's eyes widen as though a revelation has just hit him.

Paul chuckles. "We're just messin' with you. I'd be a lonely man if it weren't for Linda and the kids and grandkids."

Russ runs up to Paul and dances around him until the leash snaps back on. "Good boy, Russ."

Russ pulls Paul toward the wooded side of the road, barking up a storm. He'd better not dig up a bag full of mice and drop them on my front lawn.

Frickin' dog.

"Let's get back to the furniture." I lead the way to the door.

Only when we're alone in the entryway does Craig speak up. "A gun? On your property? Why didn't you tell me you found a gun? And money? In the toilet?"

"Must have slipped my mind. Are you sure that's the best place for the sofa? Mallory will kill me if it's not arranged properly."

Chapter Thirty-Nine

Somehow, he managed to get it right. The family room furniture is in place, and even the table is moved to the dining nook by the patio doors, the new stools set in front of the kitchen island. Perfect. The yard work is ongoing, and the front looks fabulous. I step out the back door to check on the progress there.

The grass is cut. They seem to be working on finishing touches like edging, raking, and general cleanup. No big rainstorms are forecast for the next few days. Fingers crossed. I don't need mud trailed into my new addition. If Saturday turns out to be as nice as today, it'll be smooth sailing.

I can't be bothered to fuss with supper, and Beth hasn't been interested in food anyway, so I decide to fix a salad and pop it into the fridge. I'll boil some pasta when she comes home and toss in a jar of sauce. I reach for a knife to chop the veggies and notice one is missing from the wooden block. In the dishwasher? No, it doesn't seem to be there. Not in the sink, either.

When Beth walks through the front door, she finds me lounging on the living room sofa, feet tucked up, with Nellie nestled next to them. She looks like I feel. Exhausted. Dark circles under her eyes, shoulders slumped, vacant stare. She drops her purse by the bookcase and eases herself onto a chair.

"If I didn't need the money, I'd just give up. Get in bed and stay there till Jason comes back." Beth closes her eyes, and her head lolls to the side.

"Why don't you go up and get ready for bed. I'll bring you supper on a tray, and you can nap after you get some food into your stomach."

With great effort, she pushes herself up and climbs the stairs, setting one foot beside the other, and it takes forever before she reaches the top. In the kitchen, I boil pasta and glance through the bay window as the landscapers continue perfecting our yard. It's a good thing Vicky offered to pay for professional services. I'm not up to doing yard work, and Jake's too busy with the renos. I could get used to having someone do the work for me while I sit back and watch. Must be nice to have enough money to be able to do that on a regular basis.

Once the pasta is al dente, I add sauce and stir, take out the salad and mix in the dressing, grab a ginger ale, and make up a tray for Beth. Not only is she physically worn out, she's dealing with financial ruin and the stress of a missing husband. There's nothing I can do to make it any easier for her, but simply be there. I carry the tray up, stepping as Beth did, with extreme care.

She's lying on her side, facing away from the door. Sun filters in from around the closed curtains. Outside, voices travel through the partly open window, the thin material billowing, allowing more light in. The steady rise and fall of Beth's shoulder and the rhythmic breathing tell me she's asleep. I set the tray on the dresser and pull the covers over her. She doesn't stir.

Light reflects off the night table on her far side, projecting on the ceiling. I reach across Beth's body to find the source of the glistening.

Laid across the night table, handle facing Beth, is the paring knife from the butcher block in the kitchen. What is it doing here? Why would Beth leave it beside the bed? I pick it up and place it on the tray, returning to the kitchen to put the knife in the dishwasher and the plate in the refrigerator. At the kitchen table, I eat alone, my eyes on the activity in the back yard.

They appear to be packing up. After placing my empty plate into the dishwasher and wiping the table, I go out to speak to the workers. The crew of four has been busy. The yard looks immaculate, weeds and dead blooms removed from edged flower beds, trees and bushes neatly trimmed, the grass evenly cut and clippings and fallen leaves removed. I thank each of them personally and remark on how nice it looks.

One of the women says to let her know if I find anything that isn't done to my satisfaction, and they will come back tomorrow to fix it. "But it looks lovely, if I do say so myself. A perfect venue for a wedding. Like a fairytale."

"Yes, it is, isn't it?" I marvel at the beauty of nature, tamed by man.

The afternoon sun warms my face, and I curl up on the rattan sofa after the workers leave, the throw over top me. When I wake, I shudder, a chill coursing through me as the sun sets. Through the bay window, the interior lights illuminate Beth as she warms the plate of pasta I left covered in the fridge, a note attached on the door. Her wan face and bleary eyes tell me she's not looking forward to her meal, but the baby needs nourishment.

When will the police bring news of Jason? Not knowing is the worst.

No. Not knowing is not the worst. The worst is knowing your husband is dead and there's no chance of him coming back.

Chapter Forty

The closing credits wake me. I must have fallen asleep again as soon as my head hit the living room sofa pillow. Ten o'clock. Now that I've had a couple of naps, will I be able to sleep through the night? Beth must have gone up to bed. She joined me for the movie, but I guess she was too tired to see it through. The drapes are open, allowing darkness to intrude into the room, the television the only source of light. The thought of the woods looming beyond our lawn unnerves me. My mind conjures up all sorts of creatures that might leap out at any moment. Like a pack of hungry wolves. I'm not sure where that image comes from.

A cup of calming tea would be nice. Then, up to bed. One more day and the week will be done. All four of us are taking Friday off to check on last-minute details for the wedding, and then to spend the night relaxing in the hot tub with a movie on our outdoor screen.

I feel my way through the hall into the kitchen, and as I'm about to flick on the kitchen lights, voices stop me. Coming from the yard. I can't make out the words, but someone is having a heated argument just beyond the back door. I creep toward the mudroom and find the door slightly ajar. When I reach out to close and lock it, I recognize one of the voices. The words become clearer as I strain to listen, hidden behind the door.

"You're going to get caught."

"The job's done now. I just need to get my hands on that money, and it'll be over."

"That was a stupid place to hide it."

"How the fuck was I supposed to know she was going to break the damn

189

toilet?"

"Forget the money."

"Are you nuts? A wad of $500 bills? Have you got another wad? 'Cos if you do, I can forget about the one that's missing. It's got to be here somewhere. I just need to keep looking. If you'd help me, we'd find it twice as fast."

"I can't involve myself any further. I'm not going to jail over this. Besides, maybe she took it to the bank and deposited it when she found it."

"Then I'll have to convince her to un-deposit it."

I can't stand not knowing. Terrified as I am, rooted to my spot, I peer around the door, hoping to get a glimpse of the two people out there. A gasp escapes me as my fears are realized. I remain hidden as they continue their conversation.

"Shh...what was that? Did you hear something?"

Yipping and barking, getting closer.

"It's those damn coyotes."

"Coyotes! I'm heading inside."

I take the opportunity to skulk away from the door, tiptoeing back to the living room, where I curl up on the sofa and pretend to sleep. When Jake comes through the front door more than an hour later, he asks me what's up.

"Nothing. Just really tired tonight." I smile, not letting on that I witnessed something odd in the back yard earlier.

Jake takes me by the hand. "Not *too* tired, I hope." He leads me up to the bedroom.

My mind's elsewhere as he undresses me, but I soon lose myself in the sensation of his kiss as he caresses me with his hands. Afterwards, as I lie with my head on Jake's chest and his arm around me, he asks if I'm happy with the landscaping job.

"It's amazing. We should have them do it regularly."

His chest jolts up and down as he chuckles. "Sure, hon. I'm expecting a big pay raise anytime now. We'll hire a whole staff to take care of the chores."

I know he's kidding. I also know I need to return the money I took from the toilet and slipped unnoticed into my pajama pants pocket when Jake came home with the new toilet.

Trust is crucial in a marriage. Without trust, things fall apart.

Chapter Forty-One

I need to stay out of the way. In my own damn house.

Since seven a.m., they've been at it. Worse than yesterday. At least, that was confined to the outside. Now, the place is buzzing with vacuums, carpet and floor cleaners, drape and upholstery machines. You'd think the Queen was coming to visit. Scrubbing, polishing, shining everything to perfection. Not that we keep a dirty house, but this crew means business. They're not leaving a square inch untouched.

After showering and getting ready for our day, Mal and I abandoned the bedroom for the kitchen, where we maneuvered our way around the staff polishing the countertops and appliances. Mallory even had to ask a cleaner if she could use the powder room before leaving for work.

I'd go outside, but the forecasters, who promised a nice, sunny day, got it wrong again. Drizzle and wind don't entice me to sit outside. That leaves the garage and the shed. They won't be cleaning there.

I grab a windbreaker out of the front closet and take a tour of our property. Nice job on the landscaping. Mal and Vick should be happy with what they've done. At the far end of the back yard, I open the shed door and let my eyes adjust to the interior. The large wooden floor, walls, and shelves are half full, but neat. Mal's gardening bench and stuff, birdseed, my mowers and lawn tools, camping gear...

Someone's been in here. The rope hanging on the wall isn't coiled properly. Its unraveled end lies loose, nearly touching the floor. On the bench, pruners are left carelessly open. Upon further inspection, I notice a few things askew on the shelves. Nothing seems to be missing. Mallory must have been doing some work on the flowerbeds to have them ready for the landscapers. Just like she wanted the house clean before the cleaners came.

"We don't want people to see the place a mess," she'd said.

I straighten things up, recoil the rope, and realize I've seen this rope in my basement cistern not long ago. Wrapped around Mal's rug.

If Dom is going to dump bodies on my property, the least he could do is use his own materials. He owes me the price of a new rug, if nothing else.

Looks like I'll be leaving early for work. Got a stop to make. I pull out my phone and send a text. When a reply comes through immediately, my eyes nearly pop out of my head. Seems he's taking me seriously.

Fifty minutes later, I walk through the casino entrance and head straight for his office. I figure we're on good terms now that he's relocated the bodies off my property. Three-quarters of the way there, Nick intercepts me.

"Do you have an appointment?"

"I don't need one. Dom and I are friends. He'll see me."

No response. But I know he's rolling his eyes without actually doing it.

Nick speaks into his phone, and seconds later, he escorts me the rest of the way to Dom's office. Dom, a grim expression on his face, lips tight and eyes drawn together, stares at the door as we enter.

"You've got your nerve," he says, cold blue eyes locked on mine. "Demanding to see me on such short notice. But I'm sure it must be extremely important. Sit. We've got some things to get straight." He indicates one of the chairs in front of his desk. Nick takes the other.

Not quite on friendly terms. I might have misinterpreted Dom's feelings toward me.

Since I initiated this meeting, I start. "You're right. If you think I'm going down for these murders, you'd better think again. I'll cover for you, but no way am I going to prison." Dumping bodies on my property. Using my rug, my rope. Leaving the gun behind. Stuffing a wad of cash in the toilet for my silence.

I could swear the corners of his mouth turn up in a smirk. And I remember something Craig said to the cops. Maybe someone *is* framing me.

"I'm going to let you in on a little secret, Jake." He motions for me to lean

193

in closer, and meets me partway across the desk, hand on his chin, elbow on the mahogany.

"Things always work out exactly the way I want them to." The smirk widens to a grin. And he reaches over to slap me on the back. "I'm so glad you and I are such good friends. You scratch my back, and I'll scratch yours."

Oh. Shit.

Chapter Forty-Two

Something is happening.

As I near home, a line of police cars sits along the road a mile from our turnoff. Right about where I walked into the woods to bury the gun.

What are they looking for? Russ already found the gun. It's not like there's going to be a body there as well.

I keep driving, passing by with only a curious glance, like any other motorist. If I seem too interested, they might think I had something to do with it.

In front of our house, more action is taking place. Several cars are parked along the road behind a van with a sign along the side. *Keep it Clean. Ontario's favorite clean freaks.*

Right. I'm not going to mess with that. Beth and I will eat out tonight. Save the kitchen from unnecessary filth. Then we just need to get through tomorrow without any disasters, and the big day will be perfect.

On the porch, I wipe my feet, then remove my shoes and place them on the mat in the front entryway. My first impression is that it smells nice. Fresher than when I left this morning. And a whole lot more pleasant than it has been the last couple of weeks. I move past a couple of the cleaning staff, through to the kitchen, and open the basement door. Nothing. Just fresh and clean.

"Excuse me. Did you clean the basement, too?"

"Something smelled down there. So, we wiped the shelves, mopped the floor, disinfected," says an older woman. "And used some heavy-duty freshener in the far part."

"Wow, you're thorough."

"We aim to please. Straightened up, dusted, and mopped down your garage and shed, as well," a young man added. "Took that pile of junk to the dump, like your husband asked."

"You're amazing. Thank you so much."

"They don't call us the clean freaks for nothing."

I am one hundred percent sure this house has never been so clean in all its one hundred and some years. Jake will love it.

Not wanting to interfere with whatever still needs to be done, I sit on the living room sofa, feet planted on the floor and wait for Beth. My paperback book isn't on the coffee table. Turning my head in all directions, I spot it on the bookshelf, tucked in with other books. Exactly where it belongs.

Beth arrives not long after me, and I tell her we're going out. "Let them finish up here. We'll go to the diner in town."

"I'm not feeling like going out." Beth's face is even more drawn than it has been the last several days. "I think I'll go straight to bed."

"I think they're still cleaning upstairs. Why don't we walk to town? The fresh air will do you good." It's not the nicest weather, but at least the rain and wind have let up. A nice, long stroll will give us a chance to unwind. And maybe she'll confide in me. Let me know where exactly her husband is. She's been keeping something from me.

"You're right. The exercise might be better than moping around."

From the closet, I hand my windbreaker to Beth to wear over her sweater. Jake's jacket isn't there, so I grab his hoodie and zip it up over my knit tunic. We begin the trek to town.

If I expected conversation along the way, I soon discover Beth is in no mood. She keeps her head down and moves at a good pace.

"Have you heard anything at all?" I ask.

"No."

"No new developments?"

"No."

"No one's heard from him?"

"No."

At the restaurant, she focuses on reading the menu, then on eating. Or moving her food around, giving the illusion of eating. But every time I ask about Jason, she brings a forkful up to her mouth. If nothing else, I might get some food into her with my persistent drilling.

"You must have some idea where he could be."

She chews and swallows a piece of her grilled chicken sandwich.

"The police must have some clues."

A fry finds its way into her mouth.

"Have you spoken to anyone lately?"

She sips her cola.

"I know you'd do anything to have him back."

She twirls her fraternity ring.

"I know you're involved in something you shouldn't be."

That gets her attention. Her eyes pop. "I don't know what you mean."

"Did you have him killed?"

"What??"

"Jason. Did you pay someone to kill him?"

"Of course, I didn't. Why would you ask that?" Her mouth slightly open, eyebrows drawn together, Beth shakes her head. "I love Jason." Then her mouth opens wider. After a moment, she whispers, "Why? Do you think he's dead?"

Tears spill onto her plate. What have I done? Accused the poor woman of murdering her husband. I pull out a tissue and wipe her eyes, then dab at the tears on her plate next to her chicken with my napkin. "Eat. The baby needs to be fed. That's your priority. I'm sorry I suggested you would hurt Jason. I'm sure he'll be home any time."

Not sure in the least. The opposite, actually.

"I owe you an explanation. And an apology. You've been so kind to me," Beth says.

I sit up straight, ready to listen. She's about to confess.

"I'm so sorry. I didn't know what else to do. I couldn't turn him in."

Turn Jason in? For what?

"And it was a lot of money." She twirls her fraternity ring. "I didn't want any part of it, but he convinced me no one would be hurt. So, I helped him…"

"Jason?"

"Jason? No, my cousin."

"Your cousin?"

"Jethro. We grew up together. Used to be close. But he's the one involved in something he shouldn't be. I hadn't spoken to him for a few years, not since I found out about his illegal activities. I didn't know, honestly, Mallory. I was absolutely shocked when I saw Jake with him in the back yard. I had no idea they even knew each other. So, I called Jethro and asked what he was up to."

I should be shocked as well. Yet, somehow, I'm not. My husband has several acquaintances who are up to no good. Why would one more come as a surprise? "What did Jethro say?"

"He's working in your cornfield. But it's not corn he's harvesting." Beth stops to gauge my response, to see if I know what's hiding amongst the corn.

"Oh?"

"He and some other guys have been growing marijuana."

"Really? In our corn? Oh my!" I set down my fork on the plate, my mouth open in feigned astonishment. "I'll have to tell Jake. Maybe I can convince him not to call the police, since it's your cousin. As long as they get it out of there right away."

"Mallory," she touches my arm. "I hate to be the one to tell you this, but Jake knows. Jethro rents the field from Jake. He and Jethro have a business arrangement about the marijuana. I'm so sorry Jethro dragged Jake into this."

I don't know how to respond. Is Beth going to call the police and report Jake and Jethro?

"But that's not the worst of it. There was something else in the field, Mallory."

I put my hand to my heart before hearing 'the worst of it'.

"Jethro told me that while they were checking the crops, they found a body."

I gasp, my hand moving to my mouth. "A body?"

"And my first thought was that…oh, Mallory, I thought it could be Jason. Jethro assured me he didn't know the guy, but he said they didn't want anyone else to find him and have the police coming around asking questions. So, they decided to hide the body till Jethro (he has more muscle than brains) had a chance to speak to Jake about it, since it was on his property. Then he got a phone call ordering him to move the body to another location."

"Who called him?" My hands grip the table.

"He just told me it was his boss."

"His boss?" As in Jake?

"But as they were moving the body, Jethro found something in the guy's pockets. A wad of money. He didn't want the guys helping him to know about it, so he excused himself to use your bathroom and put the money under the toilet lid. Later, when he came back to get it, the money was gone."

"But," Beth continues, "you had a new toilet. Jethro asked me to search the house for the money. I didn't want to do it. But he offered me a share of the money, and I…I'm so sorry, Mallory. When Jake nearly caught me in the garage, looking through the broken toilet pieces, I didn't know what I was going to tell him if he confronted me. And I was afraid. So, I haven't said anything to anyone about it. Are you okay, Mallory?"

"Yes, yes, I'm fine." Which is far from the truth. The erratic pounding in my chest beats a rhythm with the waves pulsing through my body, threatening to overpower me.

Our walk home is a slow one. I'm quiet as I process what Beth told me about Jethro and Jake and the money. Beth looks down at her feet, dragging herself along. When the drizzle starts up, I pull the hood over my head, tuck Jake's takeout meal into the front of his hoodie, and trudge forward.

When we arrive home, the cleaners' vehicles are gone.

A row of police cars have replaced them. Officers and their canines exit the vehicles and head into the woods across from our home.

Beth freezes.

"Oh, no. No, no." Her body crumples. "They're looking for him, aren't they?"

Chapter Forty-Three

Mallory calls during supper break as Craig and I are polishing off the bacon-stuffed pork tenderloin and scalloped potatoes Vicky made last night. He must have said something to her when I teased him about Vicky stealing Mal's lasagna recipe.

"You need to come home. Now." Mallory sounds frantic, her words running together.

I drop my fork. "Is it the baby? Mallory? Are you okay?" We can't lose this baby. Please, God.

"No, we're fine. It's the police. They're across the road. With police dogs."

Crap. Stupid dogs. What do they expect to fi—

"I'll be right home, Mal."

"Police dogs are across the road from our house looking for something," I tell Craig, who swallows, then stares at me with his mouth open.

"For…?" His hand motions through the air as though he's trying to come up with a possible answer.

"What do you think?"

He's not clueing in.

"In the woods. In a garbage bag. Buried in the ground," I elaborate.

"Mice?"

"Yeah, mice."

"Is it a crime to bury mice?"

My eyes dart around the room, looking for an escape. "It's what might be with the mice I'm worried about."

He finally gets it.

"The body? Come on. You're not serious," Craig pales. "Oh, man. You *were* serious about the body, weren't you?"

"I need to get home."

"They won't find anything, will they?"

"I'll call you when I know something. Keep an eye on things here."

"You're leaving me in charge?"

With his skill at asking questions, he'd make a good candidate for a career in interrogation. I shut down my computer, scramble down the stairs, and run toward the parking lot. If the cops find something, I want to be there.

The exterior lights illuminate the front of the house. Mallory and Beth are on the front porch watching when I pull into the driveway. Three police vehicles line the road. I run up to Mallory and take her in my arms. "You're okay? You and the baby?" This stress can't be good for them.

Beth is shaking like a leaf.

"We're fine. What are they doing, Jake? What are they looking for?"

"I don't know, hon. Let's get you inside. I'll talk to them."

Once I have the women situated on the sofa, where they can still keep an eye on the action outside, which seems to be what they want, I head across the road.

Two familiar faces greet me before I get into the woods. These guys again.

"Officer Heinz. Rombough. Is there something I can help you with?"

"Mr. Shelton. We received an anonymous call that someone was seen burying something in these woods," Officer Heinz informs me.

"Really? Well, wouldn't that be the gun Russ dug up?"

"This was a bigger bag. Last Tuesday."

"And you're just looking now?"

"The caller said they weren't sure it was something worth notifying the police about. But, it kept bothering them, so they eventually called it in." Officer Heinz says. "Wouldn't say exactly where in the woods, though."

"Huh. That's strange."

"Given that a gun was found in this area, we're doing a search of the surrounding woods." He draws his brows together. "It wouldn't happen to be Mrs. Shelton who called us, would it?"

Why the hell would she do that?

"I don't believe so, Officer. She seemed genuinely shocked to see the police and their dogs here. And I'm sure she would have said something to me if she had seen someone burying something in the woods. That seems like an odd thing to do."

Officer Rombough turns toward the woods. "It sounds like they've found something."

We all face the team coming out with the two police dogs. And a garbage bag.

"What did you find?" Officer Rombough heads over to investigate.

He plugs his nose, peers into the open bag. "Oh, shit!"

Officer Heinz runs over to see what's inside. "Oh, shit! All this for a bag full of mice?" He shakes his head. "You didn't mention you'd buried the mice in the woods."

"I guess it slipped my mind," I say. "But, yeah, Craig and I buried them the morning after you were here. Thought it would be better than having them sit in the garage decomposing till I had time to go to the dump."

Mallory and Beth come trotting out as I explain to the officers I've been busy with renos and the wedding, not leaving time to think about the mice I bagged and buried more than a week ago.

"What...what did they find?" Beth asks. "It's not Jason, is it?"

Why would it be Jason? I'm pretty sure he's a few hundred miles away from here. Still waiting for some dumb cop to put two and two together and identify him as the missing husband.

"Mice," I blurt out.

"Jason?" Officer Heinz raises his eyebrows.

"Mice?" Mallory asks, peering into the bag, nose plugged. "Why are they buried in the garbage bag?"

"Oh, thank God," Beth exclaims, collapsing to her knees.

Officer Rombough helps her up. "Are you okay, ma'am?"

"My husband...he's missing. I thought..."

I scratch my head. "Well, honey, I didn't want you to know this. But we had an infestation in the basement. That was the smell. You know, the stink you noticed one day last week?"

I catch her before she hits the ground. "Honey?"

"An infestation?" Mallory holds her stomach. "I feel sick."

"Keep it down, honey."

"An infestation? Oh…the smell…" Beth vomits on Officer Rombough's shoes. Chicken and fries, by the look of it. He rubs his shoes into the grass, trying to clean off the half-digested meal. I pull a tissue out of my pocket and pass it over to Beth.

"Oh, I'm so sorry," she says, looking mortified. "Maybe I should go stay with my cousin."

"We're going to have to take this into evidence." Officer Heinz indicates the garbage bag. "Write up a report." He motions for Officer Rombough to take the bag into the back of their vehicle.

Officer Rombough looks a little green around the gills, his shoes still slimy.

"Uh, sure. Knock yourselves out," I say.

We head back inside to watch the cops pack up and drive off.

"There's a chicken burger and fries for you in the fridge," Mallory says. "I can heat it up for you."

"That's okay, hon. I'll maybe save it for lunch tomorrow." The sight of Beth's meal on the cop's shiny shoes is too much for even me.

"I'm going to bed," Beth says, white as a sheet. "I'm sss…o…tired."

"House smells fresh," I say to Mal once Beth is gone.

She glares at me. "You said a few mice. Not an infestation. You lied."

Yeah. I lied.

And I've got a feeling the shit's about to hit the fan.

Chapter Forty-Four

We sleep in on Friday morning. When you've got an extra day off work, might as well enjoy it. Mallory seems to have cooled off about the mice situation. Especially since I assured her they're all gone. Every single last one of them. Which reminds me. I'd better check the traps.

First things first. I kiss the back of her neck. She giggles and tells me to stop tickling. Then she makes little purring noises, and I turn her around to face me, claiming her mouth. My hands slide the silky fabric of her pajama top upward.

"Craig and Vicky are coming soon," she murmurs. "We better get ready."

"There's time. Everything's spotless. Nothing to get ready. Just me and you."

I convince her to stay in bed a little longer, trailing kisses down to her slightly round belly. Is there actually a kid in there?

By the time we're out of the shower and dressed, it's almost noon. Mal says she's fine with cereal, and I can heat up the food she brought home last night. That sounds good until I remember what happened to Beth's chicken and fries last night.

At the kitchen table, Nellie winds around my legs, looking up expectantly. I throw a few pieces of chicken on the hardwood.

"The floor!" Mallory jumps up to grab a wet paper towel and swipes the hardwood after Nellie gobbles her food. "I don't want things to get dirty again."

"Sorry, I forgot."

After we eat, she wipes down the table and sweeps the floor, puts the dishes in the dishwasher, and tells me not to mess up anything else. She's getting worse than I ever was for obsessive cleanliness.

"I'm going to sit and read till they get here," Mal says, heading to the living room.

"Why don't you sit on your new window seat and look out on the yard?"

"I don't have the pillows for it yet."

"Bring the pillows from the living room for now."

She scrunches her face. "I don't want to make a mess."

I nod and head off to the back bathroom. Women are a whole different species.

I do my business and flush. The toilet whooshes and keeps running. Seriously? Can't they make anything to last these days? I don't think my parents *ever* had to buy a new toilet when I was a kid.

I flip the lever. It keeps running. I lift the lid, careful not to drop it, and set it on the toilet seat while I stick my hand in and jiggle the chain. Water starts to fill properly. I lift the lid to replace it, then hoist it higher.

And peer underneath just in case the money has magically reappeared.

No way!

My fingers slide like jelly, and the lid slips from my grasp. A quarter second goes by in slow motion.

I lift up one knee as though that might catch it. But there's no need. My fingers secure their grip around the rim. I turn it over, gently placing it on the seat, and peel off the bag of money.

Once everything is back in its place, I stuff the money into my pocket and stroll through the hall, whistling. Mallory doesn't bother to glance up from her book as I climb the stairs. The money goes into my safe. For safekeeping, obviously. Not because I'm trying to hide it from my wife. Unless...did she put it there? Took it from the old toilet, then hid it in the *new* toilet? Why on earth would she do that?

Deciding that if anyone asks where it disappeared to, I'll return the money to its rightful owner, whoever that may be, I skip down the stairs. The doorbell rings, the front door swings open, and Craig and Vicky stroll in as though it's their house. Mallory must have unlocked it after breakfast. We're going to have to start keeping the doors locked night and day. You never know what riffraff might walk right in.

"So, you've got about 24 hours of freedom, buddy." I greet Craig with a wink.

Vicky casts a warning look my way, eyes narrowed. As if he'd back out. Gorgeous woman like that. Lots of earning power, too. Lucky schmuck.

But I've got Mallory. It doesn't get any luckier than that. I hit the jackpot when she said 'I do.' What I did to deserve her, I'll never know, but I'll do whatever it takes to keep her. Till death do us part, as the vows go.

Mallory slides off the sofa and suggests we sit at the kitchen table to go over the details for tomorrow. I nudge Craig to remove his shoes, and Vicky does the same. Don't need Mal having a fit about the floors. It'll be a different story tomorrow, with guests wandering all over the place. She'll play the gracious hostess, insisting they keep their shoes on.

"I brought a checklist for us to go through," Vicky says once we sit. She pulls a notebook and pen from her purse.

"Great," I say. "A checklist. Wouldn't want to miss anything, would we?"

Craig rubs his chin as if considering other options.

"I'm sure I've got everything covered. But it's been busy at work." Vicky opens the book, exposing a long list. "I know you guys have the place looking great. Thanks for that."

She gazes out the bay window toward the furnished white tent they installed yesterday morning while I was paying a visit to Dom. "This is much better than a banquet hall. It's beautiful here. Just like your wedding."

"Only now it's reversed." I nudge Craig again. Cat seems to have got his tongue. Craig and Vicky, getting married. Mal and I, best man and maid of honor.

"Okay, so the venue is perfect. Guests have sent their RSVPs. Marriage license, check. The officiant is confirmed, as is the photographer." She checks off a few items, then stares at Craig till she finally gets his attention. "DJ?"

Craig bobs his head up and down and opens his mouth. "He's coming early tomorrow to set up. I gave him our playlist."

"Flowers?"

Mallory says, "Potted and hanging plants, bouquets, boutonnieres, all coming in the morning, along with staff from The Party Shop to decorate."

Vicky checks more items. "Catering?"

"Michaels' staff is serving at six o'clock. The menu was approved a while ago. And drinks will be on ice, ready for toasting after the ceremony." Mal looks at me and Craig as though that would interest us.

"Good. Someone needs to pick up the cake in the morning." Vicky glances my way.

"Sure."

"Rings?" Vicky smiles at Craig.

"Rings?" Craig appears dumbfounded, eyes searching the kitchen. "Don't tell me..."

"I'm just kidding, Vick," he manages to chuckle. "I gave them to Jake for safekeeping."

"You what?" Vicky slides down in her chair, head tilted toward the ceiling. "You have *got* to be kidding me."

"Don't worry. He's got them in his safe, right Jake?"

I give Vicky a thumbs up. She shakes her head.

"Vows?" Vicky turns to Craig.

"Memorized, but I printed them out just in case I get nervous."

"Honeymoon?" Vicky flashes Craig a smile.

"Ready to leave Sunday morning. My first time out of the country."

A three-week tour of Europe. Must be nice.

"Okay, we need to pick up our dresses this afternoon and you guys get the suits. Our hair, nail, and makeup appointment is set for nine. I think we're good to go. Anything I forgot?"

What else could there be? She's hired half the city for the event.

"I'm glad we decided on a small, intimate wedding," Vicky says. "There's so much less to worry about."

She puts the checklist away, and we follow her outside to see if the tent meets her expectations. "It's lovely."

Ten wooden round tables are arranged to the sides. Clear lights hang, strung up around the tent and on the colorful young maple tree (Mal said that was instead of a Christmas tree), with mesh for windows and a see-through ceiling (hopefully, there are stars that night, Mal said). Rows of wooden chairs face the wedding arbor; a white carpet runner lines the length of the tent.

Tears stream down Vicky's face.

What? She's not happy after everything we've done for her?

"It will be a lot nicer with all the decorations and flowers and lit up." Mal waves her arms around as if to apologize that it's not good enough. Vicky's face crumples, and she sobs as Mallory continues. "And after the ceremony, they'll set up the tables with pretty tablecloths and candles and flowers. And fine china and crystal. It'll be nice. Remember our wedding?"

"I'm just so…happy. You guys are the best friends anyone could have. It's beautiful already. More than I ever imagined. Thank you so much." Vicky hugs Mallory, then me.

Craig stands to the side and gawks at the wedding arbor, looking like a duck out of water.

Mallory and I take separate cars to pick up the wedding attire. Craig sits in my passenger seat. "This is it," he says. "I can't believe I'm doing it. I never thought I'd get married. Not after living through my own parents' miserable marriage."

"I hear ya. Fortunately, our parents don't determine what kind of marriage we have. Treat Vick real good. Don't cheat on her. Give her what she needs. She's a gem."

"I know that."

"Don't forget it."

"Did you ever cheat on Mallory?'

I gulp. "Once. When we were dating. Never again."

"Did she find out?"

"Yes. I almost lost her." Since it's confession time between best buds, I ask him, "What about you? Did you ever cheat on Vick?"

He laughs. "We were on and off so often. Of course, there were other women in between. But none of them were Vicky."

"What about when you were together? Any other women then? Anyone tempt you?"

"No. None. There was no one." His eyes bore a hole through the windshield, avoiding mine. "I wouldn't hurt someone I care about."

"You're the better man, then."

He says nothing more. I guess best friends aren't one hundred percent truthful with each other.

After leaving the men's shop, suits hanging on the side doors, we meet up with the girls at an Italian eatery for dinner. Full of chicken and pasta, a couple of drinks (soda for Mal), and a lot of laughs later, we drive back to our place.

Half-naked in the hot tub, a chick flick on the screen to suit the women, the four of us relax, happy as clams, Craig and I downing a couple more beers.

What the hell was I thinking, inviting them into our hot tub the night before the wedding? Since Mal's birthday in June, things have been a bit uncomfortable between the four of us. Even though we've never been closer as two couples. Two best friends whose wives are best friends.

Vick sure looks hot in that bikini. Mallory is so cute with her little belly. God, I love that woman. They call this a four-person hot tub? It seems kinda tight in here. If he starts playing footsies with my wife, I'll cut off more than his feet.

"Are you sure you don't mind sharing a bed with a stranger?" Mallory asks.

What?? My head whips from Craig's feet to Mallory's face.

"No, it's not a problem. Really," Vicky laughs. "I've slept with other women before. Roommates in university. Small dorms, bunk beds. Sharing beds during the summer with my friends when I went to Europe. I can handle a queen bed with another woman in it for one night."

Am I missing something?

"You can sleep in our bed. I'll sleep on the sofa."

Huh?

"Jake can sleep on the floor next to me," Mal continues. "Oh. I forgot. We have a new sofa in the family room now. He can sleep there."

"No. I'm not going to put you out. I'll be fine in the guest room with your friend, Beth."

Oh, okay. Vicky, in the guest room with Beth. Craig, in the den on the couch. Sleeping apart the night before the wedding. Tradition.

It's nearly midnight when Mal and I are in bed together.

"Do you think everything will work out tomorrow?" Mal asks.

"Sure. What could possibly go wrong? Everything's organized down to the last detail."

"You're right. I hope it all works out for them."

"If they're half as happy as we were on our wedding day, half as happy as we've been since then, it'll be fantastic." I kiss her, rolling over on top of her.

"I love you." She kisses me back, her fingernails tickling my back.

Wait till she sees the surprise I have for Craig and Vicky tomorrow night. For her.

Chapter Forty-Five

It turns out to be a beautiful day. The morning sun brightens our room early, waking me just before the alarm I had set for 7:45. Leaving Jake to doze a little longer, I reset it for 9 a.m. and take a long shower, brush my teeth, dress in jog pants and a sweatshirt, and head down for my morning tea and cereal.

Vicky is already up, lounging on the window seat with a cup of coffee. "Good morning. I peeked in on Craig, and he's still here, so I guess that's a good sign." Her smile doesn't hide her worry that he might still take off before the vows are said.

I plug in the kettle. "He loves you. If he has cold feet, it's because he's scared. Just wait till he sees you in that gown coming down the aisle. I always remember the look on Jake's face when I headed toward him on our day. Whenever we hit snags in our marriage, I think about that, and I know how much he loves me. It will be the same for you. There won't be any doubt left after today."

"I just hope we're not rushing into this."

"You've been together for more than three years."

"On and off. A lot more off."

"You've stayed friends through it all. That says something about your relationship." Although she and Jake have remained friends, too, since their breakup almost four years ago. What does that say about *their* relationship?

"What I feel for Craig goes *way* beyond friendship," she says. "But you're right. We've never been able to completely give up on each other."

"Like Jake and me."

Vicky laughs. "You've put up with so much of Jake's shit. He got the better deal in that partnership. But you're right. You and Jake are the perfect couple."

If she's mocking me, I choose to ignore it. It's her wedding day, and she's got enough to worry about.

"I don't know. Maybe it's too much to expect that level of devotion from Craig," Vicky continues. "Maybe I'm just not enough for him."

No, Vicky. No backing out. It'll crush Craig. So, I break Jake's confidence. "Jake told me Craig's afraid of rejection. Your break-ups were hard on him."

"They were hard on me, too," Vicky sighs. "Every time things started to get serious, he pulled away from me."

"Jake said Craig's scared of losing you because you're too good for him. That you'll get tired of him and leave for someone more exciting."

"I'm too good for *him*? More like the other way around. Craig is the sweetest, nicest man I've ever met. Not to mention the hottest. There's nothing I want more than to be with him for the rest of my life."

A creak in the floorboards draws my attention, and I see Craig standing in the doorway between the den and kitchen, listening in on our conversation. His eyes are on Vicky; his smile is for her. "There's nothing I want more, either," he says.

Vicky turns, and their eyes meet. Craig pulls her into his arms, and time stands still. Except the clock ticks away the minutes to their wedding. And there's no way I'm going to allow Vicky to be late and have Craig wonder if she changed her mind.

Seeing the time on the stove advance, I pour water for my tea into a travel mug and shovel spoonfuls of cereal into my mouth while Craig and Vicky make out in my kitchen as though they've forgotten I'm still here. "Save it for later, you two. Don't want to be late for our beauty treatment."

By 8:40, we head out to the city to meet Cindy and Moira at Cleo's Beauty Bar. Vicky is already glowing, Craig's kisses bringing out a natural flush. We're scheduled for three hours of manis, pedis, waxing, facials, eyebrow sculpting, hairstyling, and makeup, each with our own beauty consultant.

I could get used to this kind of luxury.

My mind wanders to the money I put under the tank lid of the new toilet. Hopefully, Jethro will take another look and find it and not come after me. After overhearing Beth talking to him in our back yard, and the threat to make me un-deposit the money, I had a crazy thought that she put it there to pay off Jethro. For killing Jason? For keeping quiet about something? Now that Beth has confessed that Jethro stole it from the dead man, I'm sure of one thing. That money was not honestly earned or legally obtained. Maybe I should have called the police.

By the time we arrive home, Craig's groomsmen are in the den getting ready. Jake comes out as I put my travel mug in the dishwasher and does a double take when he sees me. "Wow! Just wow!"

"Wait till you see me in the dress." The sweats aren't doing much for the overall look.

Vicky and her bridesmaids are already heading upstairs. We'll put on our dresses, shoes, and jewelry in our bedroom and wait to be called down for the ceremony by Gloria, who offered to help with small details so Vicky and Craig's parents could relax and enjoy themselves.

Gloria comes up an hour later to check on things. "Gorgeous. Vicky, you look amazing. So do all of you. The men are all set. Everything's ready. Guests are arriving. It won't be long now. I'll be back soon with your dad."

Vicky takes a deep breath and exhales. "It's really happening, isn't it?"

"Nothing is going to stop this wedding," I say.

And nothing does. Until…

We walk down the aisle, Vicky accompanied by her dad. Classical music plays as the guests turn toward us, smiles on their faces. The interior of the tent is magical, from the white and burgundy decor and flowers to the candles and twinkling lights. Jake waits for me, that charming smile and those sparkling green-blue eyes fixed on me. I glance at Craig just long enough to make sure he's there. Obviously nervous, he cranes his head to see past me as though I'm not worthy of his attention, and he lights up at the sight of Vicky as I take my place beside the bridesmaids. Perfect. His face says it all, his brown eyes soft, and his smile warm.

The officiant welcomes everyone, says a few words, and reads a few inspirational quotes. Craig and Vicky exchange the vows they wrote, Craig stumbling through, but his words are heartfelt, without the use of his prompt. 'I do's' are said. Rings are exchanged. Jake has managed not to lose them, which I know was one of Vicky's worries. No one objects at any point.

And it's over and done in fifteen minutes. The crowd applauds as Craig and Vicky engage in a long kiss and are introduced as Mr. and Mrs. Dunsmere. Jake turns to me and winks, as if to say, "Told you it would be perfect."

The traditional Wedding March plays as we prepare to follow Craig and Vicky down the aisle, and I grab hold of Jake's arm. I feel him tense and turn to face him as he stands still. "Jake?"

The smile on Jake's face has been replaced by disbelief. Mouth wide open, his eyes focus toward the back of the tent, beyond Craig and Vicky's backs. I follow his gaze.

Jason Barlett stands just inside the entrance to the tent, clothes disheveled and face bewildered, scanning the crowd.

"Has anybody seen my wife?"

Chapter Forty-Six

Heads turn toward Jason, staring at the man who interrupted the recessional, those who know him clearly surprised by his sudden appearance, here, of all places.

"Let's go." I nudge Jake to follow Craig and Vicky.

As we approach the exit, Jake catches Jason's eye. Tilting his head to indicate he'll talk to him once we're out of the tent, Jake mouths, "Outside."

Guests spill out of the opening onto the grass, congratulating the newlywed couple. Jake leads Jason away from the crowd. A moment later, Jason runs toward the back door of the house.

I raise my eyebrows when Jake returns to my side.

"Don't ask. I have no idea. I told him Beth's up in the guest room."

"I thought he was dead. In Kingston," I whisper.

"So did I," he whispers back. "But I guess he isn't."

"Then who is?"

"Beats me."

"Everything *did* work out perfectly, didn't it? Not just for Craig and Vicky, but for Beth and Jason." I smile, the sun warming my bare shoulders. "It's the best day."

"Not as good as our wedding," Jake beams.

Once congratulations are out of the way, the caterers bring out trays of champagne and make the rounds. Jake makes the first toast to the happy couple.

"To our best friends. Mallory and I brought these two together. We hope you guys will be as happy as we are. Here's to the next sixty years or more of wedded bliss." Jake raises his glass, his smile spread wide.

After the toasts, the photographer gathers the bridal party and family members together to take formal pictures. Vicky asks for a photo in front of the house, with just the four of us.

That done, Jake and I hug the two of them once more, congratulating our best friends, and leave them to socialize with their guests while we check on the progress inside the tent.

The open bar is set up, with several guests already imbibing, the DJ piping music out to the lawn. The staff confirms dinner will be served on time.

"Did you get the cake?" My voice rises in panic. Jake has forgotten.

"Of course, I got the cake. I took some shelves out of the fridge to make room. The caterers will bring it out later."

"Oh, sorry. I guess I'm still expecting something to go wrong." I shudder as though someone has walked over my grave.

"Relax, Mal. Everything's going really well."

He takes off his jacket and places it over my shoulders. "You look a bit peaked."

"Maybe I'll go inside and sit down for a bit."

Jake escorts me through the front door. Some of the guests have made themselves at home in our new addition, as well as the living and dining rooms. "Upstairs," Jake motions.

As we turn into our bedroom, Jason's voice travels through the closed guest room door. "I'm not kidding, sweetheart. Five hundred thousand bucks. We're set for life."

Beth's response isn't clear.

"No, never again. I promise. It was a one-time thing."

"What do you think that's about?" I ask.

Jake shrugs. "Maybe he had a big win at the casino."

"And he went into hiding for two weeks?"

"I don't know. Why don't you go ask him?"

"I will. After they've had some time to themselves. Let's give them their privacy."

I lie on the bed, spreading out my dress so as not to wrinkle it, and Jake closes the door.

"What's the surprise?" I ask.

"What?"

"You said you had a surprise."

"No, I didn't. When did I say that?"

"In your sleep last night. You mumbled something about a surprise at the wedding."

"Did I? Must have been dreaming. Anyway, I'd say a lot of people were surprised today with Jason showing up out of the blue after all this time. Get some rest. I'll be back to get you in a while."

I yawn and close my eyes as Jake closes the door behind him. Voices from the front lawn travel through the open window, lulling me to sleep.

A knock on the door wakes me. The clock on my night table illuminates the hour. 5:05. It must be time to get ready for the dinner reception. Why is Jake knocking?

The knob slowly turns.

"Beth?"

"Mallory. I'm sorry to disturb you. Do you have a few minutes?"

"Of course."

She closes the door behind her and sits on the bed next to me. "I want to thank you again, properly. You've gone out of your way to help me when I didn't have anyone to turn to."

"I'm glad I could be there for you. And I'm so happy it all worked out for you and Jason. I know what's it like, not knowing where your husband is. I was lucky to have Vicky and Craig's support when Jake went missing this summer."

"I knew you would understand. I can't talk to anyone else about our problems. I don't socialize outside of work. I'm embarrassed by Jason's gambling, our debt, all the time he spends at the casino instead of with me. My sister says I should leave him. She always makes me feel like I'm too weak to stand up for myself. I haven't spoken to her for months. The last time I saw her, she told me to pack my bags and get my shit together, stop letting him walk all over me. Maybe she's right. But I love him. And when I thought something might have happened to him…" Beth chokes up, a tear hanging on her lower lid.

"You're not weak, Beth." I lay a hand on her shoulder as she trembles. "Jason is weak. He has an addiction. A problem he can't deal with on his own. It takes a strong woman to support a weak man."

I'm a fine one to be handing out advice. I know exactly what other women would say if they knew what I put up with. But if Jake can't depend on the person he loves most to keep him upright, then who can he turn to?

Beth wipes the tear away and blows her nose, sitting up straighter. "He promised me he was going to get help. And he's made a good start. But these last two weeks, not knowing if he was safe…" She chokes on her words again, and I give her time to compose herself.

"Did Jason tell you where he was all this time?"

"Rehab."

"Rehab? Why wouldn't he be safe?"

Beth swallows and takes my hand in hers. "There's something you should know. About what happened to Jason last Friday night. I know Jake's tight with Dom."

"Jake and Dom? I'd hardly say they were tight. But Dom does have a hold on him."

"I'm so sorry for involving you in this mess. Taking advantage of your hospitality. Rummaging through your house, looking for the cash Jethro stole from the dead man. Having you worry about Jason alongside me. And Jason made me promise I'd keep quiet…but I'd blame myself if anything happened to you because I didn't speak up and warn you."

"Warn me? About what?"

Beth lowers her voice. "There was a *body* in your cornfield. *Jake's* cornfield. And Jason knows how it got there. Watch your back, Mallory."

Chapter Forty-Seven

The bedroom door swings open. "Hey, hon, you're not gonna believe this. I just talked to Ja…" Jake stops when he sees Beth. "Sorry, didn't know you had company."

"Can you just give us a couple of…?" But I don't get the opportunity to have any more alone time with Beth.

Gloria sweeps into the room. "There you are. People are asking for you. Both of you. You *are* the hosts, not to mention best man and maid of honor. They'll be serving dinner soon. You should be down there; guests are already starting to take their seats."

"We were just on our way, Mom." Jake offers his arm to help me off the bed and escorts me toward the door, leaving Beth on her own.

"You must be so relieved to have Jason back." Gloria turns her attention to Beth. "I'll talk to the catering staff and have them bring in a couple more chairs and place settings so you can join us."

"Oh, that's not necess…" Beth stands and follows us to the hallway.

"Nonsense. You have a lot to celebrate. Might as well do it with the rest of us."

"Yes, please stay," I agree. Maybe she'll talk to me later, tell me what she meant.

"We're not dressed properly. And I don't even know the bride and groom," Beth says.

"Jason and Craig work together, right, Jake? And they're friends."

"Uh…yeah. They kinda know each other." Jake shrugs. "The more, the merrier."

Gloria leads the way down the stairs, ushering us through the hall toward the back door. Jake pops his head into the den and tells Jason dinner is about to be served and they're welcome to join everyone in the tent.

"Oh no, we couldn't intrude," Jason says. "We'll just head home."

"Yes, we really should…" Beth agrees.

"Free gourmet meal, buddy. And dancing under the stars. You and Beth can celebrate."

Gloria takes over, telling Beth and Jason to come with her. Turning to Jake, she says, "You two need to get lined up, ready to make your entrance when the DJ announces the head table."

As we head outside to join the rest of the bridal party, Jake stops to kiss me. "I told you everything would work out perfectly. Just like our wedding."

We make our entrance into the tent, guests standing to applaud the newly married couple once more. I breathe a sigh of relief. Jake's right. It all worked out perfectly. Once everyone is seated, Jake takes the podium and welcomes everyone, making another toast to the bride and groom. He ends with, "Here's to your happily ever after, guys." As he raises his glass and sips champagne, something at the back of the tent catches his attention.

The smile remains on his face, his expression betraying nothing, but I know my husband. The look in his eyes tells me something's wrong. Without being too obvious, I turn my head from Jake to whatever has him rattled.

White fairy lights twinkle at a fairytale wedding, with a predominately white decor, burgundy accents, and fall florals adding a splash of color. In a room of one hundred well-dressed, well-wishing guests, three are out of place.

I'm not sure what their presence means, but I now recognize the look in Jake's eyes for what it is because the same emotion courses through me.

Fear.

Chapter Forty-Eight

What the hell are they doing here? First, Jason turns up alive. I was sure he was dead and buried. Or dead and dug up. And now *they* show up?

They've at least had the decency to back out of the tent entrance as the caterers begin to deliver the first course, distracting most people who are eager to dive in after a long afternoon of ceremony, socializing, and trying not to get plastered before the evening begins. But I hear the whispers between mouthfuls of tomato bisque and mini grilled cheese finger sandwiches.

How in the blazes am I supposed to deal with them without causing more of a scene? Ignore or confront them? Craig's oblivious, too busy making googly eyes at Vicky and smooching every time people clink their glasses together. Probably best to pretend I'm not bothered. Eat, applaud, smile. Maybe they'll figure out we're in the middle of a wedding dinner and get lost.

As the plates are collected and everyone awaits the main course, Mal rises from her seat. What is she up to? Whispering something to Vicky, she picks up her teensy purse, then heads to the exit, one hand lightly rubbing her belly, fake smile planted on her face as she passes guests. Should I follow her?

I nudge Craig and whisper, "Where's Mallory going?"

He turns to Vicky and relays my question.

"Bathroom," he reports back. "The baby..."

I nod and chuckle loud enough for those near me to hear. "Yep, the baby needs a lot of bathroom trips."

Why aren't they serving the main course? People are getting restless, heads turning in the direction of the exit as though they expect the festivities to come to an end anytime now. I motion for one of the caterers.

A young guy in black pants and a white shirt rushes over. "Yes, Mr. Shelton?"

"Can we move ahead with the meal? What's the hold-up?"

"Oh, of course, sir. We were just waiting on Mrs. Shelton, out of courtesy."

"Mrs. Shelton won't mind. She'll be making frequent trips with her condition. Serve the damn chicken. Now."

"Yes, sir." His face reddens, and he scurries off to get the rest of the staff moving, offering guests a choice of ham and Swiss stuffed chicken breast and pan-roasted potatoes or mushroom risotto and green beans to satisfy the non-meat eaters.

As food lands in front of people, their eyes focus on the meal and not on the exit door. I leave my chicken untouched and down another glass of champagne while I wait for the inevitable. Any minute now, the wedding crashers are bound to storm through the flaps of the tent, causing a shitstorm. No one's likely to forget this wedding.

Out of the corner of my eye, Mal waltzes through the door, stopping to say a few words to guests, her smile still intact. The minute she sits down next to Vicky, the young guy with the red face scurries over to ask about her choice of entree.

"Oh, my. It all looks and smells so delicious!" Mal's voice carries. "I don't want to be a bother, but could I have both? The baby..." She pats her stomach and giggles. "The baby has an appetite."

The server places two plates in front of my wife. She immediately samples both meals and gives the guy a thumbs up. Once he's gone, Mal pulls back her chair and leans across toward me. "I don't think I can eat all this myself. We'll have to share. Don't want to waste it."

She heads past Vick and Craig, one plate at a time in her hands, and dumps half a chicken breast and several scoops of risotto on top of my still-full china. She's managed to get people's heads turned toward the front of the tent instead of the back exit, if only momentarily.

"They're gone. I got rid of them," she whispers in my ear and pecks me on the cheek.

Okay. Good. Now I can eat. Not that I have much of an appetite.

Because I know they'll be back.

Chapter Forty-Nine

Nothing is going to spoil this wedding. Everything is perfect. The food is delicious; the decor is beautiful; Vicky and Craig are happy.

I take my time eating my meal and a half, wishing I had skipped breakfast this morning. Eating for two doesn't literally work that way. I was full after the soup and cheese sticks. Still, I manage to eat half of what's on my two plates by the time the staff come around to clear the tables. Leaning over, past Vicky and Craig, I catch Jake's eye. He flashes me a smile. I notice he's managed to clean his plate, in spite of the stress I know he's under. He's so good at covering. What he feels and what he presents to the world are two different things. That's why he's such a good liar. He can convince himself his lies are the truth.

When the server comes to take my plate, I make a production of not wanting to give up my food. "Oh no, don't take it away. It's so good. I'll just finish it up…" I push back my chair, turn to the side, cover my mouth with my hand, make a few gagging noises, then sit back up at the table. "I'm okay. Just a bit of gas. But, maybe you could box it up and put it in the fridge for me to finish tomorrow? A doggie bag? Would that be okay?"

The server, who takes a few steps back when I burp, looks horrified, his brow scrunched and mouth agape. "Yes, of course, Mrs. Shelton."

Hopefully, most of the guests will be wondering about Jason's sudden return and my odd behavior and forget the uninvited guests who showed up earlier. Especially as the evening progresses and the drinks keep flowing.

The DJ announces it's time for speeches, and Vicky's dad takes the podium, giving a heartfelt speech about losing his little girl. Craig's father gets a few chuckles from the crowd by saying he never thought he'd see the day his son would get married. I get all teary-eyed talking about my renewed friendship with my high school best friend, Vicky, skipping the part about how she slept with my future husband first, then Craig.

When Jake stands to give his speech, I realize he's single-handedly more than capable of getting people's minds off one topic onto another. He recounts the great times he and Craig had as single men, bar hopping with their other single friends, hitting on women. "Those were the days," he sighs.

I'm nearly mortified enough to push my chair back and leave, and I sense Vicky feels the same way, but then Jake laughs and says, "We had no idea how ridiculously alone and lonely we were. How empty and meaningless our lives were. Then I married Mallory, and Craig met Vicky. Everything changed. Our lives began. So, really, Craig and I aren't even four years old. If we act kind of immature sometimes, well...what do you expect from a couple of toddlers?"

Jake recounts the antics of being a married house owner and doing renos with his best friend's help, eliciting plenty more guffaws from the crowd. "Vicky, just remember to hire a plumber and electrician when you're fixing up your own place. I don't think home insurance covers do-it-yourself stupidity."

"To Craig, my best guy friend, 'cos my wife's my very best, of course. I've never seen you this happy, Craig. But it's just the start." He raises his glass to him, everyone follows suit, and I think he's done, but no, there's more.

"I don't know if everyone here knows, but my wife and I are expecting a baby. After all the idiotic things I've done in my life, Mallory still believes in me and stands with me. And now we're going to stand together as a family. I love you, Mal." He turns to me, raises his glass again, and says, "To my wife, who has shown me the one person you can trust and rely on above everyone else is the one you married."

Oh, no. He knows I took the money.

"And that is what I wish for my buddy, Craig. Love, trust, family." He embraces Craig in a big man hug before sitting down and begins to sob. "I love you, man." After slapping him on the back, he takes his seat, wiping his eyes.

Around the room, tears glisten on cheeks, and the sounds of "Awww" mix with smiles. Jake has left everyone with a warm, fuzzy feeling.

Vicky and Craig round off the speeches with their thank-yous to the guests and to their families. "And most of all, thank you to Jake, for marrying Mallory. If you hadn't, I wouldn't have Vicky," Craig beams. "Thanks to both of you for bringing us together, letting us be part of your lives, and opening up your home to us."

"And thanks for this wonderful wedding," Vicky adds. "We'll never forget it. You guys are the best."

I'm not so full as to skip a slice of wedding cake and manage to scarf it down, looking toward the chocolate fountain table for more sweets. Jake brings me a bowl of chocolate-covered strawberries and pulls his chair up behind me. I turn to face him, and we share the sweet berries.

"That was a nice speech," I say, biting into the chocolate fruit.

Jake swipes his finger across my lips and brings it to his mouth, his tongue licking the chocolate. "Don't want to waste any."

Vicky turns to me and asks me to accompany her to the washroom. I gather up her veil and train, and we head out under a darkening sky, pink and mauve clouds creating a gorgeous backdrop. I shudder as the cool air hits my bare arms.

On our way to the back door, the stray black cat crosses our path.

"Does that mean bad luck?" Vicky asks.

"No, I think it's good luck."

"Oh, okay." She continues shuffling along, with me and the yards of wedding garb following.

We climb the stairs, and Vicky uses the ensuite in our bedroom. When she comes out, she says, "Jake's in trouble again, isn't he?"

My mouth flies open. How does she know…? Oh, of course. Craig. Jake must have confided in him. But exactly how much does she know?

"What do you mean?"

"I saw them, Mallory. When they stepped into the tent. And now their vehicles are parked out front. I saw them through the bathroom window."

They're still here?

Chapter Fifty

"What's taking them so long?" Craig looks like he's considering whether Vicky took off, on her way to get an annulment.

"Relax. Women. Baby. Wedding dress. Makeup touch-up. It takes time. And they probably stopped to chat to friends on the way."

His eyes remain glued to the exit. "What do you think they wanted?"

"Who?"

"You know who. Why would they show up at our wedding? And why did they decide to leave?"

"I don't know. The important thing is they're gone." And hopefully, won't be back till Craig and Vicky are off on their honeymoon.

Craig untenses as Mal and Vicky come through the tent opening. I nod to the DJ, indicating it's time to get the party started. Minutes later, the bride and groom float across the dance floor to the song they chose together—Just My Imagination. Twinkling lights surround them, the DJ having shut off the main lighting for the dancing.

Mal and I and the rest of the bridal party join them on the dance floor after the obligatory Father/Mother dances. Holding Mallory in my arms after a long day of best man duties, her head against my chest, the smell of her hair, is intoxicating. I just want to scoop her up and whisk her off to bed.

Mallory tilts her head up. "Look, you can see the stars. Isn't it beautiful? We should make a wish."

"I have everything I could ever have wished for," I say. "Right here in my arms."

At midnight, it's time for the big surprise. The DJ asks the single women to gather for the throwing of the bouquet, followed by the last dance. Mal and I sway to Forever and Ever, Amen.

And then comes the big finale. Guests are asked to line up to the right and left of the tent door and the DJ announces the bride and groom will make their grand exit, after which everyone should gather on the lawn for something special to end the night.

As we gather outside, Mallory asks, "What's this big surprise?"

"Yeah, Jake, what's up?" Craig adds, turning his head in all directions.

"You'll see. Wait for it. And you might want to look up." I point to the sky above the meadow.

The DJ ups the volume on the music, piping out Thunderstruck by AC/DC, Craig's favorite band. A loud whistle accompanies the start of the song, and the sky lights up in multicolor explosions, cracks and booms echoing through the night.

The gasps and exclamations of guests mingle with the sound of fireworks and rock music. Vicky throws her arms around my neck and plants a wet kiss on my cheek. Craig hugs me like a woman.

"I thought you guys should end the night with a bang. In more ways than one." I wrap my arms around Mal. "Just like our wedding."

"Oh, Jake. It's perfect." Mal confirms that the exorbitant cost was well worth the result.

The light and sound show continues as Shoot to Thrill, TNT, Highway to Hell, Money Talks, Hells Bells, and Dirty Deeds rock the night, ending off with You Shook Me All Night Long.

As directed, the DJ bids everyone a good night, packs up his sound system, and shuts off the power to the tent, hinting it's time to leave. "And it's time to rock and roll on home, folks, and give the bride and groom some private time."

Craig and Vicky graciously hug and shake hands with guests as they head toward the front yard. Beth thanks Mallory for everything, and says she'll give her a call tomorrow.

"Wait a minute, Beth. Where are you guys staying tonight?" Mal asks.

"You're welcome to stay here. Vicky and Craig are going to spend the night at their new house."

"We're okay. Jason came into some money. We'll stay in a hotel till we get a new place."

Had a big win. Could've been me if I'd played.

Mom and Steve bid us goodnight. Steve puts his hand on my shoulder. "You did good, son. It was a beautiful wedding. I just wish I hadn't missed yours." And then the man has the nerve to hug me. "I'm sorry I wasn't the dad you deserved."

I don't need this shit. But I'm not going to cause a scene on the happiest day of my best friend's life. So, I return the hug and say something stupid like, "Thanks, Dad. I know you're trying to make up for it." Best to keep the peace.

Once Vicky and Craig's parents leave, we head inside to change out of our wedding gear, leaving Craig off at the den. No sooner do Mal, Vick, and I start up the stairs than the doorbell rings.

I tell the girls to head on upstairs. "I'll get it."

They stay where they are, and I open the door to the three men who threatened to crash the wedding earlier.

"Mr. Shelton. I'm Detective Swarovski."

"Detective? What can I do for you? I obtained all the proper permits for the fireworks. Were there noise complaints from the neighbors?"

Play dumb, Jake. You're good at it.

"You put on quite the show, but that's not why we're here. Out of courtesy to Mrs. Shelton, we held back till the guests left."

By 'we', he means Officers Heinz and Rombough as well as himself. I should have known I hadn't seen the last of these guys.

"I see. Well, thank you, I guess. But what exactly can I help you with?"

"We'd like you to come down to the station to answer questions concerning the gun found on your property."

"You mean the gun found on someone else's property, dropped on my property by the neighbor's dog? I already told the police I don't know anything about that."

Vicky speaks up. "You don't need to say anything else, Jake." She turns to the detective. "I'm Jake's lawyer. He won't be coming to the station tonight. If you need to question him further, he'll be happy to do so bright and early Monday morning. Good night." She opens the front door for them.

"I'm afraid we won't be leaving," Detective Swarovski states, pulling out a piece of paper. "We have a warrant to search the property."

"Can I see that?" Vicky looks it over, then nods. Her eyes meet mine. I know exactly what she's thinking.

What the hell have you done now, Jake?

Chapter Fifty-One

"Jake Shelton, I'm taking you into custody on suspicion of the murder of Anthony Martino. You have the right to…"

That was his name. I couldn't recall it at the time, but he's the guy I saw at the casino two weeks ago.

The rest of Detective Swarovski's words floated by my ears like a foreign language. Mallory's eyes captured and held mine. She had no words. Neither did I. We were caught in a nightmare.

Vicky instructed, "I'll meet you at the station. Don't say anything till I get there."

Craig stood silently by until Detective Swarovski said he wanted him to come to the station as well, for questioning. Then Craig put his hands up, took a few steps back, and said, "Hey, I don't know anything about this."

Craig, not exactly a grand master in the art of lying, fed the suspicions of not only the arresting officers, but also of our wives.

Vicky, eyes shifting from me to her new husband, said, "Not one word, either of you."

The evening ended with one hell of a big bang.

And now I sit in an interrogation room with three cops opposite me, the discussion being recorded. They're doing all the talking. I'm keeping my mouth shut, as per Vicky's instructions.

"Shut up and play dumb," she had whispered in my ear before they escorted me to the drab room. "And no jokes, Jake. This is serious."

Play dumb, Jake. That should be a breeze.

"What was your relationship with Anthony Martino?"

I shrug. "Who?"

"You were seen talking to him the night he disappeared. In the River Grand Casino. We have video, Mr. Shelton. And witnesses who say you both frequented the high-limit room." Detective Swarovski has done his homework.

"So?" I lean back in my chair. Nothing to hide. I'm not the only one who saw Tony that night.

"So, Mr. Martino's DNA was found in the bag you buried."

"Bag?"

"The garbage bag filled with dead rodents and insects. The bag someone saw you and Mr. Dunsmere lug across the road into the woods. The bag the police dogs sniffed out. That bag."

"Huh."

The detective waits for me to elaborate on that. Of course, I don't.

"How did Mr. Martino's DNA end up in that bag?"

I screw up my face as though I'm trying to figure out an answer. Then I shake my head and raise my eyebrows.

"How did the gun end up in a grocery bag with your wife's credit card receipt in it?"

"Gun?"

"The gun your neighbor's dog dropped off on your front lawn. The Glock that matches the bullet found in Mr. Martino's brain." Not an image I really need to have in mine.

I stare past the detective to the grey wall.

The detective passes the buck to Officer Heinz, giving him a nod.

"The night Officer Rombough and I answered the 911 call," Officer Heinz says. "You and Mr. Dunsmere appeared to be nervous about something."

Yep. Dead body in the basement cistern. Stinking up the whole damn house.

"That was several days after the victim went missing," he continues. "Your house smelled of decomposition."

"Rats!"

"We found no rats. Mice and a dead possum. A lot of flies and insects."

"Skunks!"

"No sign of…" He stops to reconsider. "No skunks inside the house. Nothing that would cause that kind of stench. Perhaps you'd already removed the body. Is that what happened, Mr. Shelton? Did you and Mr. Dunsmere remove the victim's body shortly before we arrived on the scene?"

My eyes search the ceiling for inspiration.

Detective Swarovski takes over. "We found Mr. Martino's VIP card in your wallet. Why do you have it?"

Why? Because I'm an idiot.

"And the money in your office safe? Where did it come from?"

From inside my fucking toilet.

"The gold money clip bears Mr. Martino's initials. Did you steal the money from him? Did you kill Mr. Martino?"

"Have you thought about a different color scheme for this room? It's a bit depressing."

"Do you think this is funny, Mr. Shelton?"

"No, no, sir."

"We know you're involved in this. I'm going to ask again. Did you kill Mr. Martino?"

"No."

"Are you covering up for someone?"

I look down at my feet.

"Is it Mr. Dunsmere? Did he kill Mr. Martino?"

"No! He wouldn't kill a fly."

"What about your friend, Terry Cox? His construction crew dug up the body on one of his work sites near Kingston, where Mr. Cox lives. Strange he didn't mention he'd seen the victim before—with you at the casino. Why would he not disclose that to the police?"

Because he's minding his own damn business. Doesn't want to join Tony.

"Mr. Shelton, did you murder Mr. Martino?" Same old question, over and over. "Did your friends, Mr. Dunsmere and Mr. Cox, help you dispose of the body?"

It's nearly six in the morning, and I can't take this much longer. "I could use my morning cup of coffee. Do you have Starbucks?"

A couple of minutes later, I'm downing a god-awful cup of black coffee, no cream, no sugar. Then, the questions continue. Don't these guys get tired? They must be pulling a double shift.

"Records show you bought two rugs, exactly the same. There's only one in your house. What happened to the other one?" Detective Swarovski catches me off guard with this one.

"The first one was defective. I sent it back."

"There's no record of a return."

"Oh, right. I took it to the dump. Is that a crime, detective?"

"No, but murder is. The blood in your cistern, I'm betting, isn't all from rodents. And I suspect the fibers found on the victim's body will prove to be a match to the rug in your family room, and the rope in your garden shed."

Shit.

"What can you tell us about your association with Domenic Pappalardo?"

"Who?"

"This will go better for you if you cooperate, Jake." So, we're on a first-name basis now. "If you did this under Mr. Pappalardo's direction, you could plead for a lighter sentence. All you have to do is tell the truth. Did Domenic pay you to kill Mr. Martino? Is that where the money in your safe came from?"

I have nothing to say. No winning hand here. No point in bluffing. I don't even hold a single card.

Arms crossed, legs crossed and stretched under the table, I tilt my head onto my shoulder, eyes closed.

This interview is over.

Chapter Fifty-Two

They're gone. One minute, we're celebrating Vicky and Craig's wedding, with fireworks ending the day with color and sound. Next, the police are searching our home.

And once again, I find out Jake is lying.

The VIP card is in his wallet, not in the garbage where it should have gone. He planned on using it again. To gamble. The money is in the safe, not under the toilet seat, where I returned it after hiding it at the bottom of Nellie's dry food canister. What am I supposed to believe? That someone else put that card in Jake's wallet and he didn't notice? Beth said Jethro put the money in the toilet. Then why is it in Jake's safe now?

And why have the police arrested him? I consider whether it's my fault for burying the gun. Craig must know something about what's going on or they wouldn't have wanted to question him, too.

Nellie senses my anxiety, curling herself around my ankles every time I stop pacing. The house has been violated. Our home, no longer private. Every room, every drawer, every closet invaded. Our best friends, witnessing the assault on our lives.

As I wander from room to room, I try to repair the damage done to our sanctuary. It's minor, in terms of physical abuse; the police were gentle with our belongings, mindful of the turmoil we suffered a couple of months ago. The effect of their rummaging through our personal property, the most intimate parts of us, won't be easily repaired, though. And the emotional trauma of being torn from your home and family and locked up must be nearly as scarring as watching the love of your life taken.

Tidying up seems silly, but I need to do something. Vicky told me to wait for her call. What else can I do? I can't sleep. I can't sit still. I need to know Jake is coming home. I need Jake.

I peek out the dining room window, imagining Jake coming home, telling me it was all a big misunderstanding and everything has been straightened out. Darkness greets my eyes, the streetlight out again. It presses forward, squeezing the house in its grip. Stars twinkle above, reminding me of the fairytale in the back yard only hours ago, Vicky and I princesses, dancing with our princes. My head on Jake's heart, his beat keeping me alive. But the dark doesn't lie. There are two sides to each day, and at the end of the day, light succumbs to darkness.

There's no happily ever after.

Hours pass like this, wandering around the house, checking through windows, picking up my phone, petting Nellie, trying to keep calm. Jake is innocent. Of murder. Once the police realize that, he'll be sent home with an apology from the entire force.

The phone rings.

"Jake's okay, but I'm afraid he's not coming home just yet," Vicky says. "We have to wait for the bail hearing. I've been in touch with some colleagues at my firm who are experts in criminal law. They'll make sure he gets the best representation possible. Craig was questioned, and now we're going home to get some sleep. Try to rest yourself, Mallory. I'll let you know as soon as I get any news about the hearing. But for now, Jake is staying at the city jail."

"But, they *will* let him go, won't they? They can't keep him in jail. He's innocent."

"You and I know that, Mallory. And I'll make sure the judge understands Jake isn't a flight risk, that he has no prior criminal arrests, and he isn't a threat to anyone. But there's a lot of evidence against him. We need to prepare ourselves for a trial, even if they do grant bail. But, Mallory, it's likely going to be a lot of money to raise, and we want to get him out as soon as possible. We'll help, of course, but maybe you could ask Jake's parents to get some cash together." Vicky pauses before adding, "I might need to bail my husband out, too. There's a good chance they might charge him with being an accomplice."

"An accomplice? What does Craig have to do with any of this?"

"They think he helped Jake move the victim's body, for starters."

"What body? I don't understand."

"Neither do I, Mallory. I still have to get the truth out of Craig. He told the police he helped Jake scoop some dead mice and a possum out of the basement cistern and they buried the bag because of the smell. He's not saying anything else, not even to me."

Vicky ends the call, saying I will be the first to know when she finds out more. But, patience not being one of my virtues, I immediately make another call.

The person who got Jake into this mess is the one who needs to get him out of it. My calls and texts go unanswered. Undeterred, I grab my purse and jacket and head for the car, the morning sun about to break through.

I won't be meek and mild Mallory. My husband needs a hero. I'm it.

I have some information no one else does. A missing piece of the puzzle. At first, I thought it might incriminate Jake, so I kept quiet. We're long past that point now, though. And the police might not believe me.

But I know someone who will.

Chapter Fifty-Three

"You're free to go. Your ride's here."

A key turns in the lock, the bars swing open, clanging rousing me from some horrific nightmare where I shoot someone's brains out and get Craig to help me haul the body into his car.

"Hey, sleepyhead. Rise and shine." Some young uniform indicates the door's wide open, and I should get out while I can.

I have no idea how long I slept. Fatigue, stress, shock. Then, the endless rounds of questioning. Did I kill Anthony Martino? If they hadn't thrown me in a cell when they did, I would have confessed just for the privilege of falling into a bed. Thank God Vicky has talked some sense into these guys, and they realize they don't have enough of a case against me to press charges.

After picking up my personal effects at the counter and signing some papers, my eyes scan the lobby for Vicky.

No Vick anywhere.

What I do see is Nick. Dressed in his casual black business attire, nodding in my direction. I follow the wordless Nick out to his black sedan.

"To what do I owe this unexpected jailbreak?"

"Dom said to pick you up." He drives out of the city in silence. The clock on his dash indicates it's almost time for lunch.

My first call is home to Mal to let her know I'm on my way. We do more crying than talking. Nick's eyes shift from the road toward me, and he shakes his head. No comment, just a smirk.

My second call is to Dom to thank him for getting me out. "I appreciate the get-out-of-jail card, Dom. My lawyer said I'd have to wait for a bail hearing. Did I sleep through it or something?"

"Or something."

"Don't worry. I'll pay you back as soon as I can."

"I'm not worried in the least. You'll more than pay me back. The judge and I came to an agreement. You're out on your own recognizance. A couple of life lessons you might want to learn, Jakey boy. Money talks. A lot of money talks louder. And it's not just who you know; it's *what* you know."

"Well, thanks again."

"Don't thank me. Thank that pretty little wife of yours. That woman has some balls. Came to my house and practically knocked the gate down, yelling and waving her arms in the air. That's one scary woman you married. Don't underestimate her." And he hangs up.

The minute I'm through the front door, Mal runs into my arms, sobbing. "Oh, thank God you're okay. Vicky called to say they decided to let you go for now. I thought...I thought..."

"I know. I know, honey. But everything is going to be okay. Dom's taken care of it."

She pulls out of my embrace. "Dom? He's the one who caused this. Incriminated you."

"Yeah. He's got my back, though, for some reason."

Mal opens her mouth to say something, but changes her mind. Instead, she leads me upstairs to our bed and we fall asleep in each other's arms after making love. So much more comfortable than a cell cot.

Ringing in my ears and a growling stomach wake me up sometime in the afternoon. Mallory moans, rolls out of bed, and heads downstairs.

Moments later, she comes back into the room. "Jake, get up! Your Mom and Steve are here. They brought food."

We dress quickly and greet them in the kitchen, where Mom is stacking plastic containers into the fridge. "I made a huge roast for lunch and thought we could share the leftovers. Mallory, you must be exhausted after all the excitement from yesterday. It'll save you cooking dinner."

"That's so thoughtful of you, Gloria," Mallory says.

"That was some shindig last night," Steve says. "You gave Craig and Vicky one heck of a memorable wedding."

You have no idea.

Don't need Steve finding out I spent the night in jail. Or that I might be spending a lot more time there. Following in my old man's footsteps.

No sooner do we settle into the living room than the doorbell rings again. Craig and Vicky, with more food containers. Finger to my lips, shaking my head, I hope they get the idea—mum's the word about last night's search and arrest. They nod, peering into the living room where Mal has my parents engrossed in her talk about upcoming renos for the nursery.

"I'll put this in the fridge," Vicky says. "Michael's had extra food left over from the reception, so there's plenty for everyone."

"Vicky!" Mom exclaims as Vick heads to the kitchen. "I thought you were leaving for your honeymoon today."

"Change of plans. Some work stuff came up this morning, so we're delaying our trip for now."

"Oh, no. That's a shame."

"It's okay. We can go to Europe any time. Vick's work is important," Craig says.

Sticking to safe topics, like the wedding, the baby, and how nice the house looks with the current renos done, Mallory and I entertain our guests, both of us hoping my parents won't outstay their welcome. Near dinnertime, several things happen almost at once.

Mallory goes to the kitchen to pop the food into the oven. The doorbell rings. My phone indicates I have a text message. Through the front window, Paul can be seen chasing his terrier across our lawn. And Dad turns on the television to the six o'clock report. Five of us listen to the local breaking news.

A local man, with possible connections to organized crime, was taken into custody last evening for questioning in the murder of businessman Anthony Martino, a long-time resident of Brampton Heights. Martino's body was found buried on a construction site near Kingston last week. The suspect was detained following an

anonymous phone call from a witness who saw the man burying garbage in the woods across from his house. DNA evidence shows Martino's remains may have been in contact with the contents of the garbage bag at some point. At the present time, it is unclear how the DNA came to be in the suspect's possession. He has been released on bail pending further investigation.

"A murder! It isn't safe to live in the city anymore. Honestly, we really should move back to the country," Gloria says to Steve.

Steve shrugs. "It's probably gang-related. Or drugs. We're not likely targets. The guy must have been high to bury evidence across from his house. Nobody in their right mind would be stupid enough to do that."

Craig and Vicky nod as I rise to answer the door.

"Yes, it would take a real idiot to do that," Vicky agrees, her eyes flitting between me and Craig.

"Sorry to interrupt. We can come back another time," Jason says as I open the door. "I see you have company."

"No problem. Come on in." Need to get everyone's mind off the news.

Beth thrusts a pizza box at me. "We brought supper. We wanted to thank you again for helping me through last week."

"What are friends for?"

It's like Grand fucking Central Station around here.

Jason and Beth join the gang in the living room. Paul lopes up to the door before I get a chance to close it. "Hey, Jake. I just want to apologize for my wife."

"Your wife?"

"I *told* her to mind her own business. A man's got a right to bury his garbage wherever he wants. Sorry she called the cops on you. She promised me she wouldn't, and she swears she didn't. But after seeing the cops around your place so often, I guess she thought she had a civic duty. I'm glad to see they let you go, though. I guess they need more evidence than just DNA and the gun?" His voice travels through the open door into the living room.

"Jake?" Mom shrieks. "Please tell me you're not the man they took in for questioning last night. Is that why the police were at the wedding?"

But I've got other things to worry about besides Mom finding out I was arrested for murder. Dom's text requests my presence bright and early tomorrow.

8 am in my office. I've got a job for you.

Mallory strolls into the room to witness everyone's eyes on me. "Dinner will be ready in fifteen minutes. I hope everyone's hungry. There's a ton of food."

Chapter Fifty-Four

Something has happened. Jake looks…I don't know. I can't quite read him. Annoyed? Embarrassed? Shocked? Scared?

"Honey, is everything okay?" I touch his shoulder as he stands in the entryway.

"Yeah, sure, hon, everything's great," he quips. "There was just a local news report about a murder, and the suspect was released on bail."

Uh oh.

"Oh. Well, I'm sure we're safe here. Those kinds of things only happen in the city."

Paul calls for Russ. "Here, boy, let's go home and heat up a TV dinner. Mommy's out with her friends tonight." He turns to leave.

"Wait. We have more than enough food here. Why don't you stay for dinner?" I'm not sure what possesses me to invite our neighbor to stay when Jake is clearly upset. But maybe it'll take some of the pressure off him if there are more people to contribute to the conversation. Make him forget about the murder.

"Oh, no. I couldn't impose on your party."

"It's not a party. Just a few friends dropped over with food."

"Yeah, sure. Come on in. Of course, you'll stay for dinner, Paul." Jake opens the door wider and Russ bounds past, nearly knocking Paul to the ground, darting after Nellie. "Hi, Russ, old buddy, nice to see you again. The more, the merrier, that's what I always say."

I'm no longer sure whether he's being sarcastic or polite. In any case, I need to set the table for nine. "Beth, could you help me out in the dining room, please?"

If I can get her alone, she'll hopefully continue the conversation we began last night. I close the oak pocket doors to allow us some privacy.

"Jake got arrested last night?" Beth's hand flies up to her mouth. "Do the police have enough evidence against him? What about Dom? Is he still a threat?"

Too many questions for me to process. Does Beth know something about the murder? "You were trying to warn me last night. Do you have information that could help Jake? If you do, you need to go to the police."

Beth places her hand on mine, and her voice is barely a whisper. "I haven't told you the whole truth about what happened to Jason when he was missing. He did go to rehab. And he did buy a winning lottery ticket. But something happened before all that. I'm sorry. You have the right to know, especially now that Jake has been arrested," Beth continues. "I know Jake has...a relationship of sorts...with Dom."

"No. He just frequents his casino." I find my voice, shaky but audible. "There's no relationship."

"I don't know how *well* Jake knows him. But I do know Dom is up to no good. Jason went to rehab for more than one reason."

"What do you mean?"

"That Friday night when he went missing, Jason was with Jake's friends. He saw something he shouldn't have seen. He'd been gambling away the last of our money—the trust fund gift for the baby that my parents in Australia set up—when a fight broke out in the high-limit room between a couple of high rollers. It got out of hand, and they kicked everyone out.

"The fighting continued outside, behind the casino. Jason headed to his car and was halfway home when he realized he'd left his bank card on the gaming table. So, he turned around to go back for it. When he pushed open the door to the high-limit room, he found the cleaning staff clearing away broken glass and mopping up after the fight. He picked up his card and left.

"But for some stupid reason, he drove around back to see if the fight was over. He said he didn't know why. It was a gut feeling that something was wrong. No one was there. But he heard a loud motor running and saw lights up ahead on the service road. He turned off his headlights, pulled over into the employee parking lot, walked in the direction of the sound, and watched."

Beth stops for a moment, as though considering what to say next.

"What did Jason see?"

"A helicopter. And a couple of guys carrying someone aboard. By the arms and legs. Someone who wasn't moving. At first, he thought the guy must be drunk or something."

"But he wasn't?"

"Jason wasn't the only one watching them. Terry Cox, Jake's friend, came along in the dark and clapped a hand over Jason's mouth. Scared him to death."

"Terry? What was he doing there?"

"He told Jason if he was smart he'd forget what he saw and leave town for a while."

"Why would he do that?" Nausea takes hold, and I clamp a hand over my own mouth, swallowing the rising bile.

"Jason thinks the guy wasn't drunk; he was dead. And Jason thought *he* might be dead, too, if he told anyone what he saw. So, he told Terry he didn't see anything and ran back to his car. Then, he decided to disappear for a while. He'd been looking into a two-week addiction retreat in cottage country, and this seemed like a good time to go. He used the rest of the baby's trust fund on rehab. When he called me early the next morning, using his one allowed phone call from the clinic, he told me what he'd witnessed and said not to worry. Of course, I couldn't stop worrying. I thought they'd go after Jason, find him, and kill him to keep him quiet. And I couldn't contact him because he lost his cell phone at the card tables. I lied to you about calling the police. I didn't know if he was safe or dead, but I didn't want to point anyone to the rehab clinic and put him in danger if he was okay."

"He thought the guy was dead? And Terry threatened him?"

"He's still scared. Especially after the police found that body in Kingston. But Jason decided he couldn't stay in hiding forever, and he thinks if he keeps quiet about it, they'll leave him alone. I don't know, Mallory. This is really messed up. My cousin, Jethro? I didn't want to incriminate him, but the call he got to move the body told him to transport it to Kingston."

"Who told Jethro to take the body to Kingston?" I don't want to hear the answer, although burying my head in the sand isn't a way to live.

Beth grips my hand tighter. "I'm worried for you, Mallory. Because either Jake is involved in this somehow, or he's in danger."

Chapter Fifty-Five

"Everything okay, hon?" I put my hand to her belly, checking on the baby. Mallory's face is white as a sheet.

"Just a bit of nausea. I'm fine. Dinner is ready. Everything is set out on the kitchen island, buffet style. Just grab a plate from the dining room table and help yourselves." She attempts a smile.

Food temporarily becomes the focus as people pile their plates and gather in the dining room. Conversation consists of how great everything tastes and how we lucked out with the weather last night, as flashes of lightning bolts pierce the evening sky, followed by the rumble of thunder.

"Looks like we've got another thunderstorm coming," Steve remarks.

"By the way, that was some fireworks display you put on last night," Paul says. "We had a great view out of our bedroom window, over into your meadow."

"Yep, we had quite a night." I hope to God no one mentions the police visit. "Lit up the sky. Hope the noise didn't disturb you."

"Naw. We were up anyway, wondering what the cops were doing, sitting down the road…" Paul reconsiders, seeing me shake my head. "…in the series we're binge watching. Some cop show; I forget the name of it. Anyway, it was a good show. The fireworks, I mean."

"Speaking of which, I'll bet Jason and Beth are going to be shooting off a few themselves. Tell them what happened, Jase."

Jason jumps in with a news headline that almost rivals **Suspect detained in murder investigation.** "I won half a million bucks in the lottery."

"Half a mill? You lucky dog!" Paul throws a piece of roast beef under the table as Russ runs in, tired of searching for Nellie, whom Mal has locked into our ensuite. "How'd you manage that?"

"I played our numbers—our anniversary date—on ten tickets. I bought them a few weeks ago, but didn't check them until a couple days ago."

"I guess it pays to gamble, eh?"

Beth shoots Paul a look that says it doesn't.

"No more for me. I promise, sweetheart." Jason assures his wife. "I learned my lesson."

"What are your plans for all that money, Jase?" If I can get him talking, we can avoid the whole murder thing.

"A house for the three of us," Jason grins. "We're having a baby. And I'm going for more rehab next month. I promised Beth I'd keep up the counseling and rehab so I'm clean by the time the baby comes."

Congratulations lead to talk of babies and houses and renos. Safe topics.

No mention of me seeing Jason at the casino that Friday night when he joined Terry and the guys in the high-limit room.

As we retire to the living room for coffee and leftover wedding cake, I let out a yawn, hoping people will get the idea. Mom catches on quick.

"We'd better head out soon. Looks like the rain is getting heavier." She nods toward the window.

Beth joins in. "We'll be on our way, too. I could use a good night's sleep after all the excitement last night with Jason coming back. And your wedding, of course. I'm sure you're tired, too, with the baby and all." She hugs Mallory and whispers something in her ear.

Thank you, Beth. Let's get everybody out.

Russ yips and makes a beeline for the door as soon as it opens, and our guests head for their vehicles. Paul yells a final 'thanks for the meal' as he runs after his mutt. My phone rings.

"Saw the news tonight, Jake," the voice on the other end states. "About some body being found and a local suspect in the case. Janice and I don't agree on much, but we're on the same wavelength about this. We don't want to be involved. I talked to Sid, and he and Gail agree."

"What's this about, Rod?"

"Don't play dumb with me, Jake. That gun your neighbor's dog dug up. Seems like a helluva coincidence, if you ask me. If the cops ask you any more questions about it, seeing as there's been a body found and the suspect is local, make sure you let them know we had nothing to do with it. We don't want to be charged as an accessory or something."

"No problem, Rod. I know how to keep my mouth shut."

As I hang up, I notice I missed a text during dinner. From Terry.

They have a suspect? How much do they know?

I text back.

Plenty but not enough. I'll be in touch.

Vicky and Craig, still in our living room, watch as I return the phone to my pocket.

"Time to tell the truth, Jake. Out with it. All of it." Vicky speaks for everyone. "We can't help you if we don't know what's going on."

Eyes drifting from one to the other of them, I know there's only one way out of this mess. My wife, my best friend, my lawyer. I can't lie my way out. I lay all my cards on the table, hoping the four of us can arrange them into a royal flush that will beat the house and bring down its owner without taking me out of the game completely.

Chapter Fifty-Six

Am I making a mistake confiding in Brad? His hand on mine, eyes searching for an answer, he makes me nervous. I pull away, shifting closer to the car's door.

The question, and the unspoken alternative, lingers in the air. "Is this the kind of life you want for you and the baby? Because if you don't..."

Brad's hand moves across my back and rests on my shoulder, his body straining over the car's gear shift. Several other cars surround us shortly after four o'clock in the school parking lot where Brad suggested we meet. "Do you want to talk about it?" Brad had asked in the staff room during lunch. "I can see something's bothering you."

"Not now," I answered.

But my anxiety grew throughout the afternoon, and by the end of the day, Sue insisted I take the next day off and get some rest. "You're not doing anyone any good being here in this condition. A mental health day will do you good. There's nothing wrong with taking some time to care for yourself."

It would take a lot of mental health days for me to cope with my husband's lifestyle. Talking things over with a good friend whom I trust seemed like a good alternative to taking off the rest of the school year. Brad helped me out this summer when Jake and I were having some difficulties. He's smart, resourceful, and trustworthy.

And since Brad has no involvement in Jake's current problems, I thought perhaps he might offer an objective perspective on how to deal with the situation.

252

"Jake was arrested for murder last night," I said after we closed the car doors.

"Oh. Okay." He didn't appear surprised. "Who did he kill?" Brad hadn't even entertained the possibility of Jake's innocence.

"He didn't kill anyone." I protested with such conviction that I was sure Brad believed I thought there was no question he did.

"Okay…Well then, if he didn't kill anyone, who's the victim?"

When I mentioned last night's news report, Brad nodded. "I heard about that. I didn't realize Jake was the suspect, though. What was his connection to the dead guy? What was his name again?"

"Anthony Martino. And Jake barely knew him. Just one of the guys he runs into at the casino sometimes."

And now Brad's arm is slung over my shoulder as he waits for my answer. Is this the kind of life I want?

Of course, it isn't. But it's the kind of life I have. Would I be happier in a safe marriage to someone like Brad? Safe, but loveless. What would that be like? A lot less stressful, for one thing.

"It's not Jake's fault this happened." I defend the man I love and can't live without.

"Really? Then whose fault is it?" His eyebrows arch, and I can see it's going to take some effort to convince Brad of Jake's innocence. If Brad has already convicted him, what will a judge and jury do?

"Circumstances, maybe. Just bad luck. Or someone could be trying to frame him."

Brad removes his arm and settles back in his seat. "What makes you think he's being framed?"

"Someone planted evidence on our property." I tell him about the gun and the body dropped in the cornfield. "I think it's the same body Jake found in our basement cistern the next day."

Brad stares at me, his mouth open in a big 'O', wrinkles forming on his brow. "The body in the news report was found in Kingston, and the police said his DNA was in a garbage bag in our area. So, Jake *moved* the body to different locations?"

"Jake didn't move anybody. He had nothing to do with it." Once again, I'm aware that I protest too much. "Someone tried to make it look like Jake was involved."

"Why would they do that?"

"I don't know. But there's more. Someone left Anthony's VIP casino card and his money clip in our house." I don't mention Beth's cousin hid money in our toilet.

"Do you have any idea who would want to incriminate Jake?"

"Jake and I have a pretty good idea."

"Are you going to tell me, or am I supposed to guess?"

"You remember Dom?"

"Not personally, but the way you described him sounds like he's a hard guy to forget." Brad's eyes widen. "Oh, I get it. He's framing Jake. I thought Jake smoothed everything over with him."

"So did Jake. But we don't know anyone else who would do this to him." With great effort, I tell Brad what's really bothering me. "And now, Jake has decided to go after Dom and turn him in. He says it's the only way to prove his own innocence. Dom's a powerful man. I'm scared, Brad. What if Jake gets killed trying to save himself from prison?"

Brad sets his hand over mine again. "I'm so sorry, Mallory. Jake's brought this upon himself. I'm here for you, whatever you need. Just say the word. You know how much I care about you."

"Thanks, you're a good friend."

Brad removes his hand, releases a big sigh, and tells me to take care.

It feels good to talk to someone, even though there's nothing he can do. Sue's advice to take some time off bears considering. I'm going to need to keep up my strength for Jake's trial.

Assuming Dom doesn't kill him first.

As I drive home through the grey drizzle, I think about Jake's meeting with Dom this morning. I haven't heard anything from Jake; maybe he's too busy to answer my texts. My phone finally buzzes, but I decide to wait until I get home to answer. The last thing I need is to slide off the road into the ditch.

When I pull into our driveway, I reach for the phone, eager to find out what happened when Jake went to confront Dom this morning. The message is from Craig, not Jake.

Jake's late for work. He's not answering. Where is he?

Chapter Fifty-Seven

This can't be happening again. Jake is missing?

My call to Craig does nothing to soothe my fears. Craig, back at work today instead of on his honeymoon, thanks to Jake, has no idea why my husband isn't at The Auto Supply Warehouse. No call from him saying he'd be late, according to their boss, or that he needed the day off.

Inside the house, everything is exactly the way I left it, except Nellie is now at the glass patio door, nose to nose with the black stray.

My calls to Jake and Dom go straight to voicemail. I try the main number of the casino, hoping someone can put me in touch with Dom. "Hello? This is Mallory Shelton. My husband, Jake, had a meeting with Dom this morning. I was wondering if you could put me in touch with either of them."

The woman on the other end of the call tells me Dom is unavailable.

"What about Nick or Adam? Could you put me in contact with one of them?"

"I'm sorry, no. But we're open for all your entertainment needs from 3 p.m. to 3 a.m. Is there anything else I can help you with today?"

The phone slides from my hand onto the new sofa as I realize that neither Craig nor I have heard from Jake since he left the house this morning, leaving me to get ready for work.

A rubber band tightens around my chest, threatening to squeeze the life out of me as I consider where Jake could be. Have I put his life in danger by confronting Dom with the fact that I saw the casino logo on the helicopter above our cornfield and witnessed the body being dropped? Blackmailing

Dom in order to convince him to get Jake out of jail was a mistake. Was Jake safer in a cell?

My increased gulps of air leave me gasping, unable to catch my breath as the room begins to fade. Jake needs my help. I need to go to the casino and find him.

Just breathe. Slow and steady. Count, Mallory, count.

The hammering of my heart against my hands, laid across my belly and chest, refuses to stop. Nellie, sensing my distress, comes to my rescue.

"Good girl, Nellie, good girl." I stroke her silky fur, taking a breath, in and out, my hand keeping time to the numbers in my head to steady myself.

There's no way I can drive to the city in this condition. I need to calm down.

Snap out of it, Mal.

My brain functions well enough for a solution to present itself. Someone can drive me to the casino and help me find Jake.

Beth.

She knows exactly what I'm going through. Pregnant. Husband missing. Last seen at the casino.

I pick up the phone. "I'm really worried about Jake. He isn't answering my calls, and he didn't make it to work today. He went to the casino this morning to see Dom and hasn't come home. I'm too upset to drive there. Could you give me a ride?"

"Of course, Mallory. I owe you," Beth responds.

By the time she rings the doorbell, my attack has subsided enough that I'm pacing, waiting for her arrival. I swing the door open, purse in hand, and rush past her. Beth runs after me, starts up the car, and heads toward the highway.

Exceeding the speed limit by just enough to avoid being pulled over, Beth asks why Jake was meeting with Dom.

"Something about a job he had for him. I don't know. I don't think Jake knew the specifics, either. But, he felt he had to go, that he owed him, especially since Dom's the one who posted bail and got him out of jail." I don't mention Jake's plans to turn Dom into the police.

"Oh." Beth's hands tighten on the steering wheel. Her eyes hold the road, and she's quiet for the rest of the trip. I'm too wrapped up in my own problems to attempt a conversation.

The casino parking lot is already more than half full, even though it's still early, with most people at home, having supper. This time, we know exactly where we're going. Through the main double doors, down the wide corridor, and into the gaming facility. Lights and sounds accost us from all sides as we stride toward the back office.

My banging on the door brings results. Nick answers.

"Where's Jake?" I shove past him, looking around the room.

"Not here."

"I can see he's not here. Where is he? He had a meeting with Dom this morning."

"The meeting took them out of town."

"Out of town? Where?"

"Kingston."

"They went to Kingston?"

"Yes."

"Why would they go to King...?" Blood whooshes in my ears. Kingston is where the body was found. The man Jake was accused of killing.

"Business."

"That's a five-hour drive. Jake knew he had to go to work today. He wouldn't go to Kingston." Not voluntarily. "Jake isn't returning my calls. Can you reach Dom for me?"

Nick makes no move to reach for his phone. Instead, he ushers us toward the door.

"Please? I'm really worried about him. If I don't hear from him soon, I'm going to call the police to report him missing."

"I wouldn't do that. Dom doesn't care for police interference, and Jake didn't seem keen on a repeat visit to the city jail. I'm sure you'll hear something once they've completed their business."

He nods toward the hallway, where another man has appeared.

"Time to leave, ladies." The man takes me by the arm to escort me out.

"I can manage myself, thanks." I slap him with my free hand, and he releases me.

The three of us stroll through the casino, but I won't go without causing a ruckus. "What have you done with Jake? Where is my husband? Jake! Jake! Has anyone seen Jake? Where are you, Jake?"

The man accompanying us counters with a louder voice. "Calm down, Ma'am. Everything's fine. You're just confused. Too many Cosmopolitans. Your husband is waiting for you in the car."

He leaves us outside the casino entrance with instructions to the doormen. "Don't let them back in."

Halfway down the corridor of expensive boutiques, the sound of footsteps pounds the granite flooring behind us. Are they following to threaten me?

"Mallory!"

I turn around to see Jilly, Idlewood's town gossip, running to catch up with us. She stops once she has my attention, panting for breath.

"Jilly, hi. I wasn't expecting to see you here."

"Well, it's not…usual for me…to gamble. But, once in a while, after work… you know, just to let off some steam…with a few co-workers."

"Of course." I'm not sure why she feels the need to justify her gambling to me. It's not a *crime*. Lots of people do it.

"Anyway, I heard you saying you were looking for Jake."

"Yes, do you know where he is?"

"No, but I saw him this morning on my way to work, just before noon. I got a new job here, at the Galleria, a couple of months ago. When I was driving toward the employee lot, I saw Jake with someone, heading toward the helipad out back."

"The helipad? Jake got into a helicopter?"

"I didn't actually see him get on it. I had to get to work, so I didn't stop to watch. Not that I spy on people."

I thank Jilly, and she walks back toward the casino. I follow, but Beth stops me. "Mallory, don't go back there."

The corridor is busier now, with people heading toward the gaming floor. I check my phone to see if Jake has tried to get in touch with me. It's after eight p.m. Twelve hours since his meeting with Dom began. No word from him.

"I want to check out the helipad, then I'm going back to talk to Nick again. If I don't get answers, I'm calling the police."

Cold drizzle surrounds the lampposts in the parking lot, like fireflies swarming toward the light, as we run for the shelter of Beth's vehicle. A dull day has become a miserable night, no stars in the sky.

Through the darkness, light flashes. Yellow, red, green. Whirring accompanies the bright blinking.

"Look! A helicopter!"

Rows upon rows of cars line the lot, with more coming in, their headlights blinding us. One lot leads to another as we circle around the complex. Behind the enormous building, a service road leads further back. A lot, labelled 'Employees Only', occupies the space to the left, with a large open space to the right and several outbuildings.

My eyes shift from the sky to the helipad as the aircraft makes its landing, the roar pounding along with my heartbeat. Beth parks in the employee lot, and I open the car door, relieved to see the helicopter door opening as well. Throwing caution aside, I run toward the helipad. Whatever Jake's involved in, he's my husband, and I love him. And I trust him more than I don't trust him—maybe that's all that matters to make a good marriage.

Relief washes over me as a figure exits the helicopter.

The walk is all wrong. It's not Jake. This man strides confidently, but something's off. I wait for Jake to follow, but he appears to be alone. I recognize Dom as he enters a waiting vehicle and is transported to the back door of the casino.

The helicopter door closes, and the rotors wind down. A rollup door opens on one of the outbuildings, and two men exit, carrying some sort of wheels. Frozen in my spot, I watch as they roll the helicopter into the hangar.

Where is Jake?

Beth runs up to me, places her arm around me, and leads me back to her car.

"Jake wasn't on the helicopter," I say, the words hitting me with the reality that he's not with Dom.

"I'm sure he's fine. Jilly did say she wasn't sure he got on the helicopter."

Darkness presses in, despite the lampposts, the isolation of the back lot creeping into my psyche. Hundreds of yards away, the busy casino contrasts with the lonely back service road. Beth's hand brings no comfort, the chill flowing through my body in waves, drowning me. I need Jake.

I stare at the back door of the casino. "I'm going back inside. Drop me off at the entrance." One way or another, I'm going to get Dom to talk to me.

Chapter Fifty-Eight

This VIP treatment is scaring the shit out of me. Parading me around, introducing me to staff, giving me the complete tour of the River Grand facilities, describing all the equipment, the employee responsibilities. What is Dom up to?

"So, what do you think, Jake?" He steps behind the Center Bar and pours a couple of shots, passing one to me, as I slide onto a high-back upholstered barstool. Not part of my usual breakfast.

"What do I think?"

"Do you see yourself being a part of this?"

Is this a job interview? "I've been trying hard *not* to be a part of it recently. Turning over a new leaf, remember? We had an agreement. I stay out of your casino, and you stop stripping me of all my assets."

Dom snickers. "That was the old agreement. I'd say it's time for a new one, in light of the fact that I helped you to dispose of an unwelcome visitor and got your ass out of jail. I told you I expected payment for services rendered."

"And, as much as I appreciate all that, Dom, I didn't exactly ask for your help. But, I'll do whatever I can to make sure you are properly compensated for your trouble."

"I have no doubt you will."

Dom ushers me to the back parking lot, pointing toward the outbuildings, up the service road. "The next part of our tour is out of town. We'll be taking the copter."

"The copter?"

"The helicopter. Whirlybird. Chopper. You never been in one before?"

"Uh, no." There'd better not be any dead bodies on it.

As we approach, the helicopter is being pushed out onto the helipad.

"I have work this afternoon. It's not a good time for me."

"Relax, Jake. You work too hard. For way too little. There are easier ways to make a buck."

At the hangar, Nick and Adam approach to escort me aboard in case I need assistance. I lift my arms in the air. "I can do this on my own, thanks."

Leather seating for eight with cupholders, a large television screen, and a minibar make up the private passenger section of the helicopter. Dom and I buckle up. Before I know it, we're in the air, the roar of the engine and whirring of the rotors whupping a rhythm through my body.

Dom indicates I should put on the headphones, then speaks into the microphone. "What do you think of your ride, Jake?"

"To tell the truth, Dom, I've never actually seen the casino helicopter. Is this a new company purchase?"

"Fairly new. Your wife's seen it."

"Oh?"

"Flying over your cornfield a couple of weeks ago. She made out the letter C on the side. Connected it to the River Grand Casino logo."

"I didn't know about that." Why the hell didn't Mal tell me?

"She was smart to keep it to herself. Smart to wipe the prints off the gun she found in the cornfield, too."

Dom knows about the gun?

"She told me what she saw drop onto your cornfield from the casino helicopter, and how I should take responsibility for it instead of letting you take the blame, or she'd be sharing that information with the police."

Mal blackmailed Dom?

"I didn't say anything to the cops. I know how to keep my mouth shut, Dom. Mallory will, too, once I get a chance to talk to her about it."

"I'm not worried about your wife, Jake. She and I came to an agreement. I put up your bail money and arranged your quick release. In exchange, she's keeping quiet."

"Mallory was just trying to protect me. I'm innocent."

"I know you are, Jake."

"The thing is, Dom, it seems like someone's framing me. A lot of evidence has piled up."

Dom nods. "Murder is a nasty business. It's usually best to get someone else to take the rap for it." He sits back. "Try to get your mind off it for a while. Relax, enjoy the view."

Thousands of feet in the air, leaving behind the mass of buildings in the city, we follow the shoreline, patches of greenery mixed with buildings the further we travel. Through the glass, a miniature world floats by, farmland replacing populated areas. Quite the view, even through the drizzle. Mallory would hate this.

Dom removes a bottle of wine from the bar, along with some salty snacks. "Free in-flight lunch." He tosses me a bag of mixed nuts.

Crunching and sipping takes the place of conversation, our eyes taking in the sights through the glass.

Some time passes before I dare to ask, "So, where exactly are we heading?"

"Kingston. I want to show you something. And I thought we could drop in on someone while we're there."

Below us, the lake comes into full view.

"I've been thinking, Jake. If someone wanted to dump a body, wouldn't this be the ideal spot?" Dom gestures to the water.

Sweat forms on my brow, and I wipe it with my hand. Dom outweighs me in muscle by about thirty pounds. Not much chance of putting up a fight. Flight is out of the question. Nowhere to run but down.

"I should call Mallory. She worries, especially now that she's pregnant." My phone falls from my pocket, and I fumble with a shaky hand to retrieve it off the rumbling floor.

"You won't get reception up here. You can give her a call later."

Later? That's a good sign.

"Here comes the best part of the ride. You don't want to miss this." Dom stands, overlooking the lake.

Islands of green dot the blue water. Mallory and I were on vacation here once, on a boat tour. Rich people own cottages on some of the private islands. A variety of boats tour the waterway. Not much civilization out here, but it's a tourist attraction. Mallory was impressed by the beauty of rocks, trees, and water, despite her fear of the boat sinking.

"Almost there," Dom says. "Up ahead." He points to a large piece of land. And I realize he's taking me to his new casino location.

"Who are we meeting with?"

"I'm hoping to flush out a traitor today." Dom steeples his fingers, stands with his legs apart, steely eyes fixed on me.

"On an island? In Kingston?"

"On this helicopter."

I wish I'd had the chance to call Mallory and tell her I love her. And to say goodbye. Forever.

Chapter Fifty-Nine

The copter heads downward, makes a smooth landing, and the door opens. Safe and sound on solid ground. In the middle of a huge body of water. Still, better than being in a helicopter.

I need to call Mal, let her know where I am and who I'm with and that I love her. Just in case. But the call doesn't go through. I have no bars. Holding my phone up in the air, I hope to God I can get a signal.

"It's spotty, at best," Dom says, slapping me on the back. "But we'll get a tower up soon."

My eyes scan the landscape, rock, and mounds of ground surrounded by green. I take in the yellow and grey hydraulic hammers, excavators, dump trucks, and other equipment. Someone walks up to us and hands hard hats to Dom and me. The company name on the equipment doesn't escape me. Cox Construction.

"We'll do a quick tour of the area, then head to the mainland for a decent meal." Dom leads the way, navigating through machinery. "It's hard to picture now, but try to envision a five-star luxury lake resort, world-class entertainment, and a full-service casino. A playground for the rich and famous. And for the everyday Joe, of course, provided he saves his pennies."

"Nice."

"Nice? You need a better imagination than that, Jake."

He continues the tour through the trees and bushes and points out there will be walking trails throughout. "For the nature buffs and the health conscious."

We end up at the water's edge, waves lapping against rocks. "A series of pools along the water, umbrellas, loungers, cabanas, a Caribbean beach bar, and waterside food delivery from the hotel via service road access. For those who want to escape the noise and just relax. And, babysitting services, of course. We're going to keep it family-friendly. You can bring the little woman and the kids."

Dom is a family man first, businessman second. I can almost see it. "It'll be a while till it's operational. But I hope you can see yourself living and working here. We'll have first-class accommodations for you and your family, of course."

"Thanks. But, like I already told you, I have a job. Supervisor at The Auto Supply Warehouse. Remember? They'll be missing me right about now, actually. The place doesn't function if I'm not there."

"General manager of The Island Casino will be a slightly more lucrative position. With all the privileges such a position brings with it, Jake, you'd be a fool to turn down this kind of opportunity." Dom walks along the shore. "All this could be under your management. Not that The Auto Supply isn't an exciting place to work."

"Why me? I'm sure you can find someone more suitable for the job."

"You can do something for me no one else can."

"What would that be?"

"Terry Cox. I hear he's an old friend of yours. Best friend from way back."

"Terry? Doesn't he work for you? It's his construction company."

"No. He works for Marco. His crew is excavating the land. Marco's developing the property. I'll be operating the casino and facilities when it's built. We're in a partnership."

Terry, Marco, and Dom. Connected.

I turn around, taking in the scenery. Paradise. Who wouldn't want to live and work here? And be in charge, to boot.

I'm no idiot.

"What do you need me to do, Dom?"

"I suspect Terry saw something he wasn't supposed to see."

"Such as?"

Dom says we'll eat first, talk specifics later. A water taxi pulls up as if summoned. "Let's go. I'm starving."

As the boat approaches the shoreline of the historic city of Kingston, I type out a text to Mallory, explaining I'm still in a meeting with Dom. Just as I'm about to click send, Dom says, "This is strictly between me and you. But, if Terry knows what I think he knows, that knowledge just might be the end of him. That's where you come in. I figure you'll be able to get to Terry better than anyone else could."

I stand up to protest. No way am I doing Dom's bidding. I wave my hand in the air. "I don't care if you hand over this whole fucking city. If you think I'm..."

My phone slips out of my hand and sinks into the deep water.

There's a good chance I'll be joining it.

Chapter Sixty

Over dinner, Dom makes himself clearer. "I'm going to lay it all out, Jake. I trust you. You're a man of integrity. Over the last decade, I've watched you become a man. Taking responsibility for your gambling, doing whatever's necessary to pay your dues, doing an honest man's work, and looking out for your family and friends. All on the straight and narrow, barring a few minor misdemeanors and transgressions, none of which you've been caught for. I'm looking for a respectable frontman for my operations. A favor from you to me, as we've discussed previously on several occasions. But now, here you are, under suspicion of…one nasty crime." He shakes his head.

The medium-rare Porterhouse steak sticks in my throat, and I wash it down with several swallows of lager. Unsure of whether he's complimenting or threatening me, I say, "Yeah, well, that kind of sucks."

To the restaurant staff and patrons, we must appear as a couple of old friends, chewing the fat. Our table, which Dom has reserved, sits next to the fireplace, shrouded by some greenery. Dom's hearty laugh travels as he agrees that it does indeed suck.

"But I think the two of us can find a way out of this that will suit both our purposes. Keep you out of prison and lock up the scumbag responsible."

I set down my fork. "I'm listening." As long as it doesn't harm Terry.

Dom lowers his voice, mindful of a potential audience, although the steakhouse is busy. Voices mix, none of the words discernible, plates and cutlery clink, soft music flows through the dining area, people arrive, people leave.

"I believe Terry Cox holds the missing puzzle piece in this situation. Since he's your friend and you're the central piece of this unfortunate mess, I thought he'd be willing to confide in you."

"I'm assuming you mean the Anthony Martino mess."

Dom nods. "We have video of Terry re-entering the casino grounds the night we had to shut down the high-limit room, and the altercation between Tony and Marco continued behind the casino. No idea what Terry was doing when he returned. He didn't show up back inside the complex."

"O...kay." I narrow my eyes. He better not be accusing Terry of having something to do with Tony's death.

"So, here's the thing, Jake. The object in question ended up buried on Terry's construction site."

"Hold on a minute. There's no way Terry had anything to do with..."

"I think Terry's keeping quiet about what he witnessed that night. Out of fear." Dom takes a sip of his cabernet. "I had no idea Marco had hired your friend's company to develop the island property when I ordered the item to be buried there."

I gag on a piece of potato, and the coughing fit brings the waiter to our table to check if I need the Heimlich maneuver. Spitting the food into my napkin, I put up my hand and shake my head to indicate I'm fine.

"It's not what you think, Jake." Dom leans forward. "Do you remember when Marco came into my office during our meeting? And I told you I didn't trust him?"

I nod, still unable to speak.

"He proved me right. My gun disappeared out of the desk drawer shortly after that meeting. Ended up in your cornfield the night of the fight, according to your wife. Along with another entity that dropped out of my helicopter. That joint plant enterprise you and I run connects me to that field. Tony was last seen in my casino, causing a ruckus. Jethro called a couple days after that ruckus to tell me they'd found Tony in your field and moved him to a more secure location pending instructions from me. Then you called me about a rat in your cistern, and I asked our associates in the cornfield to dispose of it. In Marco's lap, so to speak. Which, for the record, should the cops ask, never happened. The police discovered it on the new casino grounds. Are you connecting the dots, Jake?" He continues his meal, allowing time for the information to settle in my brain.

"Uh, kind of. Who's Jethro?"

"Big guy harvesting the crop."

Muscle man.

"So, what does this have to do with Terry?" Or me, for that matter.

"I think Terry saw what Marco did that night. The fight became deadly. Marco saw an opportunity to frame me and get rid of me. Bring down my business and have me put away. We had a verbal agreement for him to help finance my new casino. He was in charge of developing the facility and I'd run the place. But I discovered he took out a casino license in his own name. I suspect he planned to cut me out and make the Island Casino competition for the River Grand rather than a new acquisition. I thought moving Tony onto Marco's property would let him know who's in charge. But then you got yourself arrested."

"What do you want from me, Dom? Get to the point."

"The point is you need to talk to Terry. Find out exactly what he was doing the night he came back to the casino and what he saw. Get him to point the police to Marco."

"What if he didn't see anything?"

"I'm sure you can persuade him that he did. The video shows Terry entering through the back service road on a direct course to the helipad. Unfortunately, there are no other cameras in that area. Plenty of witnesses saw Marco and Tony taking their disagreement out the back door, which connects to the service road. If you can get Terry to testify he saw Marco disposing of Tony permanently and loading him onto the copter, not only will it get rid of Marco and flush out the mole I suspect works for me, it will keep you out of prison. And you'll be my right-hand man at The Island Casino." He raises his glass in a toast. "Nice promotion from growing crops next to your farmhouse."

I raise my lager and clink it against his cabernet.

What choice do I have?

Chapter Sixty-One

"Jake! Are you okay?" My hand trembles as I hold the phone to my ear. The call is coming from Terry Cox's phone, but Jake's "Hi, hon" comes through loud and clear.

"I'm fine, Mal. Sorry, I couldn't call sooner. I lost my phone, and then I lost track of the time. Dom and I had a very productive meeting."

Beth walks next to me on our way to the casino entrance to confront Dom about Jake's whereabouts. We stop and sit on a bench in the mall corridor, mostly empty now.

Relief turns to anger when I find out he's okay and neglected to let me know why he didn't show up at work today. "Where are you? Why aren't you at work?"

"I'm with Terry. He's going to give me a lift home. I wasn't comfortable getting back into Dom's helicopter, and Terry has to go to the Brampton Heights police department anyway. You won't believe it, Mal. Terry has evidence that will clear me in Anthony Martino's death."

My anger dissipates, relief coursing through me once again. Jake explains what happened in Kingston and tells me to get some rest. "I'll be home around two. I love you."

The wipers strike a steady beat, keeping time with my heart as Beth keeps her eyes on the slick road, listening to me relay most of Jake's phone call. In the darkness of the car, the quiver in her voice tells me she's frightened. "What about Jason? Won't he be in trouble if Terry testifies? Jason kept information from the police. Now that's going to come out. Doesn't it make him an accessory or something?"

"I'm sure the police will understand if he explains he was afraid and didn't know who to trust. Terry, Dom," I swallow before adding, "Even Jake."

"And what about Jethro? Are you going to turn him in for stealing the money? And moving the body?"

"I don't think the police need to know everything. At least, that's what Jake said."

When Beth drops me off at home, I run through the rain, up to the front door, setting off the security lights, my key in hand. Beth pulls out of the driveway once I'm inside and flip the switch in the entryway. I call out for Nellie.

No answer.

Illuminating each room as I tread through the main level, my voice echoes in the empty house, the only other sound the pitter-patter of rain on windows. Nellie's plaintive meows can be heard in the kitchen.

"Nellie. Here, girl. Mommy's home." I turn on the lights above the kitchen island.

A man sits on my new family room sofa, one leg crossed over his knee, making himself right at home, flipping through his phone. At first, I think it's a trick of the lighting, a shadow, maybe my mind conjuring up what isn't there. Just like when I awaken from a nightmare and shout out, having seen a dark apparition at the side of my bed, next to the window.

But he speaks. No illusion.

"Mrs. Shelton. Always a pleasure."

My blood runs cold. My mouth hangs open, and all that comes out is a squeak. Like a mouse. A song jingles through my head, the words distorted. *They all ran after the farmer's wife. They cut off her fingers with a carving knife.*

"I locked her in the laundry room. Cats creep me out. Always staring at you." He grabs a bottle off the coffee table and gulps down the rest of his beer, patting the sofa cushion next to him. "Have a seat. We'll wait for Jake together. Nice new addition you've got, by the way."

Hand on my belly, I remain standing. The whooshing in my brain keeps rhythm with the rain pinging on the bay window. I try to clear my throat, resulting in a choking sound.

"Jake..." I gag and sputter, "will be home...any minute. With a friend."

"He'll be a few hours. Takes a little longer by car than chopper. That's why I'm here. To have a private meeting with Jake and his friend."

Jake's baseball bat is upstairs in the bedroom closet. Too far away. The pull-out drawer under the kitchen island is closer. As I take out the iron skillet, the corner of my eye catches a glint of metal on the end table.

He picks up the gun. "I know you're pretty handy with a frying pan, Mrs. Shelton. I could use something to eat. How about an omelet? Fix one for yourself while you're at it. I hear you're eating for two."

The longest few hours of my life stretch into what seems like weeks. I cook as he turns on the television, gun set down next to him, along with my phone which he has confiscated. One loud crack of a pistol follows another as the movie he has selected plays out on our large screen. Very little talking on his part, none on mine.

I've chosen the recliner, to keep my distance. My bladder twitches, threatening to soil the new fabric. "Can I go to the bathroom?"

His eyes remain fixed on the shootout.

"Can I go to the bathroom? Please?" With effort, I raise my voice barely above a whimper.

He nods his head toward the left, indicating I have permission to leave the room. When I rise, he follows me. "No. Not upstairs. Right here." He indicates the powder room. No chance of getting Jake's bat. "Keep the door unlocked." He stands outside, waiting, while I pee, flush, and wash.

The toilet tank lid. That's the answer.

It's heavy. A good weapon.

I grasp it securely in two hands, remembering what happened last time I wasn't cautious. With my hip, I rattle the doorknob and call out, "Can you open the door? It's stuck."

As he swings open the door, I bring down the lid with all my strength.

It crashes on the hallway floor, next to him, as he jumps out of the way.

"Well, that wasn't a smart move," he says, grabbing me by the arm and hauling me back to the family room. "Sit! And behave yourself."

Handcuffs slide out of his pocket, and he secures me to the recliner. "Enjoy the movie. Another Bond classic is coming up."

Metal pinches my wrists as I attempt to wiggle out of the cuffs. The sense of claustrophobia at being trapped causes me to wail. "Please, please, take them off. I'll be good."

He gives me an exasperated look. "I don't like to hurt women. So, don't make me shoot you." He tosses me the key, gun trained at my head.

The rest of the evening passes with me making no sound, my eyes on the gun in his hand. By the time Terry's car pulls in the driveway, and Jake turns his key in the front door to call out, "Honey, I'm home," I've been warned enough times not to make a sound to indicate I have company. "Terry's just going to crash here tonight instead of heading to the city to his parents' place. It was a long drive."

Jake must notice the broken toilet tank in the hallway. "Mallory? Honey? Did you have a problem with the toilet again?"

When he walks into the family room and sees me sitting on the recliner, he doesn't see the man with the gun crouched behind me. Not till he stands and speaks.

"Well, this is convenient. Bringing him right to me. Thanks, Jake." He waves the gun toward Terry. "I'm going to politely request that you keep your trap shut about what you think you saw, Terry. Now, if you don't mind, we'll continue our meeting elsewhere. I'd hate to mess up Mallory's new family room. Red doesn't fit the color scheme."

Jake and Terry stand frozen, Jake's eyes darting back and forth from the gun, to me, to the patio door. "We can talk this over. Come to a resolution that suits everyone. Maybe Terry was too drunk to know what he saw."

"This solution suits me fine. Let's go." He points the gun toward the patio door. My car's right out here, behind the garage."

"You ruined our lawn? We just had it manicured," Jake quips.

"Jake?" His name passes my lips, and I want to ask what's going on, but I'm paralyzed.

"Let Mallory go, and Terry and I will come willingly. No need for you to wave that thing around. It's scaring my pregnant wife. Let's handle this man to man, leave her out of it."

Terry inches toward the man, hands up in surrender. "I don't know what you think I saw, but I'll swear on a stack of bibles, I didn't see a thing. And with no video footage, I think we can agree nothing happened."

The man considers this for a moment before answering, his gun motioning from Terry and Jake to the patio door. "I overheard your conversation in Kingston. No way is Dom going to forgive my betrayal and new allegiance to Marco. So, he's going down for the murder as Marco planned. As well as any other collateral damage that might accumulate as a result."

Jake's blue-green eyes flit around the room. I know he's calculating the odds of overpowering the muscular man holding the gun. He swallows, having come to a decision.

"How about a new plan? I'll testify in court that I saw Dom kill Tony. That he offered to pay me off to keep quiet about it. That he tried to frame me when that didn't work. That I was too scared to come forward, for my family's sake. The police are already looking at Dom for this. My testimony will put him away. Mission accomplished. Just let my wife go."

"I wasn't born yesterday. Now…"

"My baby," I squeak, "needs his father. Do you have kids?"

"None that I know of. There's plenty of kids raised by single moms. You and the kid will survive." The burly man rolls his eyes. "As long as you're smart enough to keep tonight's little encounter to yourself."

Jake mouths, "I love you. And our baby."

A scraping, scuffing sound snaps everyone's head in the direction of the patio door. "AHHH!" Jake screams. "The alien's back!"

He dims the island fixtures, drawing attention to a set of glowing eyes against the glass.

"What the fu…?" The man raises his gun toward the patio, his eyes taking in the apparition outside the door.

Jake grabs the iron skillet sitting on the island stovetop and slams it onto the man's head.

The man drops like a fly, his gun sliding across the polished hardwood.

"Thanks, hon," Jake's voice quivers as he scoops up the gun. "You've taught me a thing or two about how to use a skillet. You never know when a cooking lesson might save your ass. It's an important life skill."

He turns to Terry. "Call the cops."

Chapter Sixty-Two

"Thank God no one was hurt! And you've been vindicated." Vicky glides into our living room, arms around Jake first, holding on for dear life, then gives me a squeeze, patting my back. "You must have been terrified, with the baby, and a killer in your house."

Craig wraps himself around me, a peck on the cheek. "We're so glad you're safe." Then he switches spots with Vicky to give Jake a big bear hug. "Don't know what we'd do without you guys."

"Well, you can go on that honeymoon now for one thing." Jake reclaims me, his arm around my waist. "This murder thing kinda put a damper on the wedding. Sorry about that."

"Just as soon as I'm sure all the charges against you have been dropped, and all the guilty parties are locked up without bail. Then it's just you and me." Vicky smiles at her new husband, arm around his waist.

"We'll be honeymooning for the rest of our lives. A few days' delay won't hurt," Craig leans down for a kiss.

"We need some time to ourselves, too," Jake says. "We'll be spending a couple weeks up north in Dom's cottage. He gave me the keys. Said we deserve a break after all this shit."

Some time off for my mental health is just what I need. In the early morning hours, Terry, Jason, Jake and I, *and* Dom went to the police station to give our statements. We all agreed beforehand to tell the truth and nothing but. Unless it incriminated one of us. That truth put Marco and his accomplice in immediate custody.

"So, let me get this straight," Craig says, as we get comfortable on the old living room sofa. "Marco double-crossed Dom. He had no intention of honoring the partnership. It was all a setup to get Dom arrested for murder and put him out of commission permanently. Marco thought he could take over the entire casino operation, in both locations?"

"Yep. But he didn't bargain for witnesses. Terry came back to the casino that night, through the service entrance. The tire on his car went flat. Said he should have kept up his Auto Club membership. When he looked in the trunk, the spare was flat, too, from the last time he ran over a nail. To top things off, his phone went dead while he was calling me for help, so he walked back to the casino to use their landline. The service road was the closest way back." Jake pauses. "He's lucky he wasn't killed, too. Marco and Tony were still arguing out back, by the outbuildings. Terry saw Marco shoot Tony. He kept hidden, hoping he wouldn't be seen himself. While Marco and Adam were loading the body into the helicopter, Jason came along. Terry warned Jason to keep quiet about it. Especially since Marco and Dom seemed to be working together, and Adam does Dom's bidding. Terry figured Dom had to be in on it, and he was too scared to incriminate him." Jake stops again, shrugs and raises his eyebrows. "Everyone knows Dom doesn't put up with shit like that."

"I *thought* Adam worked for Dom," Craig says. "So how does Dom get off scot-free?"

"Adam worked for whoever spread more cash in his path. Dom figured out he was a traitor when he didn't say anything about the casino helicopter detouring over my field to make a drop-off. Adam was piloting Marco home from the casino to Kingston that night. Marco had offered him a lucrative position in the new casino for switching his allegiance. When Dom discussed the same position with me, Marco and Adam planned to take me out of the picture along with Dom, stacking evidence in my back yard. The body, Dom's gun, a phone call to the police about the bag we buried…"

"So, it wasn't Linda who called the police?" I ask.

"No. She stayed out of it. Good neighbors are worth their weight in gold."

"We'll have to invite them over for dinner, the two of them this time."

"Sounds good, Mal. No, it was one of the guys in the cornfield, working with Adam for some extra cash. Some guys will do anything for money. Jethro. He's not being charged with anything, but Dom fired his ass."

"What about Tony's VIP card and the money clip with all the cash? Were Adam and Marco responsible for planting that on you? What about the receipt in the bag? They did that, too?" Vicky narrows her eyes, trying to piece it together.

"I guess."

"That must have been what happened," I add. Some things are best kept private between Jake and me. No need for her to know it never occurred to me there might be a receipt in the bag I used to bury the gun. Or that I stole the money Jethro hid in the toilet and then returned it. That Jake, in turn, stole it from the toilet and stuffed it in his safe. That the VIP card made the rounds from back door to kitchen counter to Jake's wallet.

"And they used your carpet and rope to secure the body?" Vicky continues.

"Uh, yeah, I guess," Jake says. "That's what's in the police report."

Jake's phone rings, and he looks at the caller ID. "Excuse me. I better take this." He rises and heads out of the room.

"No more secrets, Jake, remember?" Whatever this is about, I want to know. We're a team.

"You're right, Mal. I'm an open book from now on. My business is your business, hon."

He turns on the speaker.

"Jake, my man. How's it going?"

"Uh, you know, it's going okay, Dom. What's up?"

"I want to thank you again for convincing Terry to come forward. And Jason was a bonus, with his eyewitness account backing up Terry. Not to mention the casino staff and clients who saw the fight. That, and all the evidence you and your lovely wife explained away, plus Adam's plea bargain that he was working under Marco's orders, will get Marco out of my hair for quite some time."

"Too bad the island casino project didn't work out."

"Who says it didn't? I've got a new investor."

"Oh?"

"Jason. He's never been good with numbers. That's why he keeps losing at the tables. But with my guidance and that lottery win, he'll make something of himself. I'm his new mentor."

"The five hundred thousand? Isn't that chump change for you?"

"No, the fifty million of legally obtained cash he's going to infuse into my operation. Jason misread the numbers. He was off on his zeros."

"Holy shit!"

"It *does* pay to be religious. So, what about you? Are you in? The job we've been discussing? The payback you owe? Working for me as general manager of The Island Casino and all the related perks?"

Jake's turquoise eyes meet mine.

"I'm going to have to decline, Dom. Don't get me wrong. I know what a fantastic opportunity this is, but my home and family are here, not in Kingston. Family comes first."

"I understand, and I respect you for that. But I have another proposition for you. How about you take on second-in-command at the River Grand?"

"You already have a right-hand man. Nick."

"I do, you're right. And he's a good man. But I seem to have lost my left-hand man. Adam backed the wrong horse when he teamed up with Marco. So, I'm a bit short-handed at the moment."

Jake's smile and the twinkle in his eyes tell me Jake's excited about the prospect of this new career option. I shake my head and mouth, "No way."

"I think I'm going to have to pass, Dom. My wife likes the prestige of being married to a warehouse supervisor."

"I'll be interviewing for a new pilot, as well. Maybe you'd like to take flying lessons? At my expense, of course."

"Thanks, Dom, but I don't see myself in a helicopter for the foreseeable future."

"How about I leave the left-hand position open for now, give you some time to think it over? Good help is hard to find. Harder to keep. You can't trust anyone. But you've got integrity, son. It'll be a legit position, and I'll compensate you nicely. I owe you one, and I always pay my debts. Besides, we're family."

"Thanks, Dom. Appreciate it."

"Thank *you*, Jake. And that lovely wife of yours."

"Mallory."

"Mallory. Thank Mallory. But don't think you can call me Grandpa when the baby comes."

Dom hangs up, leaving Jake with wheels spinning in his head. The possibilities Dom offers exceed any promotion possibilities at the Auto Supply Warehouse.

"Grandpa?" Craig wrinkles his brow. "What's that about?"

"Inside joke. And that's all, folks. No more guns, bodies, cops. Things are going to get a lot quieter around here. Except for the baby crying." Jake winks at me.

"Ee...oww. Ee...oww."

"Oh! Did you get a new cat?" Vicky pets the sleek kitty that jumped into her lap. Her cashmere sweater is in danger of getting a few runs in it as the silky black-haired addition to our family kneads his paws.

"Yes," I say. "That's Nellie's new boyfriend. Isn't he adorable?"

"I thought you said you weren't taking in any more strays." Vicky turns to Jake, eyebrows raised.

"That was before he scared the crap out of Adam long enough for me to whack him on the head with the frying pan." Jake scoops the cat from Vicky. "He's my boy, now. And if he and Nellie want to start up a family, I don't have a problem with that. The more, the merrier."

"Ah, that's sweet. What's his name?"

"Lucky. As in, we're lucky to be alive."

Acknowledgements

I thank my husband, Brian, for his part in the creation of this book. The old homestead where he grew up sets the scene for Jake and Mallory's place. Brian's description of his childhood home, of which I only saw the exterior, helped me to create my characters' fictional farmhouse. As well as providing suggestions for their story, Brian stands by me at every book event, telling potential readers about Jake and Mallory's world. He's the one person who understands them as well as I do, or as well as is possible. Probably because he is the one who knows *me* best.

I appreciate my family for being there for me and putting up with the life of an author. Writing takes a lot of time, as does attending book events. Thanks for your encouragement and understanding as I pursue my childhood dream to be a published writer. To my son Bryant, thanks for helping with technology and promotion; to my daughter Brittany and son-in-law Eric, thank you for attending events and standing by me; to my grandson Rowan, thanks for being such a sweetheart. I appreciate my brother Joseph's encouragement to stick with it as well as my sister-in-law Audrey's support. And to my step-nephew Max, step-niece Maia, and nephews Evan and Reid, I am so happy to be your aunt. Also, special thanks to my step-niece Maia Kowalski for providing some very useful editing suggestions in my previous book, *Lost Like Me*. Thanks to my in-laws Kim, Craig, and Jody for their interest in my books. And of course, T. C. and Scruffy: thanks for sharing your lap time with my laptop.

To friends and neighbors, as well as online friends and other authors I've had the privilege of meeting, thank you for reading my books and supporting my work by promoting it to others. Special thanks to my friend Deb Robinson for being a great supporter of my books and spreading the word in our community. And Norah Blakedon, my critique partner, what would I ever do without your expert advice and friendship?

Thank you to the bookstores, libraries, and other venues that have hosted book signings and events, as well as local media who have helped promote my books.

But of course, I wouldn't be able to say I'm a published author if it weren't for my agent, Cindy Bullard of Birch Literary. The day she decided to take a chance on me was life changing. Thanks so much, Cindy, for allowing me this opportunity to achieve my childhood dream.

To Shawn Reilly Simmons, my editor at Level Best Books, thank you for your editing expertise and great covers. I am absolutely amazed by all your talents and so grateful to be a Level Best author. Thanks to Verena Rose and Deb Well, and the staff at Level Best Books for all you do.

And finally, thank you readers, for choosing to read this book. If you enjoyed it, I hope you will consider leaving a review on Amazon, Goodreads, or elsewhere. Your support means more than I can express.

About the Author

Ivanka Fear is a Slovenian-born Canadian author. She lives in Ontario with her family and feline companions. Ivanka earned her B.A. and B.Ed. in English and French at Western University. After retiring from teaching, she wrote poetry and short stories for various literary journals. *The Dead Lie,* A Blue Water Mystery, was her debut novel. *Lost Like Me* is the second book in the Blue Water series. Ivanka is also the author of *Where is My Husband?*, a Jake and Mallory Thriller. She is a member of International Thriller Writers, Sisters in Crime, Crime Writers of Canada, and Vocamus Writers Community. When not reading and writing, Ivanka enjoys watching mystery series and romance movies, gardening, going for walks, and watching the waves roll in at the lake.

AUTHOR WEBSITE:
  https://www.ivankafear.com

SOCIAL MEDIA HANDLES:
  Facebook: https://www.facebook.com/ivankafearauthor
  Instagram: https://www.instagram.com/ivankawrites
  Twitter: https://twitter.com/FearIvanka

Also by Ivanka Fear

The Dead Lie, A Blue Water Mystery

Where is My Husband?, A Jake and Mallory Thriller

Lost Like Me, A Blue Water Mystery